COWBOYS AND CUPCAKES

MERRY EVERYTHING
BOOK 3

JODI PAYNE

BA TORTUGA

THE MERRY EVERYTHING SERIES

Cowboys and Cupcakes
Copyright © 2023 by Jodi Payne & BA Tortuga

Cover illustration by AJ Corza
http://www.seeingstatic.com/
Cover content is for illustrative purposes only and any person depicted on
the cover is a model.

ISBN: 978-1-951011-93-2

Published by Tygerseye Publishing, LLC
November 2023
Printed in the USA

As always, to our wives.

1

Jax Martinez sat on the counter in his tiny kitchen and glared at Casper. They were supposed to be making profiteroles for Sunday, but the dough hadn't really gotten doughy, and the eggs had made the mixture soppy instead of something he could squeeze through his pastry bag. What had happened? He didn't get it. They'd made them a million times.

Like, a million-million times.

Maybe he put in too much butter? Maybe he didn't cook it on the stove long enough. Maybe it was bad luck.

He had a lot of bad luck.

It was Saturday, and on Saturdays, he had pizza and watched a movie on TV. That had been his plan anyway, until the profiteroles didn't work out.

"What the hell, Casper?" He glared harder, wishing his food processor could actually understand how annoyed he was. It couldn't, of course, because it was an object and objects didn't think at all, but they should know when they weren't behaving the way he wanted them to.

"You don't love me anymore," he said and hopped down

off the counter. He didn't expect a response. Food processors were kind of the strong silent types. "You can just sit there by yourself for a while and think about what you've done."

So there.

He left the kitchen—which took him about three steps —and picked up his cell phone to order delivery. He'd have his pizza and then he'd clean up and try again later. He'd made lots of sweets at midnight, or at four in the morning. He liked baking in the middle of the night.

Just as he was dialing, a doorbell sound rang, making him grin. That was his buddy Jan's ringtone. January *Bell*. Dumb as hell but the pun made him giggle every time. He tapped on Jan's text.

> JANUARY:
>
> Hawk is at the airport picking someone up.
> Want to come for dinner about six?

Dinner? Surely Jan knew he was a very busy man and couldn't just drop everything and go out for dinner.

> I could eat.

He went to find his shoes. He just needed to clean up the kitchen.

Wait.

He stopped short outside his bedroom door. Hawk was at the airport? He looked at the text again, and then dialed Jan.

Jan was laughing as he answered. "Did you forget how to get here?"

"How is Hawk picking somebody up at the airport?" Hawk Destry, Jan's husband, was a former bull riding champion and the bravest guy Jax had ever met. Hot too. Jan was a lucky bastard. But Hawk didn't see so well. As in the guy was legally blind.

"Ever heard of a taxi? It's this yellow thing that—"

"Ha. Ha, ha." Jax snorted. "By himself?"

"Sure. He has Buck with him."

"You let him go alone." Hawk's service dog was smart as hell, but January wasn't fooling him.

"He's a grown man, Jax. I didn't *let* him do anything. He insisted." Jan sounded a little defensive now.

"Ah." Uh-huh. Now he got it.

"What?"

"How worried are you?"

Jan laughed. "Well, it's his first time going to the airport alone. But I'm not really worried, I'm... I'm kind of—okay, I'm fucking worried."

"I'll be right over."

2

Saw McMahon made his way down to baggage claim. He'd texted Hawk when he left the plane, letting Hawk know it would take him a while to get there.

He wasn't in a chair anymore, but he was slow, and the walker was clumsy as fuck. Still, he wasn't in the hospital, he wasn't at Ft. Cavazos, and he wasn't going to have to worry about Hawk staring at him, right?

Right.

Not only that, but Hawk was going to help him with the whole process of getting himself a service animal. Hawk had done it. He could do it.

There were places for soldiers to get help here, and he needed someone to take care of. Focus on. Maybe live for until he could get his shit together.

Saw sighed and kept moving. He'd never believed that something so natural as walking would become something he had to focus on.

He made it to baggage claim, and sure enough, there was Hawk, sitting on a bench with the biggest German shepherd he'd ever seen.

"Hawk. Man. You made it."

"I did. My husband has only texted twenty times. We need to get your shit, and I have a car for us." Hawk rolled his eyes and grinned. "Jan worries."

It must be nice. "I'll get you home safe. I promise."

Hawk snorted at him. "I got this, man. Let's go, Buck. Where's your baggage?"

"Down here. Do you want to sit, and I'll grab my duffel? I'll be right back." He didn't wait for Hawk to sit again. He just started toward the baggage carousel, where his duffel was the sole remaining piece toodling around the belt. Okay.

Okay.

He braced himself on his good leg and reached out with his bad arm, praying he could stay up.

He knew as soon as his hand met the handle of the bag, that he wasn't going to make it. There was no way he could stay up.

About the time he was fixin' to go ass over teakettle, a hand caught him, dragging him to his feet.

"I got that." The tall stranger caught his duffel in a big hand and lifted it off the belt like it weighed nothing. "Awkward angle, huh? You want this cart?"

"Yeah. Yeah, thanks." He blinked a little, recognizing a fellow soldier without hesitation.

"First time in New York?" The guy sat his duffel on the cart and rolled it over to him. "Where are you coming in from?"

"Fort Cavazos. I mustered out of 1st Cav. I'm visiting a buddy." *Hey, I'm a fucked-up soldier meeting a blind cowboy I met when we were both rodeoing. Pleased to meet you.*

"Awesome. You're gonna love it. I'm Truman." Truman stuck out a hand to shake. "82nd, 313th. Retired."

"Intelligence. Worked with a lot of y'all on deployment. Thanks for the hand." He moved slowly toward Hawk and the dog, whose name just escaped him.

"Any time. Enjoy your visit." Truman went back to the belt.

"Okay, man. I got it and a cart. Where to?"

Hawk grinned and spoke into his phone. "We're looking for a luxury sedan, driver's name is Michael."

"Good deal. Just out this door, look for a sedan. What color?"

Hawk arched an eyebrow. "Seriously?"

"Oh. Right. Sorry." He grinned, suddenly tickled shitless. "So, sedan. Michael. Possibly rainbow colored. Got it."

The very black, very shiny sedan pulled up not a minute later, and a polished-looking man in a suit and tie got out and popped the trunk. "Destry?"

"Michael?" he asked and got a nod. "My walker folds up. Will it fit?"

"Oh yeah. No worries. I drive around those little old ladies with their giant purses and those fancy Cadillac walkers with the hand brakes on them all the time." Michael got the door for him. "Climb on in. There's a harness thing for your dog in the center."

"Yes, sir." He focused on getting into the car. One foot down, the other foot in. Jesus. He was wearing out. He'd been on standby for hours, and now he just wanted to sit and visit with Hawk. Breathe. Take a pain pill.

"Go on, Buck. Good boy." The dog climbed into the car, politely sitting beside him and didn't relax until Hawk was in the car, and the door was closed.

Hawk gave the address, and Saw leaned back, trying to relax.

"Lord have mercy, I'm glad to be here."

"Long trip, I bet. Jan's a damn good host, so there'll be food and coffee when we get back. He gets it." Hawk's hand rested on Buck's shoulders, massaging gently.

"I appreciate you letting me come out. I—I just don't have a lot of friends left in the civilian world these days."

"I think you kicked yourself over Ollie's death more than anyone else ever did."

He huffed out a surprised breath. He hadn't heard that name since he left for basic. "Too soon, Hawk."

"Sorry, man."

The car pulled out of the Newark Airport and onto the highway, and he watched the industrial scenery go by. This part of New Jersey was not much to look at.

He forced himself to watch everything, to focus, to stay right here, right now, in the present. "So what's your favorite thing here?"

"Pizza," Hawk answered quickly. "Central Park. Jan." Hawk was watching him. Maybe not with his eyes, but Hawk was paying attention. "What's your plan?"

A plan? He was still in shock that he was here. He got it, though. No one wanted long-term visitors. "I don't have one, per se. I want to get a service dog. I need to get in with the VA. I just need somewhere to stay for a day or two, buddy." The VA would help him find a hostel or a home where he could stay for a while, and if that didn't work, he'd get on a bus and ride until he ran out of money.

"You're welcome to stay. You'll need more than a day or two. I can help get you a dog too. It's a good process. I just want to be sure you're looking forward, you know?"

"I just want to get on with life. Running away from it didn't do me a damn bit of good." All leaving had done was make him hurt more.

"I hear you. We'll help get you on your feet." Hawk looked over at him. "It's good to see you."

"You're the first person to say that to me." He knew he was pretty scarred up, raw, but that was why he'd chosen Hawk to call. Hawk was living his life. Saw wanted that too.

"Then I'm glad I said it."

"Just about there," the driver told them. "Which side of the street, Mr. Destry?"

"We're next to the bagel shop and the Viet-Rice."

There were tons of little shops, interesting places, lights, and it was busy for a Saturday evening, he thought, people wandering around, going places.

"Yes, sir. I see it." Michael pulled up to the curb even though there wasn't really a shoulder, and the traffic roared by on the driver's side. Michael climbed out anyway, walked around the car and opened Hawk's door. "Best everybody get out this side."

Oh Jesus. Okay. Focus. Scoot over. Get out of the car. Stand up. Don't fall. Get your walker. You can do this.

Hawk got out, Buck got out, and he froze for a second, his muscles just refusing to move.

Come on, soldier! Move!

The drill instructor in his brain had him moving, and he made it across the seat.

Michael set the walker as close as possible to the curb, which wasn't really all that close to the car. "You need a hand up, sir?"

He looked at the ground, and he didn't want to fall there. No way. "Please. I'd appreciate it."

The driver helped get him up, supporting him on his good side like he'd done this before, and made sure he got a grip on the walker before getting out of the way.

"You good, Saw?" Hawk asked. Even Hawk's dog was watching him closely.

"Solid. What floor are you on?" If he had to do stairs, he'd just sleep in the parking garage for the night.

"Elevator," was all Hawk said as they headed into the building, which wasn't all that remarkable on the outside. On the inside, though, was a marbled lobby, art deco light fixtures, and a fancy elevator.

"Thank God." He barked out a relieved laugh. "I had a moment of sheer panic, man."

Hawk chuckled and hit the call button. "I think I'd have made January move if I had to do stairs with Buck every day."

"Oh, man. Do you have a good place to walk him?" How did Hawk know where the poop fell?

"Well, he walks everywhere I go, so I don't need to walk him as much, but he does fine on the sidewalk, and he loves the park. That's just a short subway ride."

Buck's tail thumped on the floor. And a second later, the elevator doors opened.

Okay. He got the walker in and stood, back to the doors. He'd have to practice turning around in an elevator. That was awkward as hell, huh?

"Take your time, man. And if you need help, ask. I'm telling you, Jan is good with this stuff."

The elevator bounced and rattled a little on the way up. He could feel each floor go by.

"Do you count the floors?" He kept his eyes open, forcing himself to focus and not think about how he was in a tiny metal box.

"I used to, yeah, because I had trouble seeing the numbers. But it's accessible now, so it'll tell us what floor we're on. Buck knows too."

"Yeah? He's a smart pup, huh? Has he made it easier?"

"Hell, he makes this possible. I'd be stuck in the house without him. Everything is better now."

The elevator started counting off floors, stopping at five, and the doors opened onto a narrow hallway. Hawk stepped out with Buck and held the door for him.

"Thanks." He felt like yelling "beep beep beep" as he worked his way out of the elevator.

"I bet you're ready to get off your feet. We're almost home." Hawk led him down the hall, moving more slowly than he probably needed to. The door at the end of the hall opened.

"Hey, guys." That had to be January, but he couldn't quite see around Hawk.

"Hey, darlin'. I found myself a hot young soldier."

"Yeah? Well, bring him in. I'm collecting hot men."

Hawk laughed and went inside with Buck while January held the door for Saw. It wasn't hard to see what Hawk saw in the man; Jan had that classic handsome playboy look and a genuine smile. "Welcome to New York."

"Thank you, sir. I appreciate the invite." He held out his hand to shake, pleased to see it wasn't trembling.

"Any time. Go have a seat. You want some coffee?" Jan closed the door behind him.

"If someone else is going to have one, absolutely." He moved in, shocked as hell to see another guy moving around the kitchen. Lord have mercy.

"There is always coffee going here. We have this super fancy push-button thing now. Hawk likes to shop online." January must have noticed his look. "That's Jax. He's a good friend. He's joining us for dinner."

"Good deal. Should I go say hi?" He hadn't plopped his butt down yet.

"Come sit, buddy. Jax will flutter in soon." Hawk's grin was wicked as hell.

"Flutter." Jan snorted. "You want coffee too, baby?" Jan dragged a hand over Hawk's shoulders, and he was surprised by the ease and affection in the gesture. Like they didn't give that kind of intimacy around others a second thought.

"Sounds good, darlin'." Hawk kissed Jan's knuckles. "You did good. No panic."

Wait. Hadn't Hawk said a bunch of texts had come in?

"Panic? Me?" January laughed. "I called in reinforcements. He's making cookies."

"What kind?" Hawk grinned wide. "I love cookies. Cookies and pizza and bagels. Everything."

Saw chortled, because he got that. He'd loved mess and being able to chow down on whatever they offered.

"Chocolate chip, of course. I'll be right back."

He watched January go and could see Jan laughing with his friend through the pass-through.

"If you need to lie down, you can head for the guest room any time. Do you have meds or something you want to take?" Hawk took the harness off Buck, practiced fingers moving easily.

"No. I'm good." He'd just take a double dose at bedtime. He could handle that.

Once the harness was off, Buck went from an alert working dog to a playful pet. He put his front paws on the couch and stretched up to lick Saw in the face, tail wagging happily.

"Buck. Behave," Hawk said, grinning. "Sorry, he loves new people."

He scratched Buck's ruff and rubbed his ears. "I love dogs. He's fine."

"Oh, Buck's in heaven. A new person to beg for attention." January set his coffee on the table, then took Hawk's hand. "Coffee, baby," Jan said, guiding Hawk's fingers to the handle. "I didn't ask if you wanted cream or sugar, Saw..."

"Black is fine, thanks. I'm not picky. I grew up on cowboy coffee."

Hawk hooted, and then they spoke together. "Never let the cowboy make the coffee."

"Some lessons are learned the hard way." January took a seat in a comfy chair across from the couch.

Buck turned in circles looking to get comfy, then finally hopped up between him and Hawk and plopped his big head in Saw's lap.

January shook his head. "Welcome to the family, Saw."

"I'm honored, sir." He stroked the pup's head, feeling himself begin to relax.

"Jan, I don't know what's going on in there. Did Hawk put the cooling racks away again because—" The short dark-haired guy from the kitchen stopped with a jerk as their eyes met. His were brown, and he had a piercing in one eyebrow. "Oh. Hi. Soldier cowboy, right? Jax. Making cookies." Jax looked at Jan. "Cooling racks?"

"Did you try on top of the fridge?"

"Of course I did. Not. Did not." Jax hurried back to the kitchen.

Saw kept his head down, made sure his expression was blank—God knew he was good at that. He knew he wasn't a pretty cowboy anymore, but was he that bad? He had two days' growth of beard and hair, so it wouldn't be long before he had his freedom beard.

"Hello, Jax!" Hawk called after the guy and shook his head. "Told you he flutters."

"He's baking, Hawk. Don't pick on him; you're getting cookies for dessert. Speaking of which, are we ordering pizza?"

"Found them!" Jax shouted. "They were on top of the fridge, of course."

"Do you eat pizza, Saw? The pizza here is amazing."

"I eat anything. Y'all order. I got some cash." He wasn't poor, just lazy.

Jan smiled at him and pulled out his phone. "I have a rule. No one who just got off a plane pays for dinner. What toppings do you like best?"

"Anything that's meat or vegetable. I guess my favorite is pepperoni, but sausage is good too."

"Meat or vegetable about covers it. We like pepperoni too. Not Jax. Jax is a vegetarian." Jan was tapping his phone, probably placing an order.

"Mushroom. Jax wants mushroom," Jax said from the pass-through to the kitchen.

"Got it." Jan tapped a few more times, then put his phone down. "All set. Half an hour or so. So how was the trip up here, Saw?"

"Long. I started on standby early, but the Austin airport is good for people watching. There's barbecue." And there was a military booth where a soldier could sit and rest his bones and drink coffee.

"You'll find that barbecue doesn't mean the same thing up here that it does in Texas; it's one of the things Hawk misses most. We visit sometimes just because he has a craving."

"How's it different, man?" He'd had Carolina barbecue, and that was different. Kansas City style was better, but Texas was the best.

"Well, Hawk can probably explain it better, but a

barbecue is a social event up here not a style of food. We barbecue anything you can put on a grill. Hamburgers, hot dogs, chicken..."

Ah. "Oh, a—"

Hawk's voice joined his. "—cookout."

Some people didn't understand that barbecue was a way of life.

Jan shrugged, both hands palm up. "There you go."

Jax came out of the kitchen, went back in and took his apron off, then came out again, smoothing back his hair. "My hands are clean now." One hand shot out toward Saw to shake.

Saw sat up, telling himself to stand up. He could do this. He could.

He could and he did.

Saw didn't feel super stable, but he stood and shook. "Good to meet you, man."

Jax nodded. "You too. Thank you for your service." The smile he got was kind and awkward, but real. "Sorry I was running around before. I kind of get in the zone."

"No worries, man. The cookies smell good." Okay. He was standing. He'd best do his business. "Can someone please point me to a bathroom?"

"Yeah, I got you." Jax pointed. "It's the first door on the left down that hall. You'll know you're in the right place by all the marble."

January snorted.

"Thank you." He used his walker, moving down the hall slow and easy. Soon he'd feel stronger. The doctors swore the more he worked, the better he'd feel.

He found it, and Jax was right. It was shiny. It was a good size for a guest bathroom. Still, he was going to talk to the

VA and find a place as soon as he could. Get out of Hawk's hair.

He would call first thing in the morning. No. No, it was Saturday. He'd call Monday morning and start looking for housing near the VA. Maybe he should go somewhere else. Somewhere cheaper.

He just hadn't known where to go, once he mustered out. He'd called his old friend, and Hawk had said yes.

Saw wasn't feeling like the sharpest tack in the box right now. Still, he was somewhere, and from here, he could go somewhere else.

He leaned against the wall and panted as he managed to pee. *No more thinking. You can think tomorrow.*

3

Jax sighed and sat, climbing up on the arm of Jan's overstuffed chair.

There was a reason that he mostly kept to himself and stayed in his apartment all the time. He made an awful first impression. Meeting new people was so stressful. He'd said hi to Saw in such a hurry the first time that the guy would barely look at him, and then, when he made himself breathe and shake Saw's hand, the guy excused himself to the bathroom.

He took a second and looked himself over, he wasn't covered in flour. He'd showered this morning. Maybe it was the piercing? Hell if he knew. He'd just have his pizza and head home for a second round with Casper.

It didn't help that despite the scars, Saw was hot. He had such pretty eyes. That alone would have made Jax nervous. But for a second, Saw's gaze seemed to try to pull him in, like Saw was looking for something to hold on to. It was hard to understand, but that was how it had felt, even though their eyes had only met briefly. He assumed Saw looked at everyone that way. It was hard not to know anyone or have anywhere to go. He knew because he'd been there. Not like Saw, not anything like Saw, but he understood being alone in the world.

"Jax?"

"Huh?" He blinked as his name registered.

The way Jan looked at him he knew he'd been lost for a second. "Hawk was asking what you're baking this weekend."

"Oh. Profiteroles. They didn't work out." Jax shrugged. "I'm going to try again later."

"He's scared y'all think he's a scary monster, you know. He's hurting and lost and fixin' to bounce as soon as he can. Give him a chance."

"I get it." He nodded. Except he didn't. Not really. He was ready to try though. "He'll feel better after a cookie." Cookies made everything better, right? His chocolate chip cookies tasted like home.

"He just needs a little normal, Champ. We've got this." Jan leaned forward and rubbed Hawk's knee.

"I appreciate it. He's had a tough life, y'all. Swear to God." Hawk shook his head. "But he's a good man, and funny? Whoa."

"Well, New York will challenge him for sure, but if he can do this, he can make it anywhere."

"Isn't that a song, Jan?"

Jan's eyes rolled so hard he thought they might pop out. That would be gross. Cool, but gross.

The bathroom door opened, and the sound of the walker headed down the hall. Okay, that metallic would be creepy if he didn't know what it was.

"Did you need anything you didn't find, Saw? I put some

towels and things on the bed in the guest room." Jan spoke before Saw was even in sight.

Buck got up and met Saw part-way, walking slowly alongside as Saw made his way back to the couch. How sweet was that? Buck was a good pup.

"I'm good. Thank you so much. Y'all are being dear, putting me up for a couple of days." Saw had the brightest coppery hair he'd ever seen, and pale green eyes. Striking.

"Saw." Jan got up and went to Saw, covering one of Saw's hands where it gripped the walker. "Nobody's using the room. Hawk and I already talked about it; we'll give you a key and you can come and go when you need to. Okay? We're not rushing you out. Sometimes people need a hand up, and we're happy to give that to you. Honestly."

This was one of the things Jax admired about Jan. He had room for everyone in every sense of the word. It was one of the things that made Jan such a good friend.

"Thank you, Sir. I just... I reckoned Hawk could help me figure things a little bit. Y'all are good men." That smile lit Saw's face up.

"He can. You're in the right place." Jan got out of Saw's way.

Jax racked his brain, trying to think of something to say or ask, but everything kept coming back to Saw's past or his circumstances and that seemed really... wrong. *Where are you from, what did you do in the army, didn't you used to rodeo...* nope. All bad. But when he caught Saw glance over at him, he knew he had to say something.

"Have you always had that great hair?"

What? What the hell was that? Dammit.

Saw chuckled, the sound rusty and unused. "Well, this is the longest it's been in a long time, but yes. I was born a penny top. Thanks. Are the cookies as good as they smell?"

Jax jumped on that. "You want one? I bet they're cool enough now."

"I would. Thanks. It's been a while since I had a homemade cookie."

"Cool." That made him happy. It made him feel like he was helping. He slid off the arm of Jan's chair. "You want some more coffee while I'm at it?"

"I haven't even had a sip of this one. Lord, I was just out of it for a second." Saw picked up the coffee and took a sip. "Oh. Good."

"Bring out a plate, Jax. We can have dessert first. The pizza's going to be another ten minutes or so."

"Works for me." He trotted into the kitchen and found a plate, which he piled up with two cookies for each of them. He didn't drink coffee, but he poured himself a glass of milk. He passed the plate around proudly. "Hawk is a cookie monster."

"I am. I did without for too long."

"You were always dieting, man. Always." Saw shook his head. "Tons of discipline."

"Jax does his best to fatten us up. He's a baker. That's what he does for a living." Jan took a bite and hummed. "Mmm. So good. And still warm."

"Oh, that's cool. Seriously, lots of art and science together." Saw put his mug down and picked a cookie up. "Oh... melty goodness."

Saw took a bite, and it wasn't a princess bite. No, Saw ate like it was good.

Jax climbed back onto his perch on the arm of Jan's chair and watched Saw chew, feeling like he'd accomplished something. He liked the guy's smile. Maybe he made Saw's day a little better.

Saw's one arm was all scarred and raw looking, and he

kept it close to his body. Jax wanted to look at it, but he didn't want to see it. It seemed like everything about Saw made him want to shy away and lean in at the same time. He wanted to know, but he didn't, because it had to be awful.

Still, the guy might need friends.

Jax could count the things he actually knew about Saw on one hand. Jan had told him Saw used to ride with Hawk until he enlisted in the army. He did some time overseas somewhere, then got in a bad accident. Jax had been expecting to see scars because Jan had warned him, but not scars like that. He'd never seen scars like that. Not even Hawk, who was pretty gnarly in places, had scars like *that*.

"I had a fight with my food processor this morning. The dough just didn't work out. I don't know what it was, because I make profiteroles all the time for clients. Pastry can be so fussy," he said, just to break the silence. "Anyway, I'm glad the cookies worked out. I needed a little redemption."

"What's a profiterthingy? Are they hard?" Saw asked, then took another cookie. "These are better than my granny's."

"Thank you." Everyone liked his cookies. He was the cookie king. It was kind of braggy and snotty to say so, though, so he never did. "Profiteroles are like cream puffs, only they're frozen. So they have ice cream or frozen filling in them instead of cream."

"Huh. That sounds more than amazing." Saw blinked over at Hawk like the man could see him. "Have you had this?"

"Yeah. It's fucking ice cream, buddy. Ice cream and pastry."

Jax glared at Hawk playfully. "You have no appreciation

for the subtlety of pastry. I thought losing one sense made the others stronger. Obviously, taste wasn't the one that got the boost." He kind of hoped for Jan's sake that it was touch. *Ooh la la.*

"What?" Hawk's eyes went wide. "It was a compliment. I mean, what possible bad could be in something like ice cream and flaky crust?"

Saw chuckled softly, and wasn't that a wonderful little sound?

"Okay, you're forgiven, cowboy." He'd been fishing for a compliment anyway.

"What's your favorite food, Saw?"

The intercom buzzed just as he asked, and Jan got up. His stomach growled at the promise of pizza.

"Huh." Saw waited for a second, then nodded. "Beef enchiladas. Although chicken broccoli casserole is a close second."

He smiled at Saw. "Nothing wrong with a good casserole. Super easy, reheats well, I'm a fan."

"Yeah, and there's usually cheese. Cheese makes everything better." Saw hesitated dramatically. "Well, not cookies."

"Ha!" Jax bit his lip after his outburst, but still giggled madly at Saw.

"Speaking of cheese, where do you guys want to eat the pizza? Maybe the table is easiest?" Jan set the pizza boxes down on the pass-through. "Jax, can you grab plates?"

"You got it." Jax hopped up and went to the kitchen.

Jax kept glancing over at Saw, watching Hawk help him stand and stabilize. He tried not to be a looky-loo, but...

But he was curious. Did that make him a bad person? He just wanted to understand. Saw was interesting. The most interesting person Jax had met in a while. Granted, he didn't meet a lot of new people hiding in his apartment as much as he did, but Saw wasn't your average guy.

For starters, the guy was named "Saw". Who named their kid after a tool? And a dangerous one at that. Was it short for something? Sawvania? Sawerino? Sawman?

Sawtooth. That had to be it.

He grabbed the plates and set them on the table. Saw was just getting seated so he decided he would just ask. "Hey, how did you get named Saw? I mean, you're in a room full of guys whose names are a little off the wall so you're in good company, but... Saw is different."

Saw rolled his eyes. "My momma, God rest her soul, was an English teacher in a tiny high school in East Texas. She told my Aunt Barbara to name me after Mark Twain. She was expecting Samuel Clemens on the birth certificate. She got Sawyer Huckleberry."

Hawk began to chuckle softly, and Saw kept on.

"Not Tom Sawyer. Not Huckleberry Finn. No. Sawyer freakin' Huckleberry."

He grinned. Everybody had a story, right? "I like it. Sawyer's a great name. I guess your mom had a sense of humor, huh?"

"She did, yeah. She was one hell of a practical joker."

"Did you inherit that trait from her?" he asked as Jan put two slices of mushroom pizza in front of him. "Ooh. Thank you."

"You're welcome. Stop asking questions and let the man eat." Jan winked at him, and he rolled his eyes.

"Sorry."

"No, no. It's fine. I've played a few, but I don't think you'd say that about me anymore."

Hawk nodded once. "I can remember once it might have been, huh?"

"A long time ago."

There was a look that passed between Hawk and Saw. Never mind that Hawk couldn't see. He could once, and probably didn't need to see Saw's face to hear whatever was in Saw's voice anyway.

Jax wasn't going to ask that question. It seemed like Hawk was trying to get Saw to say something, but Jax wasn't going to pry.

He was bad at awkward silence though. "Have you had New York pizza before?"

"I've had pizza that looks like this in Austin once. It was downtown on Sixth Street. It was the first time I'd seen a place you could walk up and just buy one slice of pizza."

"Seriously? You can't just buy a slice of pizza in Texas? What's wrong with cowboys?" He broke the crust and folded his slice in half, then bit off the end. Oh. Cheese, sauce... so good. "Mmm."

"I don't know, but we can buy a brisket sandwich any time, any place, so, it's a fair trade." Saw watched all of them and then followed suit, taking a bite.

For a couple of minutes, the table was quiet, and Jax was okay with that because everyone had their mouths full. He ate his first piece pretty fast, loving every mushroomy bite. Hawk looked like he was in pizza heaven too. He wasn't sure about Saw, and he kept glancing over, trying to get a read on him.

Finally, Saw finished his second piece with a groan of what sounded like pure joy. "Y'all are right. This is amazing. I love pizza."

Hawk crowed. "Told you!"

"It's the best pizza ever," Jax and Jan said at the same time. "Jinx! Stop it!"

Jax pointed at Jan. "You owe me a Coke." He couldn't stop laughing.

"Vile stuff." Jan turned his stuffy little nose up and that only made Jax laugh harder.

"Who says 'vile'? Like, for real?"

"Who doesn't like a nice frosty Coke? That's un-American," Saw pointed out, and Hawk stage-whispered.

"Here Coke means Coca-Cola. Not Dr Pepper."

"It does say 'Coke' on the can, you know." Jan was teasing now, straight-faced, but Jax could see the grin pulling at the corner of his best friend's mouth.

"Yeah?" Hawk went wide-eyed. "Show me?"

There was a silence, and then they all cracked up.

The rest of dinner was chatty and light, and they ate almost all of the pizza. Jan insisted on wrapping a couple of slices up for him to take home, and Hawk called him a car like always. He'd given up protesting.

But despite having work to do at home and knowing how tired Saw must be by now, he wasn't ready to leave. It had been a fun night.

"It was great meeting you," he told Saw, offering a hand. This time, it was way less awkward than earlier. "I'm looking forward to making you more cookies."

Oh, lord. Why did he say that?

"I'm looking forward to eating more of them. Do you make snickerdoodles?"

"I do. And they're Jan's favorite, so good call. I'll bring some over soon. Get a little rest. You're in a good place, I promise."

There, that was better. That was more... normal.

"It was nice to meet you, sir. Do you need someone to walk you down?"

That was so sweet he almost said yes. He even wanted to, which was a strange enough thing. But the poor guy needed to get off his feet, not walk that long hall to the elevator. "Thank you. That's nice of you, but Hawk got me a car. I'm all good. Night, everybody." He gave a wave to Jan and Hawk and headed home to duke it out with Casper.

4

Saw slept hard, the pain pills and the comfy bed assuring no nightmares, no waking up, and no restlessness.

When he woke up, it was light outside, and he smelled coffee.

For a second—maybe two—he wasn't sure where he was, but then he heard Hawk calling Buck away from his door.

"He's good, man. I'm just getting up." He sat up, breathing hard, because damn, he was sore. Still, it was Sunday. That meant sleeping in was okay, right?

It took him an embarrassing amount of time to go from bed to dressed to bathroom, but he couldn't make that shorter. He was doing his best, and he managed to make it out to the front room, where Jan and Hawk were watching the TV.

"Morning, y'all."

"Good morning." Jan got up. "Did you sleep okay?"

"Like the dead, yes. Thank y'all for letting me sleep in. I

was wore." And he was feeling a little beaten up, but he was alert, so he'd take it.

"Traveling will take it out of you. Hawk brought bagels back after his walk with Buck. Are you hungry? And there's coffee. I'll show you, and then you should just help yourself."

"I'd appreciate that. Thank you." The more independent he could be here, the less trouble he was. "Teach away."

January showed him around the kitchen and made him a fresh cup of coffee. "Hawk loves the people that own the little grocery on the corner so there is always food in the fridge. Just help yourself. There's a key on a purple ribbon hanging by the door, and that's for you. Download the subway map to your phone, and you'll be good to go."

"It's accessible for the walker?" That was probably important to know.

"Yeah. Not every stop, but most. The app will tell you where the elevators are, and many have escalators too once you're down to a cane. But don't stress it. Hawk has plans to show you around. He spent the morning printing out the paperwork for your service dog. Buck knows the subways as well as I do now." January set a sliced bagel and a tub of cream cheese on the counter for him and grinned. "Leftover Jax goodies live in that covered thing on the counter if you want cookies for breakfast."

"Thanks. They were great. I'll have the bagel first, though." That was one of the things Hawk went on about, after all.

"Good." Jan refilled his own mug and sat with him "What's the most pressing thing on your agenda today?"

"Well, it's Sunday. So I just thought I'd follow y'all's clues." It seemed like a nice way to spend a day.

"Our Sundays are lazy. We watch TV, sometimes a

movie, sometimes rodeo. Jax usually comes to watch a couple of baking shows and stay for dinner. But I'll ask him to hold off until next week, since he was just here last night."

"Hey, if he wants to come, that's fine with me." There was something sweet and easy about Jax, like he was someone a guy could talk to about nothing. Those dark eyes read as kind.

"You don't mind? He's my closest friend, but I know he can be a lot of company. It's fine if you just want some downtime."

"No. No, I just want whatever y'all's normal is." Hawk liked the man, and he liked the way that Jax didn't treat him like an outcast.

"Okay. Well, you'll be an asset then. We'll have bull riding on soon, and you can narrate for Hawk. He gets frustrated with me sometimes, because I'm still getting all the nuances. At least I know most of the names now. He was not impressed when I was saying things like 'the bullfighter'." Jan laughed. "Which one? Does he have a beard? Is he super skinny?"

"Oh lord. Did you get to meet Mackey and them?" He bit into the bagel, humming at the flavor. They were a little chewier than he was used to, but so much more tasty.

"I did. Quite an eclectic bunch of guys. Hawk is still friendly with all of them. We travel out when we can."

"Good deal. They're good folks, as a rule."

"They're not mad at you, you know," Hawk said, and he shrugged.

"I am." He couldn't forgive himself, so how could anyone forgive him?

"Hey, Champ. Hungry?" Jan took Hawk's hand. "We should go maybe, all of us. We could even bring Jax. It could be fun."

"Yeah, don't they have some events up this way, still?"

"They do. Usually one in Connecticut, one here at the Garden, and Skylar Paulson has his event up in Vermont." Hawk fed Buck a bite of bagel.

"Something to look forward to then." Jan hadn't asked why anybody on the circuit would be mad at him. Hawk must have told him the story.

Ollie Gruene had been his best friend, his hand-job buddy, and probably the man he'd have fallen in love with, and he'd been gone in a couple of seconds on an arena floor.

That was part of the life. Everybody told him that, but it wasn't that easy to get over.

He had lost his best friend in a minute, and he couldn't forgive himself for it.

"Saw says he's up for our usual Sunday laziness. I told him he could answer your riding questions today." Jan grinned at Hawk as if Hawk could see the knowing look on his face.

"Absolutely. We'll just chill, watch TV, eat." Hawk looked at one with the world. "Jax coming?"

"In a bit. What did you want for dinner? Are we cooking? Ordering in?" Jan looked at Saw. "We usually order ramen on Sundays; it's Jax's favorite. I don't think it's Hawk's cup of tea, but he puts up with it. We could cook... you could throw something in the crockpot, Champ."

"You cook, Hawk?" That was a trick and a half.

"Jan and I have a couple of things we do, but we need ramen. It's Sunday!"

"You're a good man." Jan kissed Hawk and smoothed out Hawk's hair. Saw tried not to stare and was saved by a text coming in on his phone. He felt it vibrate in his pocket.

JOANNA:

> Hey. Did u make it to NYC? U ok? I sat for a practice test yesterday. I think I did pretty good.

> Hey sister! Good on you. Here and safe. Love you.

His baby sister was trying to become a nurse, and he was damn proud of her. Little Jo was trying to make it without Momma, and she was managing better than anyone thought she could.

She sent him a selfie. She was in her Sunday best, all smiles with her hair done up nice, and there were a couple of other girls in the background.

JOANNA:

> Now u.

"Can y'all come take a picture with me for my baby sister? I think she's convinced I've been kidnapped." He handed Jan his phone.

"You got it. Get in there, Hawk." Hawk moved in closer, and Buck popped up between them just as Jan snapped the picture. "Oh, that's priceless. Look at that!" Jan handed him back the phone. "Buck got right in there like he was the star of the show, Hawk. It's adorable."

Hawk beamed. "Oh, good. I can't believe your sister's old enough to be on her own."

"She's all grown up." Saw shook his head. "I can't understand when that happened. She was a baby yesterday."

JOANNA:

> Looking good! Kiss the pup for me. And the Champ. Love u.

"You go overseas for a couple of tours, and time goes by, huh?"

"Yes, sir, that it does." No shit on that. Time moved different over there.

The buzzer went off. "Guess who?" Jan left him there with Hawk and went for the intercom. "Why don't you guys refill your coffee and sit?"

He made their coffee, and Hawk carried it while he made his way to the front room. They managed to sit down, both of them chuckling at themselves.

"Hey, Jax, long time no see." Jan and Jax hugged like they hadn't just seen each other the night before. "You good?"

"Yeah, I got the baking order in this morning. The second batch went fine. I guess I just bake better in the middle of the night. *And*—" Jax made his way into the living room and set a Tupperware container down on Saw's lap. "—I made snickerdoodles."

"And you're giving them to him? I feel so betrayed." Jan scoffed, taking the same chair he'd been in the night before. Hawk was in the recliner so that left a seat on the sofa next to him empty. Jax jumped onto it, crossing his legs under him.

"These were by special request." Jax smiled at him, dark eyes twinkling.

"Oh, wow. Thank you." He nodded and smiled right back. "Can I try one now?"

"I'm not the cookie police." Jax watched him, and he got the feeling Jax wanted him to try one.

"Good to know." He opened the container and took a

cookie out. He loved the smell of cinnamon. Loved it. The cookie was cakey and tender and warm, and he moaned. "Those are perfect."

Jax sat up a little straighter. "Thank you. You can have one now, Jan."

Jan laughed and stood so he could reach. "Guests first, huh? Okay." Jan hummed happily after the first bite.

Buck came over and sniffed at Jax, and Jax gave him lots of attention. "Hey, buddy. I know, there's a man in your seat. What are you going to do?"

Buck sat pretty, wagging good and hard, paws up.

"Oh, look at that!" Saw approved, all the way.

"He is the smartest dog in the world. Aren't you, pretty boy? Yes, you are." Jax shifted in his seat, giving Saw a better view of Jax's Stranger Things pajama pants. He was pretty sure those were pajamas. And fuzzy socks too, Jax must have left his shoes at the door.

"I like the socks." He might have to get fuzzy socks when he didn't have to worry about falling so much.

Jax looked down at his feet and then up at him, blushing slightly. "Oh. Thanks. Yeah, I come comfy on Sundays. I guess I should have put on real clothes for you since you're visiting and... stuff."

"I'm not real formal. I'm not in pants with buttons yet."

Jax glanced at his sweats, then chuckled. "Oh. Cool. I could do without buttons entirely really. You want me to put those on the table?" Jax gestured to the container of cookies.

"I'll steal one more first." He matched actions to words, and then leaned back into the sofa cushions.

Jax put the cookies down and got comfy. "So, Hawk, are we watching bulls today?" Buck climbed up on the couch between them, which really meant the dog was lying half on him and half on Jax.

The heavy head was warm and soft on his arm, and it was surprising and comforting, all at once.

"I believe we are." Hawk put a hand on the end table.

Jan glanced over. "About... two o'clock, baby."

Hawk slid his hand over and nodded as he found the remote. "Yep. Got it."

"They have a tricky remote with Braille on the buttons," Jax told him. "Hawk is taking lessons."

"Cool." He couldn't imagine trying to figure that out. He just couldn't. This whole 'let's learn where a new center of balance is' was hard enough. Hell, he hadn't known until the rest of the world that Hawk could hardly see, and he and Hawk had emailed a ton from the hospital, from the rehab. Hawk was loving learning things.

"It is cool, right?"

"I'm blind, not deaf, *Joachim*." Hawk put a playful emphasis on the name.

Jax snorted. "Ooh. I'm in trouble. Dad is using my real name. I hate it when you do that, you know."

Hawk waggled his eyebrows. "I know."

"Man, when you do that, it looks like you have caterpillars on your forehead. I love it." He had to tease. Had to.

"Christ, a guy falls asleep against the wrong tree once, and he never lives that shit down."

"Ha!" Jax burst into hysterical laughter. "Caterpillars. Oh, man. The picture in my head!" Saw thought maybe Jax was going to roll off the couch he was laughing so hard.

He chuckled softly, Jax even funnier than the actual event had been.

"That's enough of that, troublemaker." Hawk turned on the TV and found the right channel, no sweat.

Yeah. Yeah, that was cool. Fucking go, Hawk! He loved that—loved how Hawk was living life like he wanted to.

Jax sat up and gave Saw an evil look. "Sometimes, Hawk is just an old cowboy, sitting on his front porch in a rocker, telling me to get off his lawn."

Saw snorted. "Oh, I can see that, all the way. He's totally a curmudgeon."

Hopefully, he said that right. He'd only ever read it.

"He and Jan are going to be like those two old Muppet guys."

"I heard that," Jan said with a snort. "Don't make me send you two whippersnappers outside to run around the house."

"Whippersnappers? Seriously?" He chuckled and shook his head. "I think I'd just have to beat you, man. I'm too tired to run."

"Okay, you get a pass. For now." Jan winked at him. "Who's up, Champ?"

"You tell me, baby."

Saw bet he wouldn't even know any of the guys riding. He'd stopped riding eight years ago. That was a lifetime in bull riding. He'd know some of the bull fighters, but that was all.

He found his chest growing tight.

"Well, we're a few rides in already. I think that's Dalton in the chute."

"I'm going to hit the head. Excuse me." He stood and headed down the hall to splash water on his face. He could learn how to be someone new again. He would. He didn't have a choice.

"Is he okay?" He heard Jax ask before he closed the bathroom door.

He was okay. He was going to be fine. *You breathe, you focus, and you get back out there.*

Saw did his business and washed his hands, then headed back out into the fray. *Bull riding. You know this.* "Did Dalton ride?"

"Two pretty quick buck-offs in a row." Jan shrugged, eyes on the TV.

Jax was watching him though. He glanced over a couple of times like he wanted to say something but didn't. Not right away anyway. Before the next rider left the chute, though, Jax cleared his throat. "You want to help me make some banana muffins?"

He met Jax's eyes, part shocked, part pleased, and part embarrassed. Still... "I'd love to. I can mash bananas like a pro."

"Good. I noticed these guys had a few dead bananas on the counter last night. I hate to see them go to waste, you know?" Jax got up. "We're off to save your bananas, guys."

Jan nodded. "Go for it. No nuts."

"No nuts." Jax sighed. "Like you needed to tell me."

Maybe this was just something Jax did all the time. Jax was in the kitchen baking when Saw had arrived last night too.

"He doesn't like nuts?" He could make about thirty dirty comments about that, but Jan seemed vaguely fancy, so...

"He does. He just has enough on a regular basis—sometimes for breakfast even—that he doesn't need more." Hawk didn't even crack a smile.

"Ah. Well, some guys get tired of them, buddy. You got to watch that..." He had to. Had to.

"Not any time soon." Jan deadpanned without taking his eyes off the TV.

"Good grief, the unbridled testosterone in here is

enough to smother a guy." Jax tossed his head and took off for the kitchen.

"Is that bad?" So maybe it was Jax who didn't like teasing. Good to know. It was weird, because he'd never felt alone once—not at home, not on the circuit, not in his unit —but after he'd hit that mine, no matter how many folks were around, he felt like the only person he could talk to was in his own head.

"No. I'm teasing them because they're so fucking adorable it's disgusting. I love them together." Jax grinned. "Bring on the testosterone."

Well okay then. Fucking adorable sounded about right. "They are a match. Which bananas do you want me to smoosh?"

"The three brownest ones. Have a seat at the counter and take a load off." Jax sat a fork and a bowl in front of one of the stools. "I was going to make these after the movie, but... no time like the present, right? I'm more into the baking shows we watch after riding anyway."

He had to wonder whether that was really true. But Jax was cool not to say he seemed uncomfortable, or really anything other than Jax wanted company.

"I haven't watched in a long time. Everyone is new." That seemed like a harmless truth.

"I can never remember their names." Jax moved around the kitchen like he knew it well. He got the feeling Jax didn't sit still much. "I guess you couldn't get bull riding over in... in, uh." Jax stopped and turned endlessly deep brown eyes on him. "Where were you?"

"Afghanistan, once. Iraq, once." He'd slept a lot. He'd played a lot of basketball and baseball and football and cards.

"Wow. Twice?" Jax's head tilted curiously. "On purpose?"

"You don't get a choice. Your unit goes, you go." He'd known he was going to be deployed, of course. He had been trained as a mechanic. It's what happened. "But I knew when I enlisted that it was a definite probability."

"I couldn't do it." Jax shook his head as he whisked batter in a big bowl, dark bangs falling in his face. "No way. I'm not brave enough."

"It was a way to try and make a difference." It was a lie, and he knew it. He'd run away from Ollie's death. He'd run away from the pain.

"That's cool. Slightly lunatic, but cool. I guess the world needs brave, crazy people." Jax put the bowl down. "Are those pulverized?"

He looked down, surprised that they were mushed. "You know it."

"Scrape them into this bowl, will you? I'll get the muffin tin." Jax turned his back and went digging in a cabinet.

Shit. He scraped the banana into a pile toward the edge of the plate. Then he put the fork in his left hand, using his right hand to close it around the goddamn thing. Now hold it. Don't drop it.

He picked up the plate with his good hand, hoping everything would just slide...

"Jan's muffin tins are—oh. Do you need... uh. Sorry. I can..." Jax reached across the counter and grabbed the fork, not pulling it out of his hand but helping to steady it and scraped the banana goo into the bowl. "Sorry. I should have... I wasn't thinking." Jax blushed and let his hand go.

"Thank you," he murmured. "You're the first person that wasn't a medical professional that's touched my hand since."

"Shit. Did I hurt you? God, I wasn't..." Jax sighed heavily. "That was stupid of me. I'm sorry."

"No. No." Fuck, he was an idiot. "Your hand was warm. It felt good. Thank you. Seriously."

Jax looked up at him and smiled, his whole demeanor changing, his shoulders relaxing. "Oh. Well, then you're welcome." Jax took the bowl and stirred again. "You're right. You're a pro masher."

"It's totally a skill. They need something mashed, they call me." Was he flirting? Was he allowed to flirt?

Jax glanced at him a couple of times. Saw knew now that meant Jax wanted to ask him something but wasn't sure he should. He also knew Jax would, so he waited.

"Does it hurt still?" Jax paused in the middle of putting little muffin cups into the pan. "I mean, you said I didn't hurt you, but does it just... hurt?"

"Sometimes. Mostly when I forget it's been tore to hell and try to use it like I'm used to or after PT." It wasn't embarrassing to answer. It was a little bit of a relief to acknowledge it was real.

Jax nodded. "PT is tough. I saw Hawk do it for his shoulder, and it sucked. It helped, but it sucked." The batter went into the cups one by one with a cookie scoop. "It feels neat. Is that weird? The skin felt interesting under my fingers. The texture is kind of cool. I guess that's... is that okay to say?"

"Yeah." God, yes. It was okay. "It's better than pretending it's not different. I keep expecting it to feel like... plastic. Weird, huh?"

Jax shook his head. "It doesn't. I can see that, but it doesn't." Jax touched him again, fingers tracing lightly over his scars. "I don't know what it feels like exactly, maybe... like a soft leather? I don't know. It's different, but it's not bad different." He got a playful grin. "I mean, I don't know what it looked like before, maybe you had the most handsome hand known to man, but this one seems perfectly good to me."

The touches made his fingers twitch and curl. It was electric, but it wasn't bad. "It was probably more sexy than this one, but I'm working hard on making it functional. Workable."

"Jan said you came up here to find a therapist and stuff through the VA, huh?" Jax gave his hand a pat and then picked up the muffins to put them in the oven.

"Yes. I need more help, so I'm going to go tomorrow and see if the VA has a group home or some such. Some sort of old soldiers' hostel. Then I'll get me a dog."

Jax closed the oven. "Do you have to stay in a group home to get help?"

"No, but I don't want to impose on the guys." He had a goodly amount in savings, and his disability, but he wanted to be frugal, careful.

"Oh." Jax laughed. "Yeah, they're not going to let you do that. I mean unless you insist and have some very good reason why you can't stay here."

"No?" That gave him a little warm feeling, Still, fish and guests, right?

"Nope. You're not their first house guest. I suggest you invest in some ear-plugs though." Jax winked. "The walls are kinda thin."

"I lived in the barracks. I brought some." Exploded, not stupid. Hawk had been notorious before he went exclusive.

"So smart." Jax put his palms on the counter and pulled himself up to sit on it with ease, showing off some muscle. The baker was built. Pretty. He would have torn the man up six months ago.

"So, now we wait for the muffins." Jax kicked his

dangling feet and smiled at him. "Tell me something about you I don't know yet."

Apparently, he was allowed to flirt because that was pretty unmistakable.

"I know how to crochet." True story. He'd had a girlfriend teach him, and the physical therapist had loved that little bit of information and used it. "Your turn."

"No way. What do you make? Afghans? Trivets? Scarves? Teapot cozies?" Jax was teasing him, but it was fun, not mean.

"I used to make hats. A lot of winter hats." Now he made granny squares. Slowly.

"Oh neat. Those will come in handy up here for sure. Okay. Something about me. Hm." Jax looked thoughtful. "I'm not that interesting but... my favorite thing right now is my Great British Baking Show coloring book."

"There's a coloring book for that? Huh. That's actually pretty damn cool." Wow. He had colored a ton in occupational therapy. Those little fucking things were hard to hold.

"Right? I didn't either. It was a present from Jan for my birthday." Jax leaned closer. "Which was last week."

"Happy birthday!" He chuckled softly. "Congratulations on making it another circle around the sun."

"Thank you." Jax looked pleased with his reply, even if the guy had been fishing for it. "What is something you've always wanted to see in New York?"

"Central Park. You see it in so many movies, and as a ranch kid, it seems so... foreign." Everything used to seem bigger than life. It was smaller now, but no less cool.

"Oh, that's easy. Hawk walks there all the time with Buck. Just get up early one morning. It's a bit of a walk though. I could take you on a rolling tour. They have pedicabs that go through the drive."

"Pedicabs? No shit?" That was cool. "If you have time, I do. Thanks. Are you from here? Like originally, I mean?"

"As much as I am from anywhere, yeah. I moved around a lot." Jax hopped down and poked his nose in the oven. "Soon."

"Ah. I lived in one place for eighteen years; then I been on the move."

"Texas, right? What part? How long were you riding?"

"I grew up in Emory. That's northeast." He counted. "I rode junior rodeo for six years, then got my card and rode two and a half." It had felt like a lifetime, a second, all at once.

"That's a lot to give up. Why did—"

"Those muffins smell so good." Jan interrupted, going to the coffee pot for a refill. "Was he helpful?"

"He is a first-class pro banana masher." Jax winked at him.

"Good to know. Life skills."

"I'm gathering them like a squirrel stuffs in acorns."

Jax's giggle filled the kitchen. "Next up, measuring one-oh-one."

"See? Gaining skills like I got nothing else to do." Saw chuckled softly. "I'm going to be marketable in no time."

"I measure things for a living, you know. I'm my own boss even. Everyone starts out mashing bananas." Jax pulled a couple of mitts from a drawer.

"Well, when you two are ready to binge some baking shows come on back." Jan took his coffee and left the kitchen.

"So did your profit-deals come out?" He was actually

interested, if for no other reason than Jax had gone home late to start them.

"Profiteroles!" Jax laughed. "Yes. They turned out just right. I made four dozen of them, and then I made two big trays of éclairs and two batches of oatmeal raisin cookies."

"And you said the éclairs were using the same goo?" There was nothing wrong with his brain, he guessed. "And you made snickerdoodles."

"Oh, the snickerdoodles are so easy; they didn't take any time. I can make those in my sleep." Jax pulled the muffins out and set them on the stove. "I almost did."

"They're the best. Thank you." Okay, those muffins looked delicious.

"You're welcome. I felt like you needed a little... home."

"Yeah. Last night was rough. I slept hard, though, and I'm more solid today."

Jax finished setting out the muffins to cool. "I'm glad. You do look better. Traveling had to be tough."

"Do I need to clean the pan?" He wasn't sure he could do it, but he was too well raised not to ask.

"You don't need to." Jax studied him for a second. "If you... you can if... I'm sorry. I don't know how to answer that question." Jax bit his lip.

"I don't know if I can either." He went with honest. He liked Jax; there was something kind about the man. Genuine. "There's a lot of shit I don't know how to do now, but I'm learning."

Jax looked relieved. "You want to try? I guess you have to do it to learn, right?"

"I can't break it, right? I mean, it's not glass. Glass, I'd worry about."

"Nope, it's metal. It'll make a nice loud noise if you drop it and that's about it." Jax gave him a toothy smile.

"Then I'll try before I sit down." He walked to the sink and leaned hard, focused on the project at hand. At hand. He cracked himself up.

Jax came up and stood with him, close to his bad side. "You've got this. And if you don't? Nobody wants to wash dishes anyway, right?"

"No, but life skills. I'm learning how to make this work." He didn't have a choice.

"Dude, you got the banana thing down, what more do you need?" Jax chuckled and handed him the sponge.

"I'm shooting for being about to pick things up and button my jeans." He chuckled. The hot water felt good, he had to admit.

Jax shrugged. "I guess those are good skills too. The weird dispenser thing is the dish soap. A plastic bottle isn't good enough for Jan, apparently." Jax teased January an awful lot. They had to be pretty damn close.

"No shit?" He pressed it and, sure enough, soap splurted out. "Fancy!"

"Silly. But so very Jan. Gotta love him."

"He's been good to me, and Hawk loves him. That's more than enough." There was something likeable about Jan, something basically happy. Maybe that was being in love.

Jax leaned toward him. "Are you going to wash that or just play with the sponge?"

"I might just play with the sponge for hours." He managed not to blush or grin. "It's nice and squishy."

Jax laughed out loud, scooped some of the bubbles off his sponge, and put them on his nose.

He cracked up, just laughing so hard he had to hold onto Jax to stay upright.

"Nice and squishy?" Jax was giggling pretty hard but still

managed to hold him steady. "I mean, whatever turns you on, man."

"If I was turned on, it wouldn't be squishy, now." Hell, it might not be nice either. Well, for him it would be wonderful.

"This is good to know." Jax snorted and helped him back upright, still giggling in short bursts. "I think you're procrastinating."

"Right. Scrubbing. Bubbles. Cleanliness and godliness and all that shit." He balanced with his bad hand, scrubbed with the good one.

Jax gave him a pat on the shoulder. "I think you've got this. I'm going to just wipe the counters down and stuff, and then we can go sit."

"Good deal." He did the best he could, and he hoped it was good enough, because he was wearing down a little bit.

Jax flopped a dishtowel over his shoulder. "Come on, soldier cowboy, let's get you off your feet."

"Yeah." He pushed himself to his walker and made his way across the floor.

"Okay, breakfast, or a midnight snack or whatever, is cooling for you guys. Is it baking show time?" Jax shooed Buck off the couch to make room for them.

Jan looked between them. "Sounds like you guys were having fun in there."

Jax blushed hard; there wasn't any way of hiding that color. "I told you, Saw is a natural."

"We had a ball." At least he had, and he thought Jax had too. He sat slowly, easing himself down. Okay. Okay, that was good.

"You comfy?" Jax sat with him, closer than before. Too close for Buck to hop up between them.

"I am." He let their legs touch, all the way down. He needed to let his muscles ease, and Jax was easy to touch.

"So... porn?" Hawk asked, pointing the remote toward the TV.

"Wha...?" Jax stammered, voice cracking.

"Food porn. Baking show?" Hawk shrugged, looking innocent but was likely anything but.

"Oh!" Jax tossed his head. "Oh. Yes. Food porn. Haha."

"So when you color Paul Hollywood's eyes, what color do you make them?" He had watched a ton of the baking stuff in the hospital. A ton.

"I don't think there are any people in the book, but if there are, I'll make them blue." Jax shrugged. "Because they're blue. A really nice blue. He's handsome, right?"

"He's got bright ones. My roommate in the hospital thought he was mean. He would have colored them red." He didn't care, one way or the other. He liked watching people make things.

"He's a perfectionist. I get it."

"Don't let Jax talk your ear off. It's Sunday. One of us is always dozing off at one point or another." Jan patted Hawk's arm. "Turn the volume up a little, Champ."

Jax just waved Jan off. "I don't talk over Paul."

"Understandable." He winked at Jax, relaxing deeper into the cushions. "You can explain all I don't know in between."

Assuming, of course, he could stay awake.

5

January was either worried or bored. It didn't take a genius to figure out which, given that Hawk had taken Saw to the VA and to see someone about a dog, and was out in the city unsupervised.

Still, Mondays were almost always a dead day for him, and Jax was getting free sushi out of the deal, so he agreed to meet Jan for lunch. He even put on actual jeans and real shoes.

Jax was late, though, and Jan hated that. He couldn't help it. He ran into Mrs. Schwartz outside the building and she proceeded to tell him all about the roach she killed in her bathroom this morning and how he needed to move because his cooking at all hours was bringing the bugs and the rats.

No one had ever seen a rat in the building, but whatever.

"Jan!" He shouted from halfway down the block as soon as he saw his friend hanging out on the sidewalk waiting for him. That was two fewer seconds he was late, right?

"Hey, Jax." Jan nodded to him, slipping his phone into his pocket. "How's it going?"

"Okay. Good." He sucked in air. "Out of breath. Sorry I'm late."

"What happened? You look aggravated."

I ran from the subway so you wouldn't be annoyed with me? He sighed. Jan would forgive him. "Dragon Lady Schwartz." He pulled open the door. "After you."

"Oh, man. She's a bitch. Are you causing the plague this time?" Jan winked at him, and yeah, Jan forgave him.

"Rodents. Roaches are invading. Invisible rats are coming out of the kitchen sink or something. I wanted to say, lady, I bake for a living. My kitchen is my office. It's so clean you can eat off the floor. Ugh!" She made him insane. He wouldn't be surprised if she had it out for him.

Jan rolled his eyes. "She grinds that axe, doesn't she? You ought to set Hawk on her."

"Yeah? Is he mean? You think Buck would eat her for me?" He let Jan pick a booth, then slid in and crossed his legs under him.

"Buck is good, but he'd destroy anyone that hurt Hawk. And Hawk loves you to death. You know that." Jan handed him a menu and a pencil. "What do you want today?"

"Everything." Jax licked his lips and narrowed his eyes at the menu. "Mmm... spicy tuna roll... eel and avocado? Seaweed salad. God, I'm hungry." He tapped the pencil on the table. "You?"

"I'm going for spicy salmon and a miso soup." Jan rolled his eyes. "I promised the guys they could pick dinner. Neither one of them are interested in baked chicken anymore."

Jax snickered. "No, I bet not. Saw can put it away after two tours, huh?" And Saw still looked good. Beat up, okay, but the not-beat-up parts were in good shape and he had great eyes and a kind smile. "Did he like the muffins?"

"He did. He ate all of them." Jan wagged his eyebrows. "*All* of them."

"What's with the eyebrows? So he was hungry. I'm glad he liked them." He blushed, though, because that made him happy.

"What's with the blushes?" Jan shot back.

He didn't know, and he wasn't looking at it too hard. "Saw liked my muffins. It's nice, that's all." He sat up straighter in his seat. "Where is the server? Aren't you hungry?"

"Starving." Jan peeked at his phone. "I wish he'd check in."

"Seriously? Give me that." Jax reached over and yanked the phone out of Jan's fingers. "He's a grown man! He has Saw and a dog and money. What are you worried about?"

Saw was slow, but he was focused. Jax admired that about him. He was all about rehab and getting better.

"You make him sound like a... a... circus performer."

"Well? You make it sound like he's flying without a net." Jax shot back, daring Jan to take the analogy any further.

"I—Shut up." Jan started to laugh, though, good and hard, just a big belly laugh.

He grinned and nodded. He'd done his job. Get Jan's mind off worrying over nothing. Jan's laughter brought the server over with tea and they placed their order.

Now onto his agenda. "Saw and Hawk seem friendly but they don't seem all that close. Has it just been a while?"

"Apparently, Saw had a breakdown. Like a total breakdown, and disappeared. No one knew where he went. He just went away. Then, about eight months ago, Hawk gets this email from him in Germany, in the hospital."

"Whoa." Saw hadn't even hinted at that. "That's... wow. Why Hawk?"

Jan shrugged. "Hawk's out of the closet, blind, and knew the guy that died. Saw's friend, Ollie."

"Oh, damn. Overseas? Was it the same explosion?" Man, that had to be hard—making it when your friend didn't.

"Bullriding. Ollie died saving Saw's life."

He found himself staring at Jan. "Shit. Really?"

Jan nodded. "Hawk showed me online. The guy covered Saw and got trampled. His head. He was dead before he even knew it. Terrible, man."

His eyes went wide and covered his gaping mouth, horrified. "Oh, god. Wait. Is that why he left riding? Is that why he enlisted?" His whole perception of Saw shifted.

Jan nodded. "He just lost it, and apparently, he joined the service and disappeared. Now he's back, and Hawk thought he didn't know what to do, you know? He doesn't have anyone to go home to—he's got a little sister in nursing school, his mom is gone, he's never even mentioned a dad."

"You're not going to let him move into a group home, are you? I told him you wouldn't. Hawk wouldn't, right?" He was suddenly worried that Saw would just disappear again. Why that worried him so much was a little hard to put his finger on, but the poor guy... Saw needed people around that would make him feel like he mattered.

"A group home? No. No, he can stay with us until he figures something out. He's not dumb or lazy. He'll get a plan fast. We might have to stress it once Saw gets a service dog. I don't think there's room for two."

He thought he remembered getting Buck took a little time for Hawk. "Saw will figure things out by then. He's, like, zeroed in on relearning useful things. He knows what he needs." Whether Saw knew what New York could offer him was another thing, but surely there were people at the VA who could help with that?

Ollie. He was going to look up that YouTube video when he got home later. He didn't want to know... but he did. Seemed like a lot about Saw was like that.

"Ooh. Food." He leaned back as the server laid out their food and refilled their tea.

"It's so pretty, isn't it? That must take a certain amount of patience, like your job." Jan looked at the sushi roll, then started with his soup.

"So pretty." He liked that, the way Jan always made his job sound important. Like what he did was more than just mixing some flour and sugar together. Jan got it.

He picked up his chopsticks and started with the avocado. "So... Saw is out? Can he be out at the VA?"

"I—Well, I know he can be. I assumed so, because he never flinched about me and Hawk. He doesn't seem like the type to hide himself."

He had no idea why he'd asked that question. None. Zero.

That was his story and he was sticking to it. He nodded and took a bite, humming at how good it was.

"God, spicy goodness. I love this shit." Jan moaned, diving into the sushi. Hawk never came with them for sushi. Not ever.

He'd never asked why. Sushi wasn't everyone's taste, and this was kind of his thing with January anyway. They'd been meeting here for sushi forever.

Jan's phone vibrated and he handed it back over. He knew Jan worried. There were worse things than wanting your lover to be safe, right?

"Is it him?"

"It is. They're there, waiting in a line. Saw's exhausted. Hawk says he's getting a car to bring them home when they're done." Jan nodded. "He's still recovering, but he's a macho little fuck."

"He was a bull rider. Isn't that kind of part of the gig?" He grinned at Jan. Hawk was the same way.

"I think so. I really do, man. There's something about the way they walk." Jan's expression went a little distant, a little moony.

He snorted. "They walk a little different with a walker." But there was still something... something he liked.

"A little, but he's walking. I don't know that I would be."

"I told him he was way more brave than me. I couldn't do it. Enlist? No way." He admired that about Saw. A lot. Saw was brave.

"I'm glad you talked to him. He likes being with you. I can tell."

He couldn't stop the blush, but he tried to cover his goofy smile. Jan would pick that up for sure. "He's easy to talk to."

"Yeah? Good deal." Jan met his gaze. "Can you come over for dinner one night? You seem to relax him a little bit."

"Yes," he said too quickly. "I mean, sure. You know me and free food. I have a big order for Wednesday morning, but I could come Wednesday or Thursday if you want." Or both.

"If you could come Wednesday, that would be amazing. We'll do something easy—burgers or something." Jan's grin spread a little. "Is it okay if I give him your number? He asked me if I thought you would mind."

"He asked for my number? Really?" Jax blinked. "I mean, if he wants it, that's fine. I don't mind. He probably just wants more cookies." Saw asked for his number. It might be cookies. He kind of hoped it was more than that. Jax grinned back at January. "Tell him he can place an order Wednesday morning."

"I don't know that he wants your cookies, Jax..." January winked at him, teasing hard.

"You think he wants more than my snickerdoodles?" he teased back. That would throw Jan off the scent, right?

"He hasn't even tried your cupcakes yet. I mean, there's icing, mousse, éclairs..." Jan's eyes danced. Asshole. "Pie."

"Okay, okay. Fine. He's sweet. And we got along pretty well. But he needs to focus on his recovery. He just needs friends right now. That's it." That was a legit worry, wasn't it? Getting in the way of Saw's recovery? "He doesn't need to be flirting with basket case midnight bakers that weren't born with a filter."

"Why not? If he's interested in flirting with a midnight baker that's flirting back, that's healthy."

"Flirting is safe." He shrugged. "I'm good at that part."

"Yeah, you are. Anyway, I'll give him your number. He'll be pleased."

He nodded. "Cool. At least he knows who he can text if he can't sleep, right?" Jax grinned. He was a terrible sleeper and he kept weird hours anyway. He finished off the last bite of his sushi. "This was so good. Thank you."

"It was perfect. Thanks for coming out. I needed this."

"It's scary, I know. But if Hawk can stay out of the way of a bull he can't see, he can handle New York City."

"I know. That's why I never say anything to him, never discourage him." Jan shrugged one shoulder. "My worry is my problem, right?"

"Mostly. But I see he knows to check in, so he's taking it seriously too." He didn't get texts that said "Mayday" anymore... Jan had come a long way. Jax uncrossed his feet and stretched them out with a groan before getting up. "So much to do later. This fueled me right up. You good getting home?"

"Sure. Do you need any help?"

"Nope. You go give your man a little love and send Saw to bed. I'll see you Wednesday. Maybe I'll bring Hawk a pie." And wait to see if Saw texted him before then.

"Ooh. Pie." Jan chuckled for him, phone going in his pocket. "Can do. See you Wednesday."

"Bye!" Jax gave January an impulsive hug because the man needed more hugs. He was so wound up. Then he took off for the subway, mind going a million miles an hour.

Pie for Hawk. Saw might call. Or text. He had to make macarons in a rainbow of colors for the next two days. But at least he didn't have to eat. And Saw. Lots of Sawyer on his mind.

6

Saw ate supper and then excused himself to go shower and sleep.

Possibly shower and stretch out and text Jax.

Was that weird? It probably was, but he wanted to say thank you for the cookies and muffins.

So he did his thing, got clean, and settled on the bed. Lord, he'd had the longest damn day, and he knew Hawk was damn tired too.

Maybe texting was a shit idea.

> thnx for the cookies

Still, he sent that, didn't he?

He'd about given up and dozed off when Jax's reply came in.

JAX:

> Hi! Sorry hands were busy making macrons. Can't text and use a piping bag at the same time.

There was a pause, and he watched the three dots dance for a second.

> Oh and ur welcome.

> Send me a picture? Those are cookies?

He hoped they were something neat. Something that Jax wanted to talk about.

What he got was a picture of Jax, grinning and flour-faced.

> Oh. Shit. Did you mean of the cookies?

He got a picture of them too. Delicate-looking things in pink and green and brown and yellow.

> Cookies are pretty. You're better.

He chuckled and snuggled back into the pillows.

> You're kind. I'm a mess right now! Did you kick ass at the VA?

> Tried. Lots of paperwork.

Lots of red tape. Still, it was started. He'd started the ball rolling. That was important. Hawk had asked him to stay until he found a safe place to live.

> Jan said you were in a line. Did you get to drop off the paperwork for your dog too?

> Yeah. Got to get more docs to sign off on that.

Because the ten thousand he had wasn't enough.

> Gotta start somewhere. You rock. I'm coming for dinner Wednesday. What do you want me to make for you?

Okay, so that made a heat in the deep pit of his belly. What did he want? To know more about Jax.

> Your favorite dessert.

> OK. That's easy. You'll be surprised though. It's not what you might think. I'm weird that way.

> Nothing wrong with weird. What do you like on your burger?

Do you like ex-soldiers that are deeply fucked up?

> Cheddar and dill pickles. Tomato. Ketchup and mustard. Are we having burgers?

> That's what January says. Burgers and tater tots.

He was a huge fan, and apparently now, so was Hawk.

> Tater tots! He's good to me. I love them. I bet he has Impossible burgers for me too.

More dots danced in a bubble at the bottom of the screen. It seemed like Jax was typing forever, but there it was, just a few words. Just a few interesting words.

> I'm looking forward to seeing you.

What should he say? What was too much? What was too little? He went with,

> Ditto. Sunday was good.

> It was fun. You didn't get annoyed with all my questions.

> I enjoyed talking to you.

He'd felt heard. Hell, he'd felt real and whole, and he'd liked that.

> I'm glad you asked for my number. I would have asked for yours eventually if you hadn't. You can text or call or whatever any time. I don't really sleep. I bake all night sometimes.

> Yeah? Now?

He let himself ask it before he talked himself out of it, because he wanted to.

> Sure. Easier for me to work and talk anyway.

Oh. Oh, okay. That was a fast yes. Not a 'gee I don't know' yes. He grabbed his earphones and dialed.

"Hey, soldier cowboy. Is everyone else asleep?" Jax sounded wide awake, and there was some soft music in the background he couldn't quite make out.

"I don't know. I showered and came to stretch out. It was a long day on my feet. How are you? The macrons are pretty."

"Thanks. They're work, but they're worth it. I'm fine. Had sushi with Jan today. Came home and watched *Tron*. Like you do." Jax laughed so easily, like he didn't have a care in the world.

"Yeah? I've had sushi a few times. Me and Hawk had a slice of pizza. It was good." What had been better was Hawk deciding they could get a car and come home. His feet were nothing but blisters. "What's your favorite movie, man?"

"Oh. Wow. That's a horrible question. I like a lot of movies. Have you seen *The Martian*? Or *The Shining*. Or *Alien*."

"No and yes and yes." He chuckled softly. "I like *Jurassic Park* and *Gladiator* and *Eight Seconds*."

Even if *Eight Seconds* broke his heart.

"Dinosaur movies and shark movies are always a yes. I've never seen *Eight Seconds*. I will put that at the top of my list." He could hear Jax working as they talked. It didn't seem to be interrupting at all.

"I love them—monsters. I even watch the old Godzilla ones." He closed his eyes, imagining what Jax was doing. "Is Halloween a big thing here? I imagine there are some wild parties."

"I guess. I always see people out in costume and the bars are packed. Jan and Hawk and I have stayed in and watched spooky movies the last couple. I'm not exactly a wild party guy. I don't have any idea what the kids do."

"Watching spooky movies is the best. Movies and Reese's and a bowl of chili." He did love a big bowl of chili.

"Hawk makes a mean chili when Jan lets him in the kitchen. Also, Reese's are God's gift to mere mortals." Jax chuckled.

"You understand me. I'm not a big partier. I think I did Austin once, when I was at Ft. Cavazos during Halloween.

That was crazy and busy and kind of wonderful." He'd laughed his ass off at the wild costumes.

"There's a parade in the Village, I've been to watch that a couple of times, but honestly, I get cold and then I get cranky, and that's totally un-fun." He could hear a whisk going a million miles an hour. "I could use your banana-mashing skills right about now. They'd translate really well into whipping cream I bet."

"Do you not use a-a-stirring machine? You know, one of the ones with the fast beaters?"

"Mhm. Bessie does the mixing and the whipping. She's been with me forever. Nine or ten years at least. I just like to start it by hand to make sure everything mixes in with the sugar and flavoring and stuff."

"Oh, cool. What color is she?"

"She's black," Jax said simply. And then like he could hardly contain himself, he added, "With flame decals. She looks like the Firebird Hot Wheels car."

"Dude! That's cool." He had to love a guy that decorated in Hot Wheels. "I have a couple of cool ones in storage. Hot Wheels, not Bessies."

"Yeah? I used to have a million of the regular ones. And I've never had a real car, so this was my gift to myself. It's fun. Where is your stuff in storage?"

"Fort Cavazos. It's outside Austin about an hour." It wasn't a bad place, but he wanted to see snow. Explore. Get away.

"Will you get your stuff when you can get your own place?"

"Yeah, the Army will send it to me. I don't have a ton—a bedroom set, a TV, some movies and books." Nothing fancy. Just stuff.

"Cool. My place is such a disaster. I have two

refrigerators in my living room where most people have bookcases." Jax laughed. "I don't need books I guess."

"I spent a lot of time on the road, so I read a ton." Nothing fancy. Lots and lots of spy novels, serial killer novels, murder mysteries...

"Oh, I read. My bookcase is just electronic. Even my cookbooks. Well, not my really nice ones, but the everyday things."

"Yeah? Tell me what you like to read?" *I want to know everything. Everything.*

"Anything that's not reality, you know? SciFi, Fantasy, epic world-building stuff. *Lord of the Rings* kind of stuff. You?"

"Spies, serial killers, murder mystery. I like David Eddings a lot, though. I read all of the Belgarath books."

"Oh, those are old classics too, huh? I liked them. We should go see a movie sometime. In the theater, you know? I love big screens."

Yeah, but they had to pick ones without explosions. He wasn't ready for that. At all. "I haven't been to one off-base in a long time. Are you pro-popcorn?"

"I am so pro-popcorn. Easy on the butter. Also, Junior Mints."

"We can totally enjoy a movie together then. Large popcorn, two boxes of Junior Mints. I'm in." Wait, were they having a date?

"Yeah? Really? So... you pick the movie. There are dozens in the city. I'm free all weekend."

"Is there a certain theater?"

"I like the big one in Union Square. The Regal. We can reserve seats. But if there's a particular movie you want to see, we'll go wherever." There was a short pause. "Do you... I mean you might be totally sick of my jabbering by then, but if you want to have a quick bite first..."

"I'd love that. I'll pick the movie, and you pick the restaurant?" He felt his heart flutter a little bit, the excitement building.

"Okay. Cool. It's a date! Or... you know, that's just an expression. Sorry." Jax stammered, sounding adorably nervous. "It's a... going out... together thing. Dinner and a movie. That some people call a date, but we don't have to."

God, Jax was cute as all get out. "I'd call it a date. I haven't ever been on an official date with a man. I'd like it if you were the first."

"If I were... oh. That's so sweet. That's amazing. Thank you."

"Thank you for asking. I appreciate it." He more than appreciated it. He was excited.

"I can't wait. Honestly. Is that too... much?"

"If it is, I don't mind. I like it. I enjoy being with you, you know?" He wanted to be interested in someone; he wanted someone to want to be with him. It wasn't practical, but it was true.

"Yeah. Yeah, I like you. I know it's been five minutes, but... well. I'm looking forward to the weekend. And Wednesday. Man, I've never had such a busy social life." He could picture Jax's silly grin. "I should probably let you go though. I have a ton of cookies to finish."

"Yeah. I need to rest. Thank you for letting me call. I'll see you day after tomorrow." He took a deep breath. "Have a productive night, Jax."

"Thanks. You rest and heal up. That's a big job. Goodnight, Sawyer."

"Goodnight." He hung up and took a deep breath. He had a date. Him. With a man. Huh.

Saw thought that was possibly the best phone call he'd ever had.

7

Blue jeans, black T-shirt, purple hoodie, Chuck Taylors. Jax combed his hair, which he only just now realized needed cutting. Damn.

Freshly showered, shaved, clean teeth, a little tiny bit of cologne. Not a sign of flour anywhere on him. In fact, he'd stayed out of the kitchen entirely because he had cupcakes to make and they were calling him.

Jesus, he was a wreck.

Wednesday at Jan's had been fun but also weird. The Impossible burgers were good, actually sitting at the table for a meal and talking like adults was okay. Sitting across the table from Saw, though, knowing they had a date scheduled and that dinner wasn't it? That was nuts.

Their quick hug right before he left had been awkward. That was his fault. He'd hugged Hawk goodbye and then Jan like always and then Saw was just... next. But he'd hesitated, and then Saw hesitated, and then they'd both gone in for it... what a mess.

He didn't mind that little zing between them though. He liked it. It was good energy, even if it was kind of out there and all over the place. Hopefully, it would settle some tonight when they were alone.

Alone. On a date. God, it had been forever. He grabbed his keys and headed for the subway, wondering how Saw was going to get to Union Square. Shit. Maybe he should have offered to meet Saw at Jan's place? Or maybe Hawk would get Saw a car. He pulled out his phone and texted Saw just in case.

> OMW. Would you rather I meet you at home?

SAW:
> On subway. Doing okay. Been practicing.

That was some walking.

> Cool. Me too in a sec. You'll come up in Union Square Park. Grab a seat, I'll find you.

That would give Saw a chance to rest and they could walk to dinner together.

> I'll be there.

Saw sent him a selfie, and the man had trimmed his beard.

He'd trimmed from a wild freedom thing to a more shapely freedom thing. Jax wasn't sure how he felt about beards. He didn't hate them, but he wasn't sure he loved them either. Still, he had no opinion one way or the other on a first date. Saw was who he was, and that was kind of the point.

The trip on the subway seemed to take forever, but it didn't actually. He was just impatient to get his evening started. He was determined to start this evening off better than the last one had ended. It didn't take him any time at all to find Saw after he climbed up out of the subway. Saw was on a nice little bench near some street musicians.

"Hey." He smiled at Saw and took a seat on the bench. He didn't make it awkward. He sat just as close as he figured he should on a first date—right next to Saw without climbing into the man's lap with him.

"Hey, you. It's good to see you." Saw smiled at him, and that was friendly and warm and not weird. Oh yay.

"You made it. How was the subway ride?"

"Less scary than it was Monday. I'm learning." Saw's grin was self-deprecating, but it made him smile back. "Did you get your baking done last night?"

"I did. I wanted to be free and clear tonight. No plans but you." He liked Saw. He wanted to be honest about that, and he wanted Saw to know this was real to him. This might be one time his non-filter might work in his favor.

"That's me. No plans but us. My first night out in New York, our first date, and I'm looking forward to it."

"Oof." He grinned at Saw to make sure Saw knew he was teasing. "No pressure."

"None. We've got this. I figure we need to tell Jan and Hawk we were abducted by aliens."

"Oh, that's a great idea. Jan's pretty cynical, but Hawk might fall for it." He stood. "Ready for some dinner?"

"I am." Saw braced himself on his walker and stood. "Lead the way."

"It's not too far. A couple blocks this way. I went back and forth about where to take you—Thai, Italian, fancy, not fancy..."

"I'm a good eater. Not a bit of fear in trying things." It seemed so strange, after knowing Hawk's riding diet.

"Well, I thought about that. And then I thought maybe we'd do a trendy New York place this time. Somewhere fun." The Union Square Cafe was busy and upbeat. He thought it would be a good first-date place.

"Works for me." Saw seemed to be moving more easily, more naturally, and the lines around his mouth were easing.

"You look good. I should have said that first. I noticed right away." Saw's gray button-down sat nicely on his shoulders. "That's a good color on you."

"Thank you. I bought it yesterday. I wanted something better than a T-shirt."

Saw had shopped for him. How sweet was that? It made him feel like a schlub in his hoodie. But the T-shirt under his hoodie fit him just right, nice and snug and showed him off well. Working out was the only thing he did regularly besides baking. "You didn't have to shop just for this, but it looks great, so I'm glad you did."

He thought Saw was moving pretty well with the walker. Slower than a New York pace, for sure, but people were being cool, and this wasn't midtown.

"Thank you. I need to get a couple of T-shirts that aren't ripped or stained or faded." Saw's gaze dragged over him. "I like the way yours fit."

Ooh. He felt that look in places he hadn't felt anything for a while. And Saw's look made his mouth go dry. "Thanks." He managed not to croak on his reply. He led Saw around some random construction that was clogging up the sidewalk. "Seems like there's always work going on down here. So, did you find a PT?"

"I start Monday. I go three days a week for physical therapy, aqua therapy, and occupational therapy." Saw shook his head, but he didn't seem upset. "It'll make for long days, but then I'll have four days a week to myself."

"Sounds like you'll need some rest in there. That's a lot. But if it's what you need, then it's worth it." He pointed to the retro neon sign outside the restaurant. "We're here."

"Oh, how cool! I like the big windows." Saw did look pleased as hell, gaze searching the place. It made Jax wonder how much of all this he paid attention to.

He opened the door and held it for Saw, and the warmth and busy sounds from inside poured out onto the sidewalk. He was even more excited now. He hadn't been out for dinner in forever.

"Hey, guys, just two?" The hostess looked at Saw, smiling. "What do you prefer? Booth? Table?"

"A table, please."

Yeah, that would be easier to get in and out of, Jax bet.

"You got it. Are you from out of town?" She walked slowly, leading them to a table in the main room but off to the side.

"I'm local. He just got here from Fort Cavazos in Texas."

"Oh, wow. Thank you for your service. You can park that right against the window. Does that work for you?"

"Perfect." Saw smiled at her, then turned to Jax. "If I sit, can you put the walker over there? There's a ton of shit for me to break if I fall."

"You're not going to fall; you've totally got this. But I am more than happy to be your knight in shining armor any day." Jax winked and pulled his chair out for him.

Saw sat with only the barest wince, then smiled at him. "Okay, Sir Jax, if you'd put that to the side, we can eat."

Jax laughed and put the walker out of the way, then took a seat. "Sir Jax. I like it." He pushed a menu over. He knew Saw had some limitations, and he was ready to help with anything. But why make the man feel... less? He kind of felt like it was his job to boost Saw up.

"So, what do you like here?" Saw looked over the menu quickly, just glancing before meeting his eyes.

He squinted. "Green. Uh... I mean, your eyes. Which are not on the menu, but they're pretty." He felt himself blush and looked down, trying to hide in the menu. "Scallops maybe?"

"Oh! Thank you. Most people don't notice. I like that. Yours are deep. I always think that brown eyes like yours feel magical." Saw just made the weird feel normal. No one else did that for him. "Do you want to share the fritti or maybe the squash one? I don't know what burrata is, but I like grapes and pepitas."

"Oh, the fritti sounds good." His eyes weren't really magical, but he liked that Saw thought so. Something about Saw definitely was, though. He tried not to think too hard about it. He had a way of jinxing things. "How hungry are you? We could split that and an entree."

"That's perfect, because popcorn and Junior Mints await us." Saw chuckled, leaning in closer. "I feel like a teenager, you know? Like I'm faking being an adult. I missed feeling this way."

"You know what I learned?" Jax leaned in too. "Everyone is faking it. I promise."

"No shit on that. I had a couple of minutes in the service where I wasn't, and I have to tell you, it sucks. This is better." Saw reached out under the table and barely touched his knee. "Infinitely."

The touch, just like the look Saw had given him earlier, went right to his balls. He couldn't even pretend it didn't. He reached under the table as well and grazed Saw's fingers, but then pulled his hand back and lay it on the table, palm up. "It's New York. We don't have to be in the closet or under the table."

"Oh. Right." Saw chuckled, cheeks going pink, but there was no hesitation in taking his hand, fingers curling around his. "I can get used to this."

He looked at their hands and brushed his thumb over Saw's fingers. "Me too."

"Oh my God. I literally just said to my coworker, if those two aren't a couple, they should be." The server smiled as he stopped at the table and lit the little candle in the center. "So what are the lovebirds having?"

"We're having the fritti and the scallops, yes?" Saw kept holding his hand. "And I'd like a glass of iced tea, please."

Oh. Damn. He was thinking about a beer. He glanced up at the server. "Diet Coke for me."

"Splitting it up, huh? Great choices. I'm Luke if you're looking for me. I'll be right back with your drinks."

"Thanks." He gave Saw's hand a squeeze. "I wasn't sure if we were drinking or not, so now I know. Is it the meds? Or do you just not drink?"

"It's the meds. I take a bunch of muscle relaxants and pain meds, and they don't mix with booze. I got a bunch of lectures about how that can shut your system down. I have to admit, I've worked too hard to be alive to accidentally die." Saw stuck out his tongue and rolled his eyes. "I'm beginning to pare down. In six to eight weeks, I'm hoping to be able to have a beer without stressing, and I'll be in a place where I take a pill when I need it."

"I'm totally supportive. I definitely prefer you over beer." He probably should let go of Saw's hand and stop looking like a moony teenager, but he didn't want to. He thought maybe Saw looked more relaxed, and that's all he wanted for the guy. A little peace.

"Cool."

They sat there for a while, looking at each other, quiet, and it was... easy.

"So, tomorrow I'm making cupcakes. Tons of them... two hundred for a wedding. Four different flavors, with white and sage green and yellow frosting."

"Two hundred? That's... there's only twelve holes in a pan. That's lots. Four flavors? Which ones?"

"Right, so I can bake forty-eight at a time, and they only bake for eighteen minutes. It's the frosting that takes the time." He loved cupcakes though. Almost as much as his famous éclairs. "I'm doing espresso brownie, peanut butter cookie dough, banana crème, and vanilla, which sounds boring but it's not."

Saw's eyes went wide. "Peanut butter cookie dough cupcakes are a thing? How has no one ever told me about this?"

"Oh, they are a thing. So evil. The last time I made them, I ate two and had to make an extra tray. Chocolate cake, peanut butter cookie dough filling, peanut butter buttercream frosting and a drizzle of chocolate ganache. So good." He'd make another tray and bring them over.

"That's like porn when you say it." Saw blinked at him. "That's the coolest thing ever. Did you invent that?"

"Oh, no. But it's my own twist on one I saw someone make on *Cupcake Wars*. The groom is wearing a kilt. Now that's porn."

"That's cool. I had a buddy that did that. I was his best man. He married a sweet little girl. Had a baby five months later."

"Hm. I'm not that good at math but..." He chuckled. "How long ago was that?"

"Oh, Bella's got to be five now? She's a sweet baby. I get

pictures every few days." Saw shook his head. "He mustered out, and he's working in IT now."

"That's neat. Are you like a godfather or something?" He had to be a good friend at least to get pictures so often.

"No, just Uncle Saw. I am Uncle Saw for a few babies, and I like it. I like sending presents."

"So, you're not quite as all alone in the world as Jan made it seem. That's good." He blinked at Saw. "Uh. Not that we were talking about you. Much." He sighed. "Okay, so I was asking about you."

Saw waited as the server left their drinks before answering him. "I had a lot of friends in the service, but they all have lives. I'm trying to figure out things like walking. And it's cool that you are interested enough to ask about me."

"I'm here, right? I'm interested. Very interested." He gave Saw's hand a squeeze before letting it go to pick up his drink. "Do you want kids?"

What? Who asks that on a first date? He sighed. "Hypothetically speaking. Just making conversation. Oh my god." He shook his head.

Saw didn't even twitch. "I love babies, but I need to know I can do what all I'd need to keep up. What about you?"

Oh. He hadn't expected that to come back to him. He probably should have. "I never thought about it. Like, never. I'm a single, gay guy living in New York, you know? I never thought about myself as a dad." He shrugged. "I think kids are cool. I don't personally know any though."

"That's fair. So did you always want to be a baker?" Okay, so that was cool. Just 'that's fair.' Saw made this talking thing so easy.

That was an easy one. "Since the first batch of cupcakes I remember making with my grandmother. They were yellow cake with chocolate frosting. Her favorite. And we put gumdrops on top." He remembered everything about it.

Saw nodded, and Jax got a warm smile. "Oh, that's cool. The spicy ones with the pretty sugar on the outside. I haven't had a gumdrop in a long time."

"Yes, those! I haven't either. I remember liking the purple ones. I don't think I've seen them since I lived with her."

"Huh. I bet you there's a neat candy store in this city we could find some."

Jax nodded. "That'll be our next date. Find gumdrops. And then make cupcakes to put them on." Gram would be proud. She'd said he could do anything he wanted to, and it hadn't totally worked out that way, but he'd made a really good run at it. And he still had a plan.

"Sounds like one hell of a date. I love classic candy stuff. I used to order it for my unit—you can get bags of candy from all these decades."

"You can? God, don't tell me that, I'll gain two hundred pounds." He sipped his drink and the server set their appetizer on the table. "Ooh."

"Oh, wow. That's pretty as all get out."

It was, the crust crispy and golden, the aioli the barest pink. It was gorgeous.

"You first." He wasn't sure how to eat it.

"I'll cut them in half and then we can share and they'll cool down faster?"

He nodded. "Sounds good to me. They're almost too pretty to cut. Almost. They also smell amazing."

"Yeah." Saw frowned down and picked up his fork, put it in the first fried chunk, then he carefully held the fork with his hurt hand, grabbing the knife with his right.

Jax didn't offer to help, not yet anyway. He picked up his Diet Coke and took a sip, letting Saw see what he could do.

He'd been listening, he knew Saw's goals. And he was determined not to be like January and worry and hover all the time. Saw was fine. He'd figure it out or he wouldn't.

If he couldn't, Saw could ask for help.

"If it goes flying, catch it." Saw glanced up and winked at him, then went back to cutting the vegetables.

"Oh, damn. I forgot my mitt." Jax set his drink down, watching. "It's just a little harder than mashing bananas."

"A little, but I got it." It took a few minutes, but Saw managed it, and he didn't do a half-bad job.

"Of course you did." Jax smiled at him and picked up his fork, stabbing it into one of the pieces. "I can't wait to try it."

Saw grabbed a bite of the cauliflower and dipped it in the sauce, popping it in his mouth and munching away. "Ooh, spicy."

"Yeah?" He popped his bite into his mouth too. "Mmm. Good." How neat was this? A first date, new food, and he didn't even know what movie they were seeing. It didn't matter. It was going to be great. "Do you cook?"

"I like to. I don't get to much, but I can follow a recipe, most of the time. I used to help my momma all the time, but it's not fancy—things like cornbread, enchiladas, brisket."

"Oh cornbread. I had never had it until Hawk wanted some for chili. Enchiladas sound complicated to me." Cooking in general was complicated to him.

"They're real simple. I can make beef, cheese, and chicken ones. They're not fancy, but they're tasty."

"I'd love to try one. Maybe we can cook on gumdrop night. I'll make dessert." God, that sounded like so much fun. "Can we?"

He got a huge, happy grin. "Absolutely. I'd love that. Can you tell me where to buy the food? Or maybe we can shop together?"

"We'll go together. We can buy what we need and then go cook it. It'll be fun." Oh, he was looking forward to it already.

They made fast work of the appetizer and their dinner arrived. He was glad they were sharing because the portion was huge. "I love scallops."

"Do you mind cutting those? They look slippery."

That made him laugh. "But that could have been entertaining! You could have shot them across to other tables." He cut them each in half, and some of the larger veggies on the plate too.

"If I'd known that was what we were doing, I would have had them seat us up higher, dammit."

"We really need to plan better." He snapped up one of the scallops. "You know Jan hasn't texted me once. He must trust you."

"I hope so." Saw took the scallop and tried it. "Oh, it's sweet. How cool?"

He loved Saw's sense of wonder—about everything from the subway to dinner to the silly gumdrop errand. It was kind of contagious, the way Saw was so in the moment and paying attention to all sorts of little details. Jax was excited about the movie and their next date, but he made himself focus and enjoy the scallops. He tried to really taste them. "I think the sweet is from the apples they were cooked with. They're so good."

"They are. It looks like it ought to be flaky, like fish, but it's not."

"Have you had them before? I haven't had them here. The menu got all fancy since the last time I was here."

"I have, but not big ones. I had the little ones."

"I didn't even know there were little ones. Cool. Maybe we can try those sometime."

Dinner was good, and he was hungry, but something about Saw kept slowing him down, like he didn't want it to be gone too quickly.

"I got us tickets to a murder mystery movie. I looked for something fantasy, but there's nothing running." Saw caught his gaze. "I'm not ready for hearing explosions and gunfire. Not like that."

Oh, man. He wanted to give Saw a hug. He was glad he let Saw pick because he hadn't even considered that. "Sounds great. And if it's too... anything... we can just go for a walk or something. No worries, okay?"

"This is supposed to be a very classic mystery. Great cast. And if it sucks, then we can heckle. Fair?"

"It won't suck. I meant if it gets too hairy for you, that's all." He smiled. "I like mysteries."

"Cool. I do too. From Sherlock to Poirot to those silly cozy things on the Hallmark channel." Saw winked at him. "Those were on a lot in the hospital."

"Wow. That's... maybe a step too far for me." He laughed and took his last bite. "Mmm."

"Yeah, hospital TV is special." Saw stretched up tall, rolling his shoulders. "That was tasty."

"It was. I'm usually the first to finish but sharing it with you was nice. I wanted to savor it a little."

Saw bobbed his head and beamed. "It was just the right size, too. I have room for the magic corn of popping."

He grinned back. "And the squishy mints of yum."

"You guys look finished." The server set the check down, and he snagged it and pulled out his wallet.

"I—thank you. I've got the movie and dessert and the ride home, okay?"

"Deal. We might split the ride home. Movies are expensive here." He'd planned to treat, this was his invitation, and he picked this place knowing it was a little pricey. So worth it though. He didn't miss the beer at all.

Huh. He didn't miss the beer. He never went out at night without having a drink. That was cool.

"We'll wing it. You and me." Saw squeezed his hand. "Thank you for supper."

"You're welcome." He squeezed back. "This is a good night, right?"

"Better than good. It's been perfect."

Jax got up and got Saw's walker. "The movie theater is back near the subway, is that too much of a hike? Should I get a cab?"

"No, we'll wander. I like walking with you." Saw stood, then got moving toward the door.

Jax held the door open. He really wanted to hold Saw's hand as they walked down the sidewalk, but that wasn't possible. Not yet. Maybe during the movie...

"It's a nice night. I love the square after dark." There were street musicians and the sidewalks were busy, but it didn't have all the neon and flash of other parts of the city.

"It's lovely. Where do you live from here? Is it far?"

"Brooklyn. Over the bridge. It's about half an hour on the subway. Not bad." It was cheaper to live outside Manhattan and he got more room too.

"Oh neat. Do you like it there?"

"Yeah, I love it. It's way more laid-back than Manhattan. And less expensive."

"Less expensive sounds good. I have a bunch of savings and my disability, but I'm hoping I can use the savings to start something, go to school, something."

"Cool. I'm saving as well." He had plans. He wasn't there yet and he wasn't sure he'd ever be brave enough, but he had plans.

"Good deal. Plans are important. I'm planning on making a plan, myself." Saw chuckled to himself.

They stopped at a corner to wait for a light and he rested a hand on Saw's. "No rush."

"No. No, right now the plan is to heal and learn, get a dog, lose the walker maybe. That's not a deal-breaker, though."

"Stick with that plan. Maybe it will take you farther than you think." He squeezed Saw's fingers as the light turned green.

8

Saw found his very best T-shirt and a decent pair of loose jeans. Jax was coming over for the standard Sunday supper, so he wanted to look his best.

The movie had been lovely, fun. They had gone for coffee after, laughing together, even playing a game of checkers.

He had wanted to kiss Jax goodnight, but he'd not been sure how or when, so he'd missed his chance.

Saw didn't want to miss another one. He was going to invite Jax to his room, if he had to.

"You look nice." January watched him cross the living room to the couch with a knowing look on his face. "Jax will be here soon."

"Good deal." It wasn't like a secret that they had gone on a date. That it had been a good evening. That they were going to do it again Friday.

"Are you guys planning to watch rodeo with us or be in the kitchen?"

His cheeks heated. Right. This was a tradition and he'd

fucked with it last week. "Sorry, man. I'll pay attention this week."

He'd shorted out a little bit last week. He'd been tired and wigged out.

"Saw, you're an adult. You can do whatever you want with your Sunday. I was just asking if you had plans, that's all." Jan put a hand on his shoulder. "Truthfully. That was all."

"No plans." Kissing Jax. That was his plan. It was a good plan.

"Okay. Well, we have a good time cheering at the TV, if you're up for it."

Hawk let himself into the apartment with Buck. "I'm home! It's beautiful outside!"

"Yeah? It looks gorgeous." He offered Hawk a chuckle so everyone knew he was grinning.

Hawk bent and took Buck's harness off, and Buck went straight for January for some love, tail going a million miles an hour.

"I got a text, Cade and his wife had baby number three this morning."

"I don't think I've ever known her not pregnant," January said, laughing softly. "Congrats to them. Is he riding today anyway?"

"Not if he wants to keep his balls." Hawk howled with laughter.

Saw rolled his eyes, but he got it. Some things were bigger than the ride.

Their laughter was interrupted by the buzz of the intercom.

"Let Jax in, love? Come on, Buck, let's get you some water." January headed for the kitchen with Buck on his heels.

"I'll go sit down." He felt a little fluttery, a little like he was running a fever.

Jax came through the door a few minutes later, all smiles and with his hands full. "Did someone ask for peanut butter cookie dough cupcakes?"

"Peanut butter... what? If that was you, Saw, you can stay." Hawk groaned and rubbed his belly.

"It was totally him." Jax laughed and put the cupcakes down in the kitchen. "Fair warning, they need milk or coffee. They're sweet."

"Hey, Jax." January gave Jax a quick hug. "I'll make more coffee."

"Sounds good." Jax caught his eye and smiled, then came right over and sat with him. "Hey, you."

Jax smelled good. Saw wasn't sure what kind of soap Jax used, but he approved. "Hey, stranger. How'd the wedding cupcakes go?"

"Great. Turned up the music and cranked them right out." Jax took his hand. "Saved a few for my favorite soldier cowboy."

"They smell good. Thank you. You spoil me." Jesus, Jax's eyes made him so goddamn happy.

"You're welcome." Jax drew light circles on his palm with his thumb, tickling slightly. "Did you have PT yesterday? How did it go?"

"I spent the day in the pool. It was actually good. I scheduled a month of Saturdays. I feel looser in my joints."

"Oh nice. I bet that was great. I'm a little jealous. I love to swim and I don't get to do it very often."

"It felt amazing. Now I know one of my wish-list items is a hot tub." He winked over.

"I like that idea. I'll put it on my wish list too." Jax leaned back in the couch, watching him. "Did you guys decide on dinner?"

"I didn't ask. I was—" Jacking off. "—dreaming about you."

Jax blushed, those dark eyes so focused on him. "About me?"

"Yes." Totally about Jax and his smiling eyes. Lord have mercy, he was a giant dork. Hugungous.

Jax swallowed and smiled. "Sawyer—"

"I made popcorn." Jan set a big bowl on the table. Buck stuck his nose between him and Jax and licked their hands. "And the coffee is done."

"Popcorn, peanut butter cupcakes, and coffee. I'll order four orders of fries and we'll have the perfect supper." Saw chuckled and took a bite of popcorn.

"It's been known to happen," Hawk found his chair and settled into it with a sigh like it knew him well. "But in a bit, you'll start to smell the brisket that I put in the oven before Buck and I went out. And Jan roasted some veggies and potatoes we'll throw back in the oven to warm up before dinner."

Jax blinked. "Jan cooks?"

"Shut up. No, I don't cook. I follow Hawk's directions."

Hawk nodded. "He does pretty well."

Saw thought that it was fascinating—the way Hawk loved to cook. The man had been on a strict diet for two decades and he was blind, but dammit, he was going to learn how to make food.

"Mmm. Dinner." As Jan handed Hawk the remote, Jax gave Saw a smile, then turned on the sofa and leaned back against his side.

"Yeah." He sat there, sort of soaking Jax in, just letting Jax hold his twisted, scarred hand.

Jax turned and smiled at him. "This okay? You're comfy."

"I am. More than." Saw grinned back, trying his best to squeeze his hand.

"Pretty good, soldier." Jax lifted his hand and kissed it.

There was rodeo on, he was pretty sure, but Jax seemed about as interested in watching as he was. Jax was way more focused on him.

He sat, feeling the soft, steady circles that Jax drew on his hand, tracing his scars, sliding on his skin.

"Cowboys are just getting tossed today, Hawk." Jax bent and reached for the popcorn.

"It happens. People aren't genetically developed yet."

Saw nodded in pure agreement. "Those bulls cost tens of thousands of dollars per straw. Us? We're just a squirt and a dribble."

Jax laughed, hard enough Saw could feel it vibrate against his ribs. "Well, we do vary in value. Guys like January came from superior squirts." Jax turned his head and whispered, "Jan's parents are loaded."

"Oh, yes." Jan snorted. "My father's sperm were raised on caviar."

"That explains that fishy smell..." he teased.

"Ha!" Jax lost it and bent over laughing, squeezing his fingers just a little bit too hard.

He grunted softly, pain jumping up his arm, and his fingers twitched.

Jax sat up, stroking his hand and sounding a little panicked. "Was that me? Sorry. Are you okay? Shit. I'm sorry."

"It's okay." *Oh, please, don't freak. It happens.* He turned his hand in Jax's. "See? I'm good. Just a little tender, that's all."

Jax nodded and sighed. "Right. Sorry. I've been spending too much time with Jan."

"I beg your pardon?" Jan pretended to be offended, but it was obviously a long-standing joke.

Jax kissed his fingers again and smiled. "There. All better."

He hummed and nodded, that little buzz of energy making his hand tingle. "Yessir. All better."

"Quit yapping, I'm trying to listen to this ride," Hawk grumbled, but gently.

"Sorry, Champ." Jan brushed a hand over Hawk's arm. "Who's up?"

"Says it's Bry Harrison. He can't be six years old." Saw shook his head. They were getting younger and younger.

Jax shrugged. "Well, he rides pretty well for a six-year-old."

"It's easier when you're younger, right, Saw?" Hawk asked, and Saw had to agree.

"You don't know how bad it'll hurt, later."

Jax leaned into him again. "Baking is way safer. And tastes better."

"Your baking tastes better for sure." He thought about kissing Jax's temple.

"Oh. Uh... hey, Saw?" Jax turned and looked at him meaningfully. "Didn't you say you had something you wanted to show me?"

Thank God he wasn't stupid enough to miss that clue. He wanted to—well, he wanted a lot, but he needed to try a kiss. "I did. Come on back, that way we won't disturb Hawk."

"Oh, sure. Good idea." Jax hopped right up and slid his walker closer.

He stood, balanced, and headed back for the bedroom, carefully not looking at January. He'd said he wouldn't do this.

Saw needed to do this.

Nobody said a word, not even January, as Jax followed him. He could hear Jax breathing behind him as they made their way silently down the hall.

Saw opened the bedroom door and ushered Jax in, closing it behind him. His heart was pounding in his ears, and he felt like he was trembling a little.

Jax swallowed, warm eyes holding his gaze. "I couldn't just sit there..."

"No." He sat next to Jax on the bed. "No, all I can think is that I want to kiss you."

"Yeah. Me too. I shouldn't have let you get away the other night." Jax cupped his jaw and stroked a thumb gently over his lips.

He kissed the pad of Jax's thumb, humming softly. "I wasn't sure how to ask for a kiss then, but I intended to ask today." He blinked at Jax, feeling like time was slowing. "Do you feel it? The electricity between us?"

Jax nodded slowly, his expression full of wonder. "It's new. Not the situation, but this... feeling. This is different. This is... more."

"Yeah. Can I kiss you now?" He leaned in, rubbing their noses together, breathing with Jax.

"Uh-huh." Jax leaned even closer, one hand sliding across his jaw. "Now's good."

He brought their lips together, in a chaste, sweet caress. Jax's lips were soft, silky, and he pressed their lips together again, harder this time. He didn't want Jax to think he didn't mean it.

The hand on his jaw slid around to his nape and Jax hummed, answering him with another kiss, firm and deliberate.

Oh, that felt like heaven on earth. He reached out,

balancing on his good hand, other one on Jax's thigh. Solid. So solid and firm.

"Yeah. That's... mmm." Jax's voice was soft like he couldn't quite get a breath. "Can I—" Jax's tongue darted out and tasted his lower lip.

"Mmhmm." He hummed and opened a little, teasing the tip of Jax's tongue with his own.

"Sawyer." Jax exhaled heavily, lips parting farther and inviting him in. His belly went tight, and he rolled a little closer, needing to deepen the kiss just a little more.

Jax slid over, closing the last few inches between their hips so they were sitting as close as two people possibly could. Jax was warm where their thighs rubbed together and Jax's musky scent was mixed with vanilla and cinnamon. Saw figured that one of the unexpected benefits of seeing a baker was the yummy smells.

When the kiss finally eased up, they ended forehead to forehead, breathing together, staring into each other's eyes. "Wow."

Jax nodded slowly and smiled. "That was a ten, huh?" Jax kissed his nose and traced a circle on his neck with his thumb.

"Yes. And this was just the first one." They could get better, which might end up making him cream his jeans, but there were worse things.

"I don't usually take it slow," Jax admitted, grinning sheepishly. "Pretty much never. But you... you slow me down. In a lot of ways."

Saw got that. His body slowed him down these days, and it made things both maddening and focused, all at once. "I am loving getting to know you, all the way to the bone."

"I am too. I'm enjoying every minute I'm with you." Jax

slid a hand over his chest. "I can't lie though. I want more. More of this. More of you."

"Yes. I—I've never done this sort of thing before. Sex, yes, but in a hotel room or a truck bed, a tent. I don't want to do this wrong." He wasn't sure if it was terrible manners to invite Jax to spend the night in Hawk's guest room, tacky to offer to get a hotel room, or weird to ask to go to Jax's.

"There's no wrong. There's just... better. Do you want to stay Friday night? At my place. After our dinner." Jax worried at his lip for a second. "Is that too forward? Too fast? It's okay. I can be patient. Not that waiting a whole week isn't patient I guess, considering but—" Jax blinked at him, puffed out a breath, and he got another sheepish smile. "Sorry."

"I'd love to. Thank you." He was discovering that straight-forward and honest worked with his Jax like a charm.

"Okay, good. I would love that too." Jax blushed, the warm color climbing up from below the neckline of his T-shirt. "I have a bed, even. It's not huge like Jan and Hawk's, but it's more comfy than a truck bed. And honestly, I crash on my couch most of the time so the sheets are clean." Jax laughed and shook his head. "That was probably more than you needed to know."

"You've seen the bed I'm borrowing right now, so no stress, okay? I am wanting you, not your place." He didn't have a pot to piss in or a window to throw it out of right this second. It would happen. Just not today.

"I'm just... I'm really looking forward to Friday." Jax kissed him again, just sweet and gentle. "And I'm not going to pretend we're not dating out in the living room. Just saying."

"No, that would be silly." And cruel, he thought. It was

one thing when you didn't have a choice, but they did. They didn't have to hide.

"Not that I'm in a huge hurry to get back out there." Jax chuckled. "This is nice."

"It is. It's a strange situation, but wonderful." He had chosen to get ahold of Hawk. He had chosen to come to New York City. Of all the coincidences and permutations, he'd landed here, now.

"So," Jax seemed to be looking for conversation that would keep them sitting right where they were. "What do you think of New York so far?"

"It's big. Fascinating. Busy. There's a lot to explore." He stroked Jax's thigh, nice and slow.

"It's all of that. Yeah." Jax's fingers slid in between the buttons on his shirt and stroked his belly, warm and soft against his skin.

"Why do you like it here?" Oh, that felt good. Everywhere. Tingles. Lightning.

"It's busy. Like you said. There's always something going on, something I need to do. It's up at all hours. It's loud. Louder than this." Jax tapped his temple. "And pizza."

"Mmm. I like pizza." He dared to lean in, nuzzle Jax's temple. "I like this more."

Jax sighed, fingers scritching slightly. "This is better than... anything."

"It is." He brought their lips together, taking another taste, dipping his tongue in to tease Jax's.

Jax melted. There really wasn't a better word for it. Jax just opened up and let his tongue in, let him taste and explore. Let him tease and play. And for a guy that was always moving, Jax was still and settled, focused on him.

They leaned over, stretching out on the bed sideways,

their legs dangling. That brought their bodies together, both of them hard and aching.

Jax rocked into him, breath coming in soft pants. "This is good, right? You're okay?"

"This is good. I'm better than okay, swear to God." He dragged his hand down Jax's spine.

"They're gonna—no, you know what? I don't care." Jax popped open a couple of his shirt buttons with one hand and slid hot fingers over his skin. "Oh, PT is good for your abs, huh?"

"Yeah. I use them to motivate myself." He was proud of how he'd adapted, how he'd learned to function.

Jax chuckled. "They are motivating for sure." Jax slid a hand lower and teased at his waistband, tugged at the snap without opening it, and traced a finger down his fly with just enough pressure for him to really feel it.

His eyes crossed, and his hips rolled, begging for more of that connection, more heat, more pressure.

"Got you. I just wanted to make sure." Jax tugged his jeans open and pushed his shirt up.

"Make sure?" He wasn't following. All he could think of was that touch.

"I'm trying not to go too fast." Jax lowered his fly and tucked his fingers under the waistband of his briefs. "Like you said, I want to do it right."

"I—There are some scars down there, fair warning." He didn't know that it was any different than the scars on his hands, but he wanted Jax to know.

"Fairly warned. They deserve a little attention too." Jax smiled and kissed him again. "Just tell me to stop if you need me to, or move or whatever. I get it." Jax wasn't stopping now though, and those fingers found his curls and slipped farther to circle the base of his cock.

"Oh." His abs clenched and his eyes rolled back in his head, because nothing—nothing—had ever felt so goddamn right.

Jax's fingers played up his length, exploring him, letting him ride the little buzz of energy between them. "Mmm. Feels pretty good to me."

"It works. That's the important part." He had worried there for a few months.

Jax chuckled and stroked him slowly. "I can see that. Really well. Roll back." Jax leaned toward him, encouraging him onto his back, then wiggled his jeans and briefs off his hips. "I'll explore more on Friday, I promise. We'll have all the time we want. All weekend if we want it."

"Sounds amazing." He gasped as the air touched his skin, the cool caress making his mouth water.

"I want to make you feel good, because I don't think you have in a while." Jax got his knees under him and bent to nuzzle where his fingers had been, dark hair hiding his curls. Jax's tongue darted out and drew a warm line from root to tip that started to cool quickly.

"Jax." His brain stopped, his body not quite used to responding to anything that felt so good.

"More? Sure. I'm on it." Jax chuckled before tasting him more thoroughly, first sweeping his tongue around the tip and then gliding it through his slit.

He could hardly breathe, he couldn't think, but he sure as hell could feel. It was stunning.

Jax seemed ridiculously cheerful about what he was doing, responding to Saw's pants and quiet moans with soft chuckles and pleased little wiggles. But the man was very serious about the way he took Saw past his lips and right down to the back of his throat.

He slammed his knuckles into his mouth, his eyes

rolling back in his head. God, he needed, and he wasn't going to be able to hold back. No way.

He figured that was okay because Jax wasn't giving him a second to think—to even think about thinking. Jax was all tongue and lips and throat and wet, wet heat.

All he could do was whimper, warning Jax that he was coming, and then he shot, his entire body convulsing.

The blood roaring in his ears gave way to the sound of Jax, giggling and lapping at his balls, his spent cock. "Oh, that was very nice. That was lovely."

"Uhn." That was the best he had. That was the very best.

Jax hummed and prowled toward him until their noses touched. "So pretty." Jax's kiss was slow and deep, and he could taste himself on the man's tongue. As they parted, Jax ground a needy cock into his thigh with a moan.

He reached down with his good hand, working to fish out the sweet prick. He wasn't a selfish man, and he intended to give as good as he got, dammit.

"Mmm." Jax stretched out on his side like a cat, grinning at him. "I like that, soldier cowboy."

"Do you? You feel good in my hand." He curled his fingers around the heavy shaft, stroking from base to tip. It was so different and yet so similar to jacking himself. "Solid."

"Yeah, I feel pretty... solid. Oh, fuck." Jax swallowed and gripped his bicep hard. "I'm not gonna last."

"I want to see you come." Jax was the prettiest goddamn thing he'd ever touched.

"Oh, fuck. That's... you will..." Jax's little laugh was cut off by a long moan. "Like, now." Jax's hips jerked and he arched hard, a beautiful grimace on his face as he soaked Saw's fingers.

He leaned forward and kissed Jax through the

aftershocks, thanking Jax the way he knew best—just loving on him.

Jax curled into him, cuddling close. "God, I've been fantasizing about that since I met you."

Oh, wasn't that good to hear? "Thank you. You—well, I'd say you blew my mind, but that might be tacky."

Jax laughed softly. "That wasn't a quickie-in-a-truck-bed thing, I promise. You know that, right? I mean... it's real. It's more than getting off."

"Yeah. This is... we got this. You and me." He couldn't stop grinning. Not at all.

"You and me." Jax smiled and kissed him. "That sounds nice. You and me. We. Us. I'm a fan."

"I've never been an us before. You'll have to tell me if I mess it up." He felt... it was like there were bubbles in his chest, like he was ten years younger.

"It's been like a week, Sawyer. There's nothing to mess up yet. But I will if you will." Jax was leaning hard, keeping him close. "I can't wait for Friday."

"Enchiladas, candy store, and us naked in a bed." He grinned and winked, trying to act a little less like a fluttering virgin.

"So perfect. We can feed each other gumdrops after." Jax sighed. "I guess we have to go back out there, huh?"

"Yeah. I think we're being rude." His momma would be horrified. Tickled as a pink twinkie, but horrified.

"It's not like they don't know what we're up to." Jax rolled and grabbed a tissue from the nightstand before tucking back in and doing up his jeans. "You might need to hit the head." Jax seemed amused by that.

"You think? I'll be out in a few. You play hazer for me."

Jax beamed at him. "Hazer. I know what that is. That's

bulldogging. Check me out. I'm a little bit cowboy." Jax's laugh was so sweet. "I've got this."

One more kiss and Jax was out the door.

Saw sat up, a little dizzy, a lot warm, and more than a touch nervous about facing Jan. Hawk, at least, was a known horndog. Not only that, but the bastard couldn't see.

That made it way easier somehow.

9

Three in the morning was a lonely hour for frosted sugar cookies. Jax didn't have to think very hard. He could just do... like a robot. Scoop out the cookies onto a baking sheet, bake them, scoop out more while those were cooking. Cool them, decorate them.

The hour was made lonelier by the fact that his project was mindless and he had too much time to think. Thinking wasn't good. Thinking made him nervous. He liked to just do things and be good at them and make his rent.

He needed a distraction. He hated late-night TV, but he could put on a movie. He wouldn't put music on because Mrs. Schwartz complained, and she'd been trying to get him thrown out of the building for two years.

He picked up his phone to find a movie and texted Saw, not that he thought Saw would be up, but just because he actually had someone to reach out to.

> I don't know why I do this. It's silly. Nobody should be a baker, it's not even a real job.

Whoa. He'd actually hit send on that. "Shit... shit." He

tapped on his text, checked all the options. Could you recall a text message? Like, oops, do-over, please? Saw was going to think he was an idiot. Or throw him a pity party. Why had he sent that?

Stupid three in the morning. Stupid brain. Stupid need to be honest with someone he thought maybe he was... maybe he was falling for.

SAW:

Everything is hard at 3 am. Everything.

Oh, okay. Sawyer was awake. That was too fast a response for just waking up.

Yeah? Maybe you're right.

He did a lot of work at three a.m. though. A lot. What did that mean?

Even sleeping.

No shit. Everything hurts more in the middle of the night. What are you cooking?

Frosted cookies for a 12yo birthday. Sports theme. Soccer balls and stuff. BORING.

He'd love to hear Sawyer's voice right now. Maybe he could call?

Lots of white & black, huh? Yay.

Basketballs. Baseballs. Tennis balls. Speaking of balls... can I call you?

It was the middle of the night. Stupid humor was expected.

Pls.

Saw picked up on the first ring. "Hey, stranger."

"You ever noticed that baseballs is one word but tennis balls is two? I've never texted them before, I guess. I miss you." That was a fact. The two-word thing was too.

"Soccer balls is two, but basketballs is one." Saw chuckled softly. "I miss the hell out of you."

"English is a weird language. You're hurting bad, huh?" Worse at night, that's what Saw had said.

"I don't feel a hundred percent, no. I think it's the darkness, the quiet. There's no distraction."

That was it exactly. "Nothing to keep you from thinking." He nodded as if Saw could see him. "That's why I texted you. Too much air. Did you have PT today?"

"Yeah. It was harsh. Lots of pick this up, put this down, squeeze this, pull that."

"Good stuff though? I mean that's the get-independent-again stuff, right?" He couldn't imagine what it was like when picking things up and putting them down was hard. Saw was amazing. "You rocked it, I bet."

"I got to be honest, sugar. It's embarrassing how hard it was. This is shit you learn before kindergarten."

"I don't think there are too many kindergarteners that have been injured defending our freedom. But you can call me sugar again. That was nice." Jax could tell Saw he was a hero, thank him for his service... but thank-you wasn't going to make it easier on him.

"Good to know. I been calling you that in my head for

days." He heard a soft sigh. "I can't get my water bottle open. Stupid hand. You watching anything fun on the TV?"

Oh that sucked. So simple and so frustrating. He wanted more than anything to help. "*Beetlejuice*. It's a favorite." He'd text Jan and wake him up, but he knew Saw would hate that. "Beetlejuice, Beetlejuice, Beetlejuice!"

"Day-o. Day-ay-ay-o."

Excellent. Saw was with him.

He laughed. Saw just made him happy. And made this sports cookie chore way less boring. "What should I bake for our breakfast in bed on Saturday? Muffins? Some kind of bread? Scones?"

"What do scones taste like?"

"Uh." What did they taste like? "Well, whatever I put in them. There are sweet ones with fruit inside and sugar on top, and savory ones with cheese and herbs... they're kind of dry like... like if shortbread were a muffin." Well that made perfect sense to him anyway.

"Like biscuits? I love biscuits. And muffins. Shortbreads."

"Oh, sort of like biscuits... a little crunchier. I'm going to make them. They go great with coffee. And tea. And cocoa. They go with everything." He'd make blueberry ones and cheddar ones and Saw could taste them.

"I love everything." Oh, that was a happy laugh. "I can't wait. Can I help? I can teach you enchiladas. You can teach me scones."

"Yeah, I'd love to." Jan would happily eat whatever he baked but never showed any interest in learning how to make anything. Nobody ever really had before. "Is it Friday yet?"

"Thursday morning. Early-early Thursday morning. I'm ready for it to be Friday afternoon, though."

"Me too. I haven't hated the last dozen cookies I've decorated while we've been on the phone. Actually, the baseballs are kind of cute. The soccer balls look a little like a snowball with leprosy though. I better get on that."

"Do you mind if I stay with you—talking I mean? I'm not sleepy."

Stay. Please stay. "I'd love the company. Do you mind if I put you on speaker? Then I can use two hands."

"Of course not. Speaker away. I want to just keep you company."

"But you go to sleep when you're sleepy, okay? I will sleep after I deliver these tomorrow. Don't worry." Because Saw might worry.

Jax tried very hard not to worry. Saw was working hard and dealing with shit, and worrying was like, wasted energy. Joking and distracting him and a little... a little... okay. Yeah. A little love. Some tough, because the temptation was to jump in and help, but Saw needed to try to do things that were hard. And some not tough at all, like the other night in Saw's room.

"I don't have any plans tomorrow. Today. Whatever. I was laying here thinking about... bad shit. You're the polar opposite of that for me."

"I don't think I've ever been someone's good shit before." He laughed, putting his phone on speaker. "Can you hear me now?"

"Yessir." He heard sounds of Saw settling, of a soft sigh. "Did you go to culinary school?"

"No. I couldn't afford it. But I don't think I really needed it. My grandparents had a bakery and I grew up in it. When my grandfather died, my grandmother sold it, and I worked in a couple of other bakeries while I took care of her, and one of them was this high-end pastry place. Really neat.

Then I moved here and I found a job for a while. And then another one, and one after that... I'm not real good at being on someone else's schedule, you know? So they didn't last all that long. Now, I do special order projects for a couple of those places and the rest is mostly word of mouth. I keep thinking I should have a website, but my email sure is busy."

Very busy. So busy he had to turn things down pretty regularly or he'd lose his mind.

"That's amazing. Seriously. It took me forever to learn to be on military time. I'm not naturally a morning person. I know country people are supposed to be, but... I'm not."

"Bakers hours are just weird. I grew up having dinner and going to sleep as soon as I got home from school. I don't know if I'm a morning person or a night person. I'm kind of a sleep-whenever-I-can person." And that wasn't much.

He pulled out two trays of cookies, put in two more, shifted the finished ones off the counter, moved the cool ones over to decorate... cookies were so easy he didn't even think about it.

"I wasn't a full-time rider. I worked night-shift at Rubbermaid." The wildly different levels of bull riders was still kind of stunning.

"You'd work all night and then ride the next day? And travel all over the place? Wow." That was crazy. Just about as crazy as he was.

"Yeah, I had an apartment early. I had to make the rent."

"I hear that. I was barely old enough to sign a lease. I had four roommates in a two-bedroom apartment. It was a zoo." Pretty typical for a kid starting out in New York though. Young, hopeful actors were everywhere. Kids with nowhere better to be were everywhere too. "I'm doing better now though. I have a little money put away and I'm making plans." He was close. Just a couple of years away from his own bakery.

"That's cool. Tell me about them? Your plans?"

Ooh. Should he tell? He hadn't told anyone yet, not even Jan. He was worried that if he said it out loud he'd jinx it, or have to admit it was a ridiculous idea. "Well... I was thinking I would open my own shop. A bakery. You know, maybe. It's an out-there idea, I know. Probably won't work out." Silly. It was silly, but he wanted it anyway.

"Oh!" God, he could almost see Sawyer's smile. "I think that's great. I can totally see that. Do you want like an eat-in one or pickup?"

"Rent is crazy on storefronts so I think I'd probably have to start with mostly a pickup kind of thing. I could maybe have one or two tables inside and a couple on the sidewalk in the summer, but a sit-down place is probably a distant future thing." Wow. Sawyer made it seem more real, not less.

"I think that's perfect, because at the start, you don't want to be spending a ton of time bussing tables. So, fancy pastries and cakes? Do you want to do bagels and bread?"

"No. Well, not bagels anyway. That's some heavy competition in this city. I think it would be better to specialize, you know? So yeah, like you said, a pastry shop or a patisserie." He could dream, right? He'd need help for sure, to run it. Someone to deal with the money and someone to help in the kitchen. "It just feels... huge, you know? It's a lot of work to start something like that."

He took the last batch of cookies out of the oven and glared at them resentfully like they were what was standing in his way. Stupid cookies.

"Yeah, it's a lot, but it's a great goal, and you're already building a clientele, so... I think it's a great plan."

He smiled, pleased with Sawyer's support. Saw was so

sweet, and it was totally real. Totally honest. "We'll see, right? It's a goal."

It was three... no, now it was four in the morning. Lots of things seemed like a good idea at four a.m. that probably would never see daylight. But Saw was right. He had a base, he had some connections... it wasn't completely out of left field.

"Basketball, baseball, tennis, soccer... that's enough, right? Am I missing anything?"

"Football?" Ah, of course the Texan would think of that.

"Hook 'em, horns!" He laughed. That was literally everything he knew about football. "No, they're not round."

"Uh...golf ball? Wiffle ball? Dodgeball? Volleyball?"

"White, white, usually white and... white. I think I nailed it. Just a few more left to decorate. I wish you were here." He could curl up and sleep with Saw right now. He really could. He didn't even need more, he just wanted Saw's warmth and... well, Saw.

Saw took a shaky breath. "I—God, me too. Me too. I could hold you."

Jax closed his eyes, heart aching for Saw. "I'd like that. Are you okay?"

"Yeah. I'm telling myself it's a bad idea to call a car and show up at your apartment."

"I was just telling myself that too."

It was a bad idea. It was a really good bad idea though. Would Jan have kittens? Okay. Hang on. Realistically, Saw had limitations that made moving around in the middle of the night maybe not the safest thing. And Saw was hurting and on pain meds... but he wouldn't discourage Saw by saying any of that. "I want to tell you to come. I do. But as much as I want you here, I do have to get these stupid cookies done and deliver them first thing and... but you don't have plans you said, right? So how about you come tomorrow instead of Friday? I have a couple things I need to make tomorrow night, but you can keep me company in person this time."

"Yeah? I can come tomorrow. You just let me know when." The eagerness of Saw's answer was gratifying as hell. He wanted to be, well, wanted.

"Okay. I will. We'll have fun." *We'll have sex. Sex is fun.*

"We'll be together. I can hold you. I can hold you and touch you and just be with you."

"Sawyer?" Jax leaned against the kitchen counter with a sigh. "I don't understand why I feel like I've known you forever."

"I don't know. Maybe it was just time for us to meet. Maybe I'm tired of waiting to meet the right guy."

He hoped he was the right guy. He felt like he could be. Like he should be. "Maybe. It's good, whatever it is."

Like he didn't know what it was.

He'd just never believed in fairy tales until he met Saw. If Sawyer wasn't his handsome prince, he didn't think there could ever be one.

"It is. We are. Good, I mean. Together." Sawyer chuckled softly. "See me. See me make sense."

Sawyer might be the only man in the world as dorky as he was. "I think you should settle down to sleep before the meds really kick in, soldier cowboy."

"You'll call tomorrow when I can come?"

"I promise. I have to drop these sportsball cookies off at ten and then I usually take a nap... you want to come nap with me? Or come after?" He'd be useless for company if he didn't close his eyes for a little while.

"If I fall asleep now, I don't know that I'll be up at ten, sugar. I'm sorry."

"No, that's good. That works. I'll call you after my nap. Okay?"

"More than okay." Saw sighed. "I'm getting stoned, sugar. I'll see you later on today. I swear."

"You will. I can't wait. Sleep well, soldier cowboy." He meant that. He wanted Saw to sleep. To heal.

"Good night, sugar. Get some rest."

They hung up, and it felt amazing, to have had this company. It turned his whole night around.

The basketball cookies were growing on him. He kind of liked the baseballs too. Jax took *Beetlejuice* off pause and got back to work.

10

Saw followed the directions to Jax's, and pushed the button to let his—his lover, his friend, his boyfriend—know he was here.

He had a bag and enough for three or four days, his meds, his chargers, and his iPad. He was exhausted and sore, but so ready to hold Jax, to hold on and rest together.

There was a crackling sound through the street intercom, and he thought he could make out Jax saying "minute" before it went dead. Sure enough, Jax appeared a minute later, and opened the door for him, beaming. "You found the ramp. Cool. Sometimes people think it's the entrance to another building... I should have said. But you found it." Jax leaned in quickly and kissed his cheek. "Hi. Come on, I'll show you where the elevator is."

"Hi. Thank you." Jax looked so good. So fucking good, and he was so glad to be here, to see where Jax lived.

"It's a weird service elevator. I got permission to use it because of all my heavy baking stuff. Mrs. Schwartz had a cow." Jax cackled and led him down the hall, walking slowly without looking impatient or anything. "Let me carry your bag?"

"You don't mind? I brought a couple of things. Some clothes for a few days." He handed the bag over. "How did the delivery go?"

Jax shouldered his bag as they walked. "Oh! Good. I got a nice tip. The mom was happy. Her friend asked for my business card. So, good stuff." The elevator was at the back of the building, a great wide thing probably used to move furniture in and out, appliances, heavy things. Jax hit the button and the doors opened slowly.

"Good deal. That's like the back of a troop loader, man." He stepped into the elevator, the big thing feeling like it would hold him.

"Yeah? I've only seen pictures." Jax curled warm fingers around his on the side of the walker.

Christ, that was warm and wonderful. "Thank you for letting me come over. I missed your face."

"Letting you? Thank you for wanting to come. I needed to…" Jax glanced at him as the elevator doors opened again and squeezed his hand. "This."

"Yeah, I needed this too. Hell, I was two shakes from coming early this morning." Waking up Hawk and Jan was his only reason why.

"It took a lot not to beg you to come last night." Jax chuckled and keyed into the apartment. "Listen to us."

Jax pushed the door open and held it, letting him into a tiny living area. Once the door closed behind him, he saw a little couch with a TV on a table between two silver refrigerators, a whole stack of unassembled pastry boxes, and almost nothing else. No knickknacks, no pictures on the walls, no… stuff.

"I love the refrigerator bookends." This was a little sad,

to be honest, how empty it was, but he couldn't wait to discover why. It wasn't like he had a buttload of shit.

"I'll put your stuff in the bedroom. Do you want to sit? Are you hungry? Sit in the kitchen. I'll be right back."

"Okay." He found a good place and sat on the seat on his walker.

The kitchen was nothing like the living room. It seemed as big as the rest of the apartment. It was bright and clean and much more home-like. There was a cute Felix the Cat clock near the door, tail swishing cheerfully and counting off the seconds. There was a collage of old pictures over the little kitchen table. The one tall window was framed by sheer curtains with petite sunflowers embroidered in them.

And it looked busy. Stacks of cookie sheets, crocks of kitchen tools, oven mitts and kitchen towels hanging on hooks. And a large white fridge covered in neon-colored sticky notes.

"Oh!" Jax hurried back in and started straightening up. "Sorry! I left all my stuff on the seats and... wow. Sorry. There. Chair. And a bench, it's comfy. Sorry."

"Easy. I'm happy, sugar. I'm here, I'm good, I'm with you." He opened his arms, needing contact, Jax's heat. "Come give me a hug?"

Jax set the stack of stuff he'd collected down on the counter and turned around. "Yeah. Please." Jax stepped into his arms and let him lean, his head resting on Jax's chest where he could feel his lover breathe. "You're here."

"Yes." He wrapped his arms around Jax and held on. His rib cage felt like it was full of butterflies, but that was okay. He was here. It was okay.

Jax took a deep breath and relaxed. He felt it; he heard that wild heartbeat settle. Jax tucked fingers into his hair and held him. "You're staying, right? A couple of days at least? As long as you want."

"I'm staying right." They could figure things out later. Right now, they were exhausted and stressed.

Jax gave him a squeeze and leaned back to look at him. "Do you like my kitchen? It's my favorite room. Do you want to go to bed?"

"I think it's amazing." He grinned at Jax, because that was right. Life was short. Eat dessert first. "And yes, please. Now is good."

Jax stepped back and let him get up. The hall was very short. They passed a bathroom and then the bedroom was right there. "This is a nice room too. It has a window and light like the kitchen. It might become my favorite room when you're in it."

Most of the room was the bed, which was cozy looking with a thick, dark comforter and at least four pillows on it. "Can you get by? I know it's kind of tight in here."

"I can. If I fall, I'll land on the bed, so that's not bad." He was pretty good at a couple of steps on his own now, especially when he wasn't scared of falling.

Jax climbed up on the bed and pushed the comforter down, out of the way. "Landing on the bed is kind of the point."

"Exactly." He left the walker and focused on one step after another. No falling. Breathing. The right foot was excellent; the left took attention.

"Hey, look at you!" Jax knelt on the bed and held out two hands for him to catch when he got close, dark eyes dancing.

"I'm trying hard. I'll have a cane for sure, maybe a walker, but I want to be as strong as I can." He took the strong hands and held on. "Here I come."

He put his hurt leg on the bed and balanced with the good.

"Well, the advantage to a walker is you can carry all the groceries in your basket when we go shopping." Jax chuckled and tried to help, tugging on him. "A cane is great for knocking out would-be muggers and blocking the subway doors open."

He made it, mostly. At least until he went over into Jax's arms. Oops.

Jax let his momentum topple them into the pillows. "Ooh. Not very many men throw themselves at me."

"No? That's hard to believe." He didn't dawdle, no sir. He took the kiss he wanted. Hard and happy and horny.

Jax returned it eagerly, fingers gripping his shoulders, lips parting with a sigh to let him have access. He moaned and licked his way in, tasting pure need in his lover.

That drew a long moan from Jax, and the kiss was interrupted as Jax tugged his T-shirt off over his head, the fabric sliding up between them and then disappearing somewhere as Jax tossed it. Then Jax pushed at his shirt. "Now you."

He hadn't been naked in front of a lover since the explosion, and he had a moment of panic. But it wasn't like Jax didn't know, right? He tore off his shirt like he was tearing off a bandage.

Jax grabbed it from him and tossed it, grinning. "Better. Warmer. God, you smell amazing." Jax explored his skin, some scarred and some not, treating it all the same. He drew lines and circles, traced ridges and valleys, chuckling softly when he got a reaction.

"It feels so different, depending where you touch." Some of the scars were sensitive, many of them were dead. It was weird, but wonderful.

"This," Jax spread his hand out over a wide patch of scarring. "This is heavy, I know. It's serious. Totally real. Something we should talk about, and I don't mean to ignore that stuff. But it's the only you I know, I've never known any *you* without all of this so it's just..." Those dark eyes found his and held his gaze. "It's all part of the guy I'm falling for, you know?"

"It's the me I am now. It's okay if I mention it? I can't ignore it."

"Mention it, talk about it, anything you want. I have questions too. Of course it's okay. I want to know everything." Jax kissed him, a quick peck that left him wanting more. "Really. Everything."

"Yeah. Everything, but this touching first?" He dragged his hand down Jax's chest, fingers exploring the sweet, ripped belly.

The muscles jumped under his fingers, and Jax gasped. "Touching first. Talking after. I've been waiting all week to touch you." Jax went back to exploring, fingers moving slowly but purposefully down his side toward his hip.

He untied his loose pants, easing them down, letting his cock breathe. "I want everything. I need you."

He didn't think he'd deny Jax anything at all.

"God, yes." Jax sat up and finished the job, tugging his shoes off for him and sliding his pants down over his ankles, before working off the rest of own clothes.

"Oh damn." He stared at Jax, who was the finest son of a bitch he'd ever seen—strong and firm, dark hair crowning the thick cock. "I could lick you all over."

"Hey, if that floats your boat, go for it." Jax climbed back up next to him, showing off a little. He could tell Jax was proud of his body. "Lick anywhere you like."

He leaned forward, propped on his good arm, and

dragged his tongue up along Jax's rib cage. That salt and sweet was the flavor of his lover.

Jax sucked in a breath, abs expanding and then contracting as he puffed it right back out. "Clever tongue."

"I like how you taste, sugar." He found a nipple, traced around it.

"Mmm. Sugar and spice and everything nice?" Jax's fingers tangled in his hair, tugging just enough that he could feel it.

He lapped at Jax's hard little nub, loving how it tightened, how Jax responded by arching into his touch and rolling onto his back.

"S—sensitive. Those are... just so you know. Extra. A lot."

They must be if Jax was already babbling for him.

"Mmm... So sucking is okay?" he teased, his lips latching on.

"Y-uh-huh. Just..." Jax hissed and rolled his hips, a hard prick stabbing into his hip. "Watch... teeth."

Like he'd bite. He wasn't going for *ow*, more *oh my fucking god yes*.

He closed his eyes and focused, sucking and teasing and playing until Jax's sounds were wild. Then he changed sides.

"Oh fuck. Evil. Love it." His lover wasn't shy with his sounds or his need. Jax's hands flailed and searched for something, finally giving up and tugging on his hair again. He paid Jax back for that little sting by rubbing his beard over one hard, swollen nipple.

"Fuck. Scratchy. No fair! I want to know what makes you crazy too." Jax pushed at one shoulder, but not very convincingly. "Sawyer."

"Kiss me, sugar." He lifted his face for a kiss, for another taste.

"Every time you ask." Jax cupped the back of his neck and kissed him hungrily, tangling their tongues. He drew Jax closer, rubbing them together and jonesing on the fire they created. It was fucking magic, the way they dragged and slid.

Jax spread and hooked his ankles around Saw's thighs, tugging them even tighter together. "You feel so good."

"I feel amazing." He chuckled, but the sound was more husky than funny. He couldn't hide how turned on he was, how much he needed Jax right now.

"Mmm." Jax chuckled, too, rocking under him, giving him a little heat. "Good. You deserve amazing. You deserve mind-blowing, incredible, nirvana amazing."

"Nirvana amazing. I like that." He found himself grinning like an idiot, pure joy just fucking flooding him.

Jax nipped at his chin. "I want to see. I promised I'd explore. Roll on your back, soldier cowboy."

"Bossy!" He laughed, easing on his back, stunned at how brave it felt, to let someone see him. It made him feel that way, though.

Jax gave him a hot look. "You're a soldier. You're used to taking orders, right?"

He saluted. "Yes, sir!"

Used to it, not particularly good at it.

Jax laughed, and combined with the flush in his cheeks, he was just beautiful. Jax pressed his shoulders flat gently and looked down at his chest, discovering Saw's skin with curious fingers like he said he would. Every scar, every patch of hair, every muscle.

Some of it was horrifying—with pink, weird, rippled scars—but a lot of it reminded Saw of a jigsaw puzzle. Of normal skin pieced together with stitches like a hundred little frames.

Jax was quiet for so long he started to worry. Was it too much? More than Jax was ready for? He wanted to say it was okay, even though it really wasn't, just to let Jax off the hook. But Jax started to move, to turn, to straddle his shoulders... and then that hot tongue that had tangled with his a few minutes ago tasted the very tip of his prick.

Oh. Oh, he got it. He craned his neck up and answered the touch, gathering up Jax's flavor on the tip of his tongue.

Jax hissed. "Yeah. You taste good." Jax moved lower, lapping at his balls with a flat tongue.

Saw hooked his right hand around Jax's hips to encourage him down. Then he played follow the leader and licked at Jax's sac.

The sound Jax made was half giggle and half groan, hips pressing down to his mouth. "Copycat."

"Is this where I say 'Mother May I?'" he teased, then turned his head to suck up a mark on Jax's inner thigh.

"Oh!" Jax gasped. "Sawyer. God." Jax rubbed a cheek along his length, and wrapped hot lips over the head.

"Mmm. Sweet." He groaned and shook his head, rubbing Jax with his beard.

"Mhm." Jax hummed and spread Saw's thighs a little, fingers cupping his balls, tongue working down his shaft as his cock disappeared into a hungry mouth. Heat surrounded him, and he gasped, taking a second just to breathe and feel every single sensation.

Jax took it slower than the other day, teasing more, testing him more, changing up hard suction and gentle licks and kisses.

He eventually started reciprocating, working the tip of Jax's cock with his tongue, teasing and dragging and licking. He drew out salty drops of need, even as Jax's mouth liked to make him dizzy.

Without someone listening in another room, Jax was anything but quiet. Saw got hums and little chuckles in response, and the occasional deep groan when his tongue got it just right.

Jax's hands slid under his ass and gripped his cheeks tight, fingers kneading into the muscle. That made him shake a little, like he'd taken earthquake pills, and he focused on sucking, on holding on. When he slid deep into Jax's throat, though, focus was damn near impossible.

He arched and grabbed Jax's leg, tugging him down. He couldn't stop moving, stop gasping for air.

Jax kept him there for an eternity, backing off every time he got close, until finally he felt Jax tapping firmly at his hole. He groaned, fastening his lips around Jax's prick and sucking desperately.

Jax released him suddenly with a loud pop and pulled in a huge breath. "Fuck. Jesus. Your mouth." The words were heated, and Jax sounded breathless.

He nodded, swallowing hard as the tip of Jax's cock slipped in deep. Fuck yes. His mouth. Jax's mouth. Their cocks.

Jax grunted and thrust into his mouth but quickly pulled up. "Shit, sorry! Fuck just feels so... sorry."

"Not sorry. Gimme, dammit." He tugged Jax back in.

"Sawyer!" Jax shouted—*shouted*—his name and took his mouth, diving in over and over. He could feel Jax start to shake before he got the warning. "God. Gonna..."

He sucked hard, feeling like a motherfucking stud. *Give me what I need, man. I want all of you.*

Jax shuddered and filled his mouth with hot spunk, hips stuttering. "Yes. Sawyer. Fuck, yes."

He swallowed hard, groaning around Jax and taking

every drop. Bitter and salty—he'd needed to know all about his new lover.

Jax lapped at him again with a satisfied hum, then took hold of the base of Saw's cock and drove his tongue through the sensitive slit, pushing in slow and deep.

His toes curled, and he cried out, his eyes flying open with the wild sensation that rocked through him.

"Hot." Jax shifted off him, settling at his side so he could watch as his cock hit the back of Jax's throat.

"Oh Jesus..." That was... he... look at that. That was the hottest thing he'd ever seen.

Jax twisted slightly and looked at him, gaze meeting his over the length of his torso. He got a wink and then Jax swallowed around him and rubbed a finger over his hole.

It was all Saw could take, and he shot, coming hard, the world going fuzzy for a second. By the time he could get a breath again, Jax had gone back to exploring, fingers moving down his bad leg, tracing his scars.

"It's ugly, but I kept most of the muscle." The doctors said that was lucky, when it came right down to it.

"Nothing about you is ugly, soldier cowboy." Jax bent and kissed his thigh, stretched up toward the pillows again and smiled at him.

"Thank you." He knew better, but it was a lovely thought, that Jax didn't know him before, so it wasn't horrifying.

"Hey. I mean that. You know what Hawk taught me? Scars are earned. They're badges and trophies." Jax kissed him gently before pulling back to meet his eyes. "They mean you didn't quit."

"No. There ain't an ounce of quit in me. Even when I try to." That was a fact, hand to God.

"See? And that's beautiful too." Jax leaned on his elbow and drew on his skin with a curious finger. "Hey, you."

"Hey. I'm here." He offered Jax a wink, because there wasn't a single other place he wanted to be.

"I'm really, really glad you are. Really. In case you were wondering." Jax leaned down and kissed his chest. "I have to make cupcakes tonight. Not yet... later. Late tonight. Wanna help?"

Did he want to help? Hell yes. He wanted to learn all about Jax's type of magic. "I do. I'd love to. You tell me what to do. I'll help."

The sun was going down, but Jax's smile lit up the room. "Yeah? Cool. We'll have fun."

"We will." He drew Jax in close. "Nap?"

He could have a nap.

Hell, he could have two.

"Is it weird that I love the idea of sleeping next to you?" Jax settled against him, all of their parts tucking against each other perfectly.

"Mmm... I don't think so." He let his eyes fall heavy. "You feel like heaven, right like this, sugar."

"I think I'm going to... sleep well." Jax was interrupted by a yawn.

"Good. If you need me, I'm right here."

"Me too. If you need me," Jax mumbled sleepily. "Me too."

He rested his temple against Jax's, and for the first time in longer than he could remember, he slept hard.

11

"You have a recipe?"

Jax shook his head. He had them, he glanced at them sometimes to refresh his memory, but he'd made all these cupcakes so many times he didn't even think about it. "Flour, sugar, baking powder, salt... it's just in my head." He put a huge bowl in front of Sawyer and dragged over a heavy five-gallon bucket of sugar and another of flour. "But since it's not in yours..." He scribbled out measurements for the dry stuff on a sticky note and handed it to Saw. "There you go. You measure those, and I'll make the filling."

It was weird having help in the kitchen. He was used to working all alone, so he didn't really know how to delegate. But he loved that Saw was interested, people were usually only interested in the finished product.

Saw seemed... happy. Genuinely one hundred percent joyful to measure and pour and stir. What was better, was that Saw paid attention.

Jax thought maybe Saw wasn't used to not having a job.

They got the batter all mixed up, and then he laid out muffin tins on the counter and handed Saw a cookie scoop. "One level scoop in each of these." He put festive little papers in each cup in the tray. "Half full, that's it, or the top gets crunchy. You don't want them to overflow, you know?"

"Right." Saw carefully, slowly did one. "Like this?"

"Yeah." He kissed Saw's shoulder. "Just like that. Are you good? Do you want to sit? I have a tall stool I use sometimes when I've had it with standing at the counter."

"That would be a blessing, yes." What a sweet turn of phrase.

Jax smiled, grabbed the stool from the corner of the kitchen and slid it up next to Saw's walker. "Here you are. I bless you with a barstool."

Saw settled in, perching and looking more comfortable almost immediately. "This works. Thank you."

"Good." He kissed Saw's cheek. He couldn't help it, Saw was just... magnetic. "These will be lemon filled, and the next batch are chocolate and cayenne, filled with an espresso cream. So good."

"Oh, spicy and cocoa and coffee. Those will be tasty. How do you decorate them?"

He grinned. "We'll be piping the frosting on nice and high, a few colorful sprinkles. And..." He opened a box and pulled out the decorations, setting one on the counter. "Gummy penises on toothpicks."

"Gummy..." Saw cupped his crotch. "Toothpicks. Ow."

He laughed, Saw was so much fun. "You should try one. They're... chewy." He giggled and put the box away.

"I've tried one. It was nice and hard." Saw waggled his eyebrows.

"All full now, huh?" Jax winked and switched trays, taking Saw's full one and trading it for an empty one.

"After you finish this, I'm going to make some frosting

and teach you how to pipe it. You can practice while I make the chocolate batter."

"I'll try, but...you know that my hands..." Saw stopped, chuckled. "Yeah, you know, sugar. You see me pretty good."

He knew. He also had no intention of assuming Saw couldn't do something. He gave Saw a warm smile. "I do. I don't see why you shouldn't try."

"Sure. Practice right, and squeezing is fucking good for the strength bit." Saw winked at him, then got back to work scooping. "So what was the first concert you ever saw?"

"Um." His total lack of a regular life was obvious when he got questions like that. "The first one you take me to?"

"Yeah? I'd like to do that. I love live music. Little venues are best, but I've heard tons—bluegrass to gospel, country to rap."

"There's places here. Lots of them. Jan and Hawk go sometimes. I just... nights are busy for me a lot." And concerts were expensive. Drinks were expensive. Every dime he spent was ten cents that could go toward the bakery. "Look at you! Those are perfectly filled cupcake trays. Impressive progress from mashing bananas."

"We can watch on YouTube." The words came out of nowhere, like nowhere.

He blinked at Saw. "Yeah. Totally. I watch stuff a lot when I'm in here." He pointed to the TV on the wall by the fridge. "Lots of Netflix... we could watch YouTube, sure."

He put the cupcakes in the oven and set his timer, then pulled Bessie to the center of the counter to start the test frosting, showing off her flames.

"Bessie!" Saw crowed. "There she is."

Saw remembered her name.

Jax smiled proudly. "Trusty Bessie. Isn't she sexy? She's ready to make some frosting."

"So, frosting is sugar and...whipped cream?" God, Saw was adorable.

He laughed. "Close! Sugar, butter, milk, and flavors like vanilla or whatever you want." He pulled over another sticky note and wrote it down and grinned at Saw. "Do you know how to make whipped cream?"

"You squirt it out of the can!" Saw threw one arm in the air, dramatically.

"Ha! Dork." Jax reached for Saw and tugged him into a kiss.

Saw hummed and kissed him back, then pressed their foreheads together. "You stir the milk a lot to make the cream, and then add sugar, right?"

"Actually, I buy whipping cream in the grocery store because this is not a dairy farm, but that's close enough. Silly." Jax chuckled, threw everything for vanilla frosting into the bowl and started Bessie up.

"That's so cool. I like this baking thing." Saw beamed at him. "I love hanging out with you."

Jax found a pastry bag and a tip and set them up. "You remember that when I keep putting you to work." He filled the bag with the frosting and set out a heavy plate. "Watch," he said, piping out a nice tall swirl of frosting into the plate. Then he put the bag in Saw's hands. "Lefty-righty, doesn't matter. Whatever is more comfortable for you."

"Can we use it again? I mean, if I fuck it up?"

"Yeah. It'll get warm but we can pop it in the freezer for a few minutes. This is totally for you to play with. It's not going on these cupcakes, no worries. You're supposed to fuck it up." Jax moved around behind Saw and guided Saw's hands through one. Jax couldn't remember learning how to do this, it seemed like he'd just done it forever. "Feel that?

Okay. You play. Don't rush. I'm going to make more cupcakes."

Saw was adorable, so focused, lips tight as he practiced one swirl after another, hands red and working.

Half an hour later, Jax had several trays cooling and several in the oven. He'd been watching Saw's progress and not saying much. Saw was his own worst critic. "That one looks great. And this one... I think you've got it. Is it hard on your hands? Take a break."

There was sweat on Saw's upper lip, tension obvious across Saw's shoulders. "This is hard."

Jax reached for the piping bag and gently took it out of Saw's hands. "It gets easier with practice. And everyone's hands get tired, even mine and I do this a lot."

"Yeah?" Saw rested one hand on his upper arm, and it was hot as a brand. "This is one hell of a forearm workout. I mean, you have to have amazing grip strength."

"You'll need less strength when you have more control. It's weird." He lifted his arm and kissed Saw's fingers, then moved around to give his lover's shoulders a little massage. "You're really doing great though. Seriously."

"Thanks. I've always liked learning stuff. This is good."

Yes, but Saw's muscles were tight, hard, and that had to suck.

"The first batch is about cool enough. You want a cup of coffee before we get started? You should probably give that arm a rest. And listen, there are other things to do, lots, so if you get sore or tired, just say so."

"I'd love a cup of coffee." Saw glanced at him. "I have to tell you, sometimes it's like—like I've lived three whole separate lives."

"Yeah? So is this four? Sawyer the Baker's Lover?" Jax cracked himself up sometimes. He snickered and helped

Saw off the tall stool and over to a more comfortable chair at the table.

"That's it." Sawyer grinned at him, the expression fond.

"Best chapter yet. Very suspenseful. Romantic. A little x-rated." Jax started making coffee. He'd sit for a minute too. This was a good time for a break.

"Very suspenseful?" Saw asked. "Are you in suspense?"

"I am. I mean, what happens next? Will Saw and Jax manage to get the penis gummies onto the cupcakes? Or will they eat them all and crash like whales on Jax's lumpy couch?"

Saw blinked, then began to laugh—loud, honest, booming laughter that filled the apartment.

There was nothing better than making Sawyer laugh. Nothing in the whole world. Seeing Saw that happy was better than orgasms.

Sometimes.

It was a tough call.

The real suspense was would Sawyer want to stay in New York? When Saw had his dog and more mobility and his confidence back, would he want to be in this crazy city? Jax wasn't going to ask those questions at one in the morning, though. Not when they were having so much fun.

"You laugh, soldier cowboy, but they're tasty!" He set down a mug of coffee and a little container of cream for Saw.

"I have no doubt." Saw pulled him down on his lap, balancing him on his uninjured leg. "Zero. I like the things you make."

Oh, how wonderful was this? He hooked an arm around Saw's shoulders and tried not to be too heavy. "You're fast, Mr. McMahon. Uh... learner. You're a fast learner, I mean.

The rest is just right." Someone should just tattoo Giant Dork on his forehead.

Saw rested against his chest. "Yeah? Thanks. I'm having a ball."

"I'm glad you came to New York. I don't know what your other ideas were, or if you even had any, but I'm glad this was the one you picked. This has been the best couple of weeks ever." He rubbed noses with Saw. "The best."

"Hawk answered my email. That's why I came. I couldn't go to my sister's—she's in nursing school. I didn't want to stay in Texas. I just rolled the dice and prayed."

It was heartbreaking to hear Saw say that. But Hawk and Jan were good people. "Lady Luck was on my side this time. I hope you stay. I mean, I guess I have to understand if New York isn't your thing, but... I'm asking you to stay."

"I need to figure out things like where to be, what to do, but I know who to be here with." Saw kissed his jaw. "I want to be useful, and I'm getting there. I learned how to try and make swirly icing today."

"You did. And you learned it fast. I'm proud of you. I think you can learn anything you want." He slid off Saw's lap and grabbed his tea. Saw needed to sit a bit, but he had work to do. "Drink your coffee. I'm going to make the butter rum frosting for the vanilla cupcakes that I'm not filling with lemon."

"Holler if there's anything I can do."

"I will."

He didn't. But Saw came over a little while later to help anyway, and made two more batches of cupcakes by himself without asking Jax for anything. Then they giggled their way through putting on all the little colorful gummy penises.

And when they were done, they had a dozen cupcakes

left over. "We're all out of penises." Jax waggled a frosting-covered finger at Saw.

"Oh no! Whatever shall we do?" Saw grabbed his wrist and sucked his finger clean.

"Clean up and have breakfast?" He wanted to say go back to bed, but had to make a delivery in a couple of hours. "Then we can nap when I get home later."

"Sounds like a plan. I know how to cook eggs if you want." Saw headed to the sink and started the water running for dishes. "I can do dishes. You worked."

"You don't mind? I can pack these up while you do that and get them ready to go." He watched Saw at his sink, looked around at all the work they'd done. Together. How much easier, how much more fun it was to do this with someone else? "I love you," he whispered, knowing Sawyer wouldn't hear him over the running water. But he'd said it. He'd made it real.

Next time he'd say it louder.

12

"You're getting stronger." Arthur nodded to him. "You're working hard. I approve."

"Thank you, sir. I'm just trying my damnedest." He was, too. He was working with Jax, fighting to get around. He was switching his sleep schedule on the three to four nights a week he spent with Jax. He was pushing.

"Have you figured out a living arrangement yet?"

"I'm working on it." Jax's place was wee bitty, but he was scared to talk to him about getting another place, so what Saw was going to have to do was find a place that was good for them in the future. At least that's what he thought he should do.

"Physically, you're doing great. So your homework this week is to work on everything else. Figure it out. Settle somewhere. They'll require it for your service animal, you know."

"Right. Right, good deal." He just needed to start looking. He'd ask Jax how that part worked. Maybe... maybe he needed to find somewhere with a yard. If he moved outside the city maybe? And commuted in to see Jax?

God, he had a headache.

Arthur didn't care, apparently, and kept on torturing him, working his hip this way and that. "Hm. You want to talk about it? Whatever is on your mind?"

No, he was good. He didn't want to chat, and— "I don't know how to do this here."

"Mm. I see." Arthur nodded. "Do you know how to do *this* somewhere else? What is *this* exactly?"

"Well... I mean, I know how to get an apartment in Dallas. I know the rules. I don't know about this with a partner. Lover. Boyfriend. You know." He hoped Arthur knew. He needed a friend that knew.

"Probably the same way it works in Dallas. Trust. Boundaries. Lots of talking. A plan. That's how it works for me anyway. Roll over."

"I hate you a little bit." Saw rolled over for his quad stretches. "I want to help him start his bakery, but I don't know if I'm big enough help yet."

Saw would be. He liked it. He liked working with Jax. He wasn't creative or anything, but he had muscle memory. He could learn.

"Well, look at that! A goal. Become big enough to help." Arthur stretched him carefully but firmly. "And you can hate me a little. You're not the first. Just bring me a muffin or something next time. Boyfriend bakes and you don't bring old Art a taste? Honestly."

"Yeah, yeah. You should see me ice cupcakes." He'd got to where he spent Thursday through Sunday at Jax's, sometimes he went Monday after therapy and stayed 'til Wednesday. Jax seemed happy, but yeah, he needed to talk to his lover, see when—if—this was going to get more permanent.

One way or the other, Hawk and Jan needed their space back. He knew that.

"It sounds great, man. No kidding. It's a solid job if you go that way too. A lot of guys buckle under all the pressure of figuring out what's next. Just keep your eyes clear; you know what I'm saying? You got enough going on. Don't go blind too."

"I'm trying. I'm trying to be..." Be what? Healthy? Okay? He was, except when he wasn't. He was great, until he was so tired that he couldn't be.

"You're doing fine. Trying is good. Patience." Arthur stretched him again. That didn't feel fab. That felt like he had a long way to go.

"Jesus. Jesus, Art. Ease up. I have to walk out of here."

"It's not my job to go easy on you. It's my job to push you. Rest up later."

"I know, but it hurts, man. Not just pulling. It hurts."

Arthur eased up, left him lying there and pulled over a chair. "What did the docs tell you? What are your expectations?"

"They think I'll be able to walk with crutches for sure. They say if the arm wasn't blown to hell, a cane would be doable, but I can't hold my weight with that arm. Not yet. Maybe not ever." He took a deep breath. "Probably not ever."

Arthur nodded thoughtfully. "Okay. I know what they think. What do you think?"

"I think I'm a stud. I think I can figure it out. I mean, I don't mind the walker; it doesn't embarrass me." He just wanted to be okay again.

"Okay. Okay good. So, if I'm hearing you right, a lot more hinges on that arm than on getting away from the walker. Right?"

He didn't have to think on that long. "Yeah. Yes, I need the arm to work more than I need to run a marathon."

"Good. Because what hurts in that leg isn't muscle, and it needs much more time. Even then... it's just going to be a hard road." Art ditched the chair. "Your arm though... sit up. You still have good motor control, and the muscle's not pretty but it works. I disagree with your doc. Just don't tell him that."

Honestly, so long as Art stopped, he didn't care. "I never bother. They don't listen. I'm a number. With you—you hear me."

"That's my job. Getting you to *your* goal. Not theirs." Art took his arm and looked it over, testing the muscle, prodding the joints and bones. "Okay. Homework. This is to work on strength and dexterity." Art handed him a contraption to work his hand, with springs for each finger. "Twice a day, every day for as long as you can stand it. If it's sore, don't skip. If it hurts, rest it for a day."

"I can do that. I've been icing and doing dishes. I know that helps." The hot water helped a lot, easing deep aches. He met Art's eyes. "I'm not asking for a miracle. I know I got shit, but I want to be as capable as I can."

He was a cowboy, down deeper than the soldier. Cowboys got hurt. They broke their backs, had their faces busted, broke necks and legs and pelvises. His injury was different, but the result was the same. He was retired. Now he had to take this body and teach it how to do other things.

Art gave him a nod. "I'm the guy that tells people that miracles only happen to people that make them happen. This is good. We've got a plan. I'm going to hook you up with our massage therapist too. Your shoulder needs to loosen up, your hip too." Art leaned closer, grinning. "I'm going to tell you a secret. Guys think the crutches look more macho than the walker, but the walker is a hundred times easier to deal with. And the one you have? You've always got a seat to wait for the subway that doesn't have chewing gum stuck to it. Score."

He chuckled, just about tickled. Obviously, he had a metric shit ton to figure out, but some of it he was doing right. That was important.

"Enough for today, yeah?" Art gave his good leg a pat. "Let me get your paperwork together."

"Sounds good." He slowly got moving, got himself ready for his trip back to... was tonight Jax's? He checked his phone with a grin, seeing if Jax left a clue.

JAX:

Miss you.

Jax's text was cryptic on the surface but very clear to him. He was off to Jax's place tonight. He was starting to think maybe he should be off to Jax's place every night, or their place, or—

He had thinking to do. They had talking to do.

He needed to know where Jax stood in all this horseshit. They needed to make a couple of decisions, even if it was that they didn't know what to do.

So. Decision one: dinner. He'd find it and bring it to Jax's. He could do that. And then they'd eat and talk and see what happened.

"You're all set." Art smiled and handed him his paperwork. "I'm going to put together our plan. You go put together yours."

"Right on, man. Plan ahoy?" He grinned, and he hoped it didn't look as unnerved as he felt.

13

"Ding Dong!" Jax shouted into the intercom, knowing full well that Sawyer wouldn't be able to understand him. Stupid intercom. He'd asked to have it fixed more times than he could count. Maybe he should protest or something? Hold back his rent and threaten not to pay it if the landlord didn't get his act together. With his luck, though, he'd get thrown out instead, and he couldn't afford to be thrown out. He'd lose his—

The door buzzed again.

"Oh. Shit. Sorry." He hit the buzzer to let Saw in. "Oops." Stupid brain wandering off without him.

He was tired. He didn't have to bake tonight, and he wanted to curl up with Saw and send the world away.

It took some time, but eventually Saw knocked on the door. When he opened it up, he found his lover standing there with bags of food, a bottle of his favorite wine, and a couple of novels. "Hey, honey. I come bearing gifts."

"How did you get all of this... let me take... wow." Jax took the bags and the wine. He wasn't sure how Saw managed to haul all of this stuff around, but he wasn't going to ask either. He loved that Saw was figuring things out. "Come in. I'm glad you're here. Thank you for the wine!"

"You're welcome. I'm glad to be here. Can I sit?"

"Anywhere your butt wants to." Saw looked pretty beat too. "What is all of this? I'm going to put it in the kitchen."

"Food for a couple of days. Some snacks. Eggplant parm subs takeout at the bottom."

"You brought dinner too?" Jax put the bags down and pulled out a chair for him. "Sit, baby. Sit and talk to me."

"I did. I didn't want us to have to cook." Saw sat, moving slow, looking a little pale. "Is that okay?"

"Oh, it's great. I'm more than okay. Thank you." He bent and gave Saw a light kiss. "You look exhausted. Tough rehab session?"

"It was. It was a bit of a bitch, you know?" Saw wrapped one hand around his hips.

"Well, I have absolutely nothing on my calendar tonight. No baking. Just rest. And you." He loved the way Saw touched him, just to connect.

"I love that idea. Rest. Hold you. All the good things."

"Exactly." He stepped away to unpack the groceries and found some plates for their dinner. "This is so domestic, right? You, bringing home groceries and dinner. I love it."

"Yeah? I like thinking I'm helping. I like being part of this. Us."

"Us." The word made Jax grin like a fool. He loved being an "us." If he could, he'd keep Saw right here in his kitchen forever. He danced around the kitchen, putting food away. "Are you hungry now? Or should I put dinner in to keep warm?"

"Can I have half an hour or so. I just need to relax my legs." Saw rolled his eyes. "Art was a demon. He gave me homework."

"You can have all the time you like, soldier cowboy. I'm in no hurry and I don't have plans. Should we go lie down? Snuggle? Curse Art together?"

"Sounds perfect." Saw had something on his mind. Jax could tell. He was worrying it like a bone. Jax put their dinner on the stove and covered it to help it stay warm. "Come on, then. I put clean sheets on this morning and everything."

"Art was a hard-ass today?" He helped Saw up, trying to distract him by being chatty. "Do I need to write you a note? Sorry, Mr. Arthur. Saw won't be at therapy today. He's... in bed. Heh."

"Oh, I like that. He's got a plan for me. A *plan*, sugar. We're going to stop pushing quite so hard on the legs, bring up the work on the arm, add in massage." They settled on the edge of the bed, and Saw took his shoes off. Then they curled together on the bed, Saw holding him. "I want to talk to you about something kind of serious, though, because I have to find a place, somewhere I have an address so I can get my service animal."

"Yes. You can move in here." That was easy. That didn't even take thought. Saw needed an address, and he needed Saw.

"I can? You want me? Here? With you and my dog?" Saw's smile was brilliant, just absolutely sunshine, even if it was a little stunned.

"Yes. I want you." Jax laughed. "Of course I want you, I —" He blinked at Saw, his laughter dissolving as quickly as it had come on. "I love you."

Oh god. He'd said it. He'd been thinking it for a while, he knew it was true, but he'd said it now and— "I know, it's too soon. It's ridiculous. Whatever. I don't care. It's true."

"It is." Saw took his hand, twined their fingers together

carefully. "I'm glad, because... well, you gotta know how I feel about you. I don't care about ridiculous. We do good together."

He nodded. "Us." Jax kissed Saw's fingers. "I breathe better around you. You... slow things down. I need that. I didn't know that was what I needed, but I do now." He glanced up at Saw. "Do we need a bigger place? I mean, a nicer one?"

"I don't know. We should decide a bunch of things, I'm sure." Saw looked at him, so serious but grinning at the same time. "First I want to just think about the fact that you love me for a minute. That we love each other."

Jax nodded. "Let's just think about that." He tilted his head back. "Can we kiss about it too?"

"Please, sugar. I want that bad." Saw drew them close together with a moan. "I was stressing all this. Thank you for making it easy."

"I should have told you. I knew before. I thought it was crazy though. I thought it would scare you off." He arched against Saw, every nerve suddenly on fire like Saw had taken a match to his skin.

"I'm your soldier cowboy. Not going anywhere." Saw dragged one hand down his back.

"Not anymore. Now I got you for half the rent!" He grinned and kissed Saw hard. Saw was his, for sure now. And he was going to hold on tight.

"You do! And I get to squeeze icing whenever I want." Saw rubbed their noses together.

"You're going to get sick of that. You're going to want to cook real food and sleep like real people do after a while."

"You let me cook whatever I want, Jax." Saw blinked at him. "And I'm a night owl. Always have been. Can't we be real together?"

He cupped Saw's face and smiled at this amazing man that had obviously dropped out of the sky just for him. "Yes. We can. Our own real."

"Oh, thank God. I want to be with you, sugar. I want to make a life. We can reckon it, together." Saw held him close, and one little kiss lingered and deepened into a bigger kiss.

That's it. He wouldn't stress it, not now. Saw said they'd do it together, and they would. Now he had his man in bed and they had all night to rest and... and not. Maybe the not part first. Jax hooked an arm over Saw's waist and rocked into him, rubbing their bodies together through way too much clothing.

Saw beamed at him, carefully, painstakingly opening his buttons.

"You can count that as PT. Buttons are hard." He grinned back, watching Saw's fingers as his cock got so hard he wasn't sure how he was going to unzip his jeans.

"They are, but I'm getting it." Saw got his shirt open, hands burning hot on his skin. It was good that they weren't baking tonight. Those hands needed a rest.

He reached for Saw and did the same, taking his time with the buttons just because it was sexy. "One... two... three. Gosh, you have a lot of buttons."

"I do. It's good practice, remember." Saw winked at him, and that was amazing, because after a bad therapy day, it could be iffy.

"Oh, I need lots of practice. Tons." He pushed the shirt open and kissed Saw's chest, then found a nipple with his tongue and played with it.

Saw had amazing hot spots, sensitive areas that were guaranteed to light his lover up. It was an easy way to make a body that was a challenge sometimes feel good.

He didn't fret over that much though. He trusted Saw to

speak up if he needed something. He didn't think much about the scars because they were just a part of the man he loved. It didn't matter if they weren't pretty or they were painful or limited things sometimes. They were just... Saw. All of them. All of this. He wondered if it was weird that he thought they were beautiful in their own way.

"You're having deep thoughts, sugar." Saw winked at him. "I saw the smoke coming out of your ears."

He chuckled and looked up from the rib he'd been tickling with his tongue. "I am. I'm thinking about you. How much I trust you."

"Yeah? Good." Saw stroked his belly with steady touches. "I want to be your good thing."

"You're my best thing." He pushed Saw's hand lower, down to the bulge in his jeans. "I'm aching, soldier cowboy."

"Ooh. I'm supposed to work on my grip." Saw squeezed in the best way, fingers rolling. "How come you're still dressed?"

He groaned, pushing into Saw's hand. "How come you haven't ripped my jeans off?"

Saw's laugh was like walking into a sudden, happy storm.

He tried to laugh, but mostly he moaned and moved both hands quickly to his jeans, wrestling them over his prick and down to his knees before kicking like a four-year-old until they went flying.

"Mine." Saw drew him in, hand working him almost immediately, thumb on his slit, easing the wetness around.

"Oh, fuck." He pushed into Saw's hand. "Sorry I'm so... you just... you wind me up."

"Not sorry." No, in fact Saw didn't look in the least bit sorry. He looked like there was nothing at all that he'd rather be doing.

"Okay. Okay, good." He fumbled between them, trying to find Saw's fly. "I want... gimme."

"One day. If you want." Each set of words was panted out. "I want you to ride me. So bad. If you like it."

Sweet man.

Sweet. And so goddamn hot. Hell yes, he wanted Saw inside him. "One day... like today? Like maybe right now? I want that too." Saw didn't have to ask him twice.

"Yeah? Today is good. Today works for me." Saw grinned at him, and that smile wasn't sweet. No, not at all. That was pure sex.

Jax humped into Saw's hand once more and then pulled away, moaning as he tugged Saw's jeans down. Socks, undies... he tossed all of them to the floor and dove for supplies in his nightstand.

He was ready. Because he'd been hoping for one day too.

"Oh, you read my mind. I was hoping you wanted me like that."

Jax pushed the rubber into Saw's palm and opened the lube. "No mind reading necessary, silly. You flat-out asked me. Which was fucking hot, by the way. Sexy soldier cowboy." He bit his lip and reached back to get himself ready.

"Oh." Saw's eyes almost burned as they stared at him, a low, wild sound on the air.

Jax gave him a hot grin. "Condom? In your... hand." Oh that felt good. He couldn't wait for Saw.

"Right. Glove up."

Had anything felt so hot as the way he distracted Saw, the way his soldier watched him?

Maybe watching Saw work the condom on with trembling hands.

"You want me, baby? I want you." He crawled over Saw

and straddled him, taking hold of Saw's cock with one hand and rubbing the head against his hole. He'd only meant to tease Saw, but damn. "Oh, fuck."

"I need you, love. You are a dream."

It hadn't been that long since he'd fucked someone. He knew where to find a guy in a bar if he needed one. But it had been forever since he'd been with anyone he was really into. Anyone he cared about this much.

Actually, he didn't think he'd ever cared about anyone this much.

And knowing that made this first time between them a big deal. He made himself slow down because for the first time ever, this mattered. "I love you." He made sure Sawyer saw him, saw his eyes, and then he guided his love inside.

Saw watched him—not his ass, not his cock, *him*—as he sank down.

"Oh." Jesus. They fit together so well. This was fucking everything. He exhaled, then sucked in a deep breath. "Oh, Sawyer. You feel so good."

Saw stared into him, nodding and licking his lips. "Beautiful. Love."

He started to move, slowly at first as he let Saw stretch him, the heat and the burn just right. He wanted though... wanted more of Saw, everything, and he took Saw in deep as he picked up a good rhythm.

"Jesus, Jax. You're burning inside. Perfect." Saw wrapped one hand around his hip, holding on.

Those were words, right? And he should say something back. Something sexy. He opened his mouth a couple of times and ended up letting out a needy sound or sucking in a harsh breath. "S... Saw... Sawyer," he managed to say, angling so Sawyer's cock hit that magic spot inside him, just... fucking... right.

He gave up on words after that because everything in his head sounded like something Dr. Seuss made up.

Sawyer kept him moving, kept him right there where they needed to be. Kept that sweet cock driving into him.

His fingers dug into Saw's chest, and he bounced hard. He was gonna lose it, and soon, but he wanted to take Sawyer with him. He arched back and grabbed Saw's thighs, cock slapping his belly and giving his man a good show.

"Jesus. Jesus, sugar. Look at you. You're a goddamn star."

"You're... too... fucking coherent." Jax clenched hard, squeezing Saw tight and making himself moan.

Saw bucked, grunting deep in his chest, and the temptation to bite out, "Bingo" was huge.

"Again!" Jax sucked in a breath and held on, trembling, so close he was ready to scream.

Sawyer grabbed him and jabbed into him, hard enough that they slapped together. Saw's lips pulled back, his lover on fire for him.

"Fuck!" He shook as he shot, balls emptying so hard it almost hurt as he painted Saw's abs. "Sawyer!" He tried to shout, but Jesus, he had to fight for a breath.

Sawyer was thrusting, fierce for a minute, then in increasingly gentler motions as he came, riding his orgasm.

The spasms didn't stop for a bit—not his or Sawyer's—and he panted through them, high as a kite. Floating on hormones and an orgasm that he wasn't going to forget. "Baby..."

"Oh, sugar. This is—I got you. Thank you."

Jax nodded because... yeah. All of that. Except the 'got you' thing because he felt like he'd shattered into a million pieces. He shifted and lay down next to Saw, curling into his side. He'd climb right inside Sawyer if he could.

Saw held him like he saw, like he understood, and Saw kept him right there close.

"You're the best thing that's ever happened to me. You're the best thing that's ever going to. I want to just stay right here for... well, forever."

"Mmm...We have to bake again at some point, and go see Hawk and Jan, but not now."

"Not now. Shhh. Casper will get jealous." Jax giggled weakly. "Oh. Tired. So well worn out."

"Mmhmm. Poor Casper." Saw kissed his temple. "Rest. We'll eat after a nap, huh?"

Jax nodded. They were supposed to be resting for Saw, and here he was the one all tired. He'd make it up to Saw later. Maybe a massage or, or a hot bath or... or... he'd think later. Thinking was hard.

The last thing he thought was how good Saw smelled before he fell asleep.

14

Saw woke up, holding his Jax, and it felt so right. So fucking right that it made the fact that he was sore as a boil okay.

Jax loved him.

Jax loved him.

Jax fucking loved him.

Jax needed him too. How incredible was that? Jax needed him despite everything about him that was broken or worn. He was enough for Jax.

Saw grinned and said a little prayer of thanks. Everybody had someone that was meant to be theirs, and Jax was his. Lord have mercy.

He needed to go get his shit from Hawk's. Him and Jax needed to chat about life and shit. He needed to do paperwork and all. First, though, he needed food. They'd slept through supper and now it was three a.m. and he was starving.

"You're still here," Jax muttered sleepily and nuzzled into him. "Yay."

"Gonna be here full-time, remember. You said yes."

"I said please." Jax kissed his jaw. "Which is the same thing only with more want."

"I like wanting." He cupped Jax's ass. "I love you."

He thought it was important to say.

Jax picked up his head and smiled, he could just make it out in the little bit of light from the window. "I love you—whoa." Jax's words were cut off by his growling stomach. "Soldier cowboy needs some food. What time is it? It's *dark*."

"Three-ish? We napped hard." Saw chuckled and shook his head. The world was a good place today, and he was going to enjoy every second of it that he could. "I do love that we have the same basic schedule."

"You mean up at all hours of the night?" Jax laughed. "I don't know why you are, but I'm so used to it I don't know if I could change it if I wanted to."

"I always was a night owl. I managed to get the night rounds a lot in the service, but I tell you—soldiers and cowboys are supposed to be morning people." But he was who he was.

Jax sat up, stretching. "Then I guess it's good you're a New York cowboy now."

"There you go." He reached out, rubbing circles on Jax's lower back.

"Mmm. Thank you. What do you think Jan and Hawk are going to say when you tell them you're moving in?"

"That I'm taking advantage of you, and it's all moving too fast." He grinned and kept rubbing. "Isn't that always what folks say?"

"That and I need to be careful, you're vulnerable, and I don't know you well enough yet." Jax looked over one shoulder, grinning back. "I know you're hungry and wanting dinner at three in the morning like I am. That's enough, right?"

"It's enough. We're both adults. We're both in our right minds. We're both happy. Joke 'em if they can't take a fuck."

Jax laughed happily and scooched out of bed, found PJ bottoms and pulled them on. "So we can order in from the twenty-four-hour Chinese place, or I can make peanut butter and bananas and, like, milkshakes or something."

"Is the chicken parm I brought home still good?"

"Oh, yeah. I forgot. So sweet." Jax turned the light on, making them both squint and Jax laugh some more. "Ooh. Light."

He chuckled, trying hard not to seem like he was hurting as bad as he was. Damn.

Jax sat next to him. "Maybe... dinner in bed? I can fluff up your pillows and get you whatever you need."

Oh thank God. "That would be decadent and fun."

And maybe he wouldn't die.

"Good. I've got this. I get to bring you dinner in bed!" Jax kissed him and that was followed by a wink before Jax left the room.

He would feel guilty, but he needed to breathe and rest, let himself relax his bones. Jax wouldn't want him to feel guilty anyway.

Jax came back before too long wearing an apron over his sweats and carrying a bed tray loaded with food. "Picnic in bed! I didn't bring beer or open your wine in case you can't have it with your meds. I'll get Cokes if you want."

"I think a Coke, please, if you don't mind. I worked hard today, you know?" He took the tray and balanced it, holding it for Jax.

"I can still write that note for Art if you want." Jax handed him his meds. "Cokes, coming right up."

"I might take you up on it." He grinned over, watching

this man that he was going to live with. "I'm looking forward to backing up off my legs for a few weeks."

"I'm excited for you," Jax said as he left the room. And then as he came back, "I do way better when I have a plan too. Mine change a lot, but it's a good start."

"It is. I like a plan. Plans. That's the best part of being a soldier. Someone always has a plan."

Jax climbed up in bed, helped settle their tray, and handed him his Coke. "Eat up, soldier. My stomach says the current plan is dinner. Your subs warmed up easy and they smell so good."

"Excellent. I hoped you'd like them." He'd thought he'd have to butter Jax up a little, ask for his place here, but he hadn't had to.

Jax took a big bite and nodded as he chewed, then swallowed. "Mmm. Yummy. Do we need to talk about stuff? Moving-in stuff?"

"Probably, yeah. I'll pay my part, I swear." And he wanted to talk about bakeries. That was what Jax wanted to do.

"Oh, I know. I didn't mean..." Jax rolled his eyes. "Thank you. But I meant things for you. To make sure you have what you need, you know? That you're comfortable."

"Well, I'm pretty comfortable with you. I want to—I think we should talk about things that we want together. I want a dog, and I want to build something with you."

"I can't wait for you to get your dog. I'll make sure the rental company knows so it won't be a thing. What do you want to build, soldier cowboy? Like some new bookshelves? I could use some, the kitchen is stuffed."

"I was thinking more like a bakery, but bookshelves are good too." Good lord, Jax made him smile.

Jax froze, mouth open, about to take a bite of his

sandwich. "A... a bakery?" Jax put the sandwich down. "A real one?"

"Yeah. A bakery. I'm not a great baker, but I can build things and do the books and things. I would be a help, I swear." He wasn't worthless. He knew how to do things, and even better, he knew how to figure out how to do things. Google was a great thing.

"Wow. That would *totally* help. That would be huge actually because I lose so much sleep already just balancing my books. We'd have so much fun! But I'm still saving startup money and then I'll have to find a location... It'll be a while before I'm ready to open anything."

"I have savings. I'd add it to yours, and we'd be partners." He had a hefty sum, and his VA lawyers to help. They could start planning. The first step was to believe.

"Sawyer." Jax whispered his name so softly he barely heard it, and then his lover started to stammer, so shocked it was adorable. "Are you—you're serious? I mean, I can see you are. I just—I..."

"I am. I can invest in us. We can have a bakery together. We can be... we are partners."

"We're going to spend so much time together we're going to drive each other crazy." Jax grinned at him, eyes twinkling happily. "I can't wait."

"We can stand a little joint crazy," he shot back, but he couldn't stop smiling. "You need to help me understand what you need in a bakery, what you want."

"I kind of want a New York version of a patisserie. You know? Specialty stuff. I don't want to compete with the bagel places and the big coffee shops. And I don't want to do little junior's *Paw Patrol* birthday cake either. Just like... cupcakes and small treats. Finger desserts. Cookies and pastries.

Maybe artisan coffees eventually, I don't know." Jax stopped talking, eyes wide. "Sorry. Babbling."

"I'm listening, sugar. Tell me everything. Every single thing." He loved it—he could bask in this excitement.

"We have to find someone we trust... a day manager. Otherwise, you'll work all day and I'll work all night and that just won't be good. Although at first, we'll probably just work all the time because getting something like that off the ground is a big deal. Oh! I can make dog treats! Gourmet dog treats? *So* New York." Jax took a bite of his sandwich and chewed it, mental wheels turning madly.

"Peanut butter ones. Dogs love peanut butter." He grabbed a notebook and started taking notes. Dog treats. Manager. Cookies. What the fuck was a finger dessert?

Jax nodded. "And busy, you know? Not too big, lots of light, displays everywhere. Glass counter, tiered trays, shelving, a cold case..." Jax went on and on. This wasn't a new idea. It was obvious he'd been thinking about it for a very long time. "I just don't have a name. That'll come."

"Do you have an idea about where you'd like to have it? Is there a situation where we could have an apartment above the bakery?" He liked the idea of just being able to go upstairs.

"We can look for that. I don't know if that's easy or not. Let's try. We might find something in the same building at least. Sawyer, this is going to be amazing. Exhausting. And amazing."

"Yes." He caught Jax's eyes. "It'll be living."

He knew all about almost dying. Living was better.

"Living. Together." Jax reached out and took his notebook. "Eat. You're going to need your strength to live with me."

"Yes, boss." He chuckled, but Jax was right. He had to eat

with his pills, and he wanted to enjoy every second of Jax's excitement.

"So what stuff do you have to move in? Where is it?"

"I have a storage space with a couple things. A chest, my grandpa's recliner, a couple boxes of things and books."

"There's a great spot for a recliner by the window in the living room. And we could put a dog bed next to it."

"Yeah." He wanted a service dog, an extra helping hand. "You don't mind it? Me taking up space?"

"No worries. If it gets crowded, we can snuggle." Jax laughed. "Silly."

"You know it." He took a bite of his sandwich, letting himself enjoy it. "I'm a damn goofball, just ask Hawk."

"We've got this. If Hawk and Jan don't kill us, we're totally golden." Jax leaned back against the headboard with his coke.

"You're in way greater danger than me. Hawk don't care." Hawk was an easygoing guy who was just tickled to be out and eating and in love.

"Well, I don't care either. Jan's happy. He doesn't get a say." Jax rested his head on Saw's shoulder. "Thank you."

"Thank *you*. I didn't know how I was going to ever be— at home. I haven't been for a long time."

"I kinda thought I was too busy and kept the wrong hours to ever meet anyone serious." Jax shrugged. "And I'm... weird. That's not a bad thing, but you have to find the right weird to go with it."

"I like your weird. It suits me to the bone." And he thought Jax just needed someone to listen. He liked that, because he needed to hear what Jax told him.

"We're going to have so much fun. I'm going to start looking for a place. Talk to some of my clients. Start thinking up names."

"I'll get an appointment with legal at the VA and find out what to do next."

"Legal. Oh man. Lawyers are scary. You sure you want to do that part?"

"Sure. I'm not worried. And it's a free service, so we might as well take advantage of it."

"That's the hardest part for me, you know? All the setup, legal stuff. I really appreciate you doing that. You're going to be so much help."

"That's what I want. To be your partner in this." That was easy.

"It's a dream come true." Jax sounded awed and far away. "For me. Imagine that."

"Yep. We are." All the way.

15

Jax was super careful with his tray of Napoleon's on the subway, and carried them like they were made of crystal all the way to Jan and Hawk's building. Thankfully, Saw wasn't speedy, so it was easy to baby them on their walk.

They were Jan's favorite, and he was all about buttering Jan up tonight. He and Saw were going to make everything official, tell Jan and Hawk together about Sawyer moving in.

He'd told Saw a bunch of times that he didn't care what Jan and Hawk thought about their moving in together, but that wasn't totally true. He did care. He wanted Jan to be happy for him. It wouldn't change anything if Jan wasn't, but he would be disappointed.

"Almost there. We're having ramen, did I tell you? My favorite. I haven't had it in a while."

"Well, we should have it more often. I was thinking about making you chili tomorrow night."

"I'd love that. That's one of those things you hear about up here—Texas chili. I could make some cornbread. Are we bringing the rest of your stuff to my place tonight?" Jax hit the buzzer to be let in.

"I am, yeah. I'll get us a car to get us home. Cool?" Saw stole a quick kiss. Those little PDAs were coming more and more often.

"So cool." He tried not to swoon like an idiot, but he probably did anyway.

"Come on up, guys!" Jan buzzed them inside. He let Saw open the door, but he put his back against it so Saw could get through with his walker.

"You nervous?" Saw asked as they headed for the elevator. "I'm excited. No more lonely nights."

"A little maybe, but I'm more excited. No lonely anything. Not even work. We're partners now, in everything." It was perfect. It was amazing. He could hardly believe Sawyer was all-in on making his dream of his own bakery real.

"Yes. Warts and all." Saw began to chuckle, body shaking. "I haven't discovered any warts on you, sugar. I need to explore more in-depth."

He laughed. "Shut up. You won't either. I am wart-free." The elevator opened onto Jan's floor. "Wartless."

"Sans warts?" Saw shot back. "The anti-wart?"

"Bereft of warts." He stepped out and stuck his foot in the way so the doors wouldn't close on Saw. "Devoid, even. I hang out with Jan, you know. He uses big words." He snorted, trying not to laugh.

"The word devoid makes me think of the sound of duck shit hitting water."

He cracked up, his laughter echoing in the hallway. "I can't say... I've ever heard that," he said, giggles interrupting his words.

"Hello, gentlemen!" Jan called from down the hall. "I knew that giggling had to be you."

"Mr. Jan! How goes it, sir?" Saw was still laughing as they headed down the hall.

"I'm well. We've been looking forward to seeing you both. You're looking good." Jan gave them both quick hugs and held the door. "Hawk will be right out. He's powdering his nose."

Sawyer gave a soft hoot. "He's got to get all prettified."

Jan closed the door behind them and winked at Saw. "I hear it's a cowboy thing. So vain."

Jax chuckled and headed right for the kitchen. "I brought a pretty cowboy of my own. And napoleons!"

"Ooh, napoleons. I love those. I ordered the ramen. It should be here soon." Jan followed him, all smiles. "Saw, you want a beer?"

"Is there a Coke?"

Jan didn't say anything, but he saw the way his friend's head tilted. "There is always Coke. Dr Pepper? Sprite?"

"Saw's been working his ass off in PT." He didn't think Saw and Hawk had talked about the new plan yet.

"Oh, good for you, Saw. How's it going?"

"Good. Hard, but it's working." Saw was getting stronger, recovering faster with the upper body work.

"I feel like we hardly see you anymore. You sort of breeze through here." Jan held up a Dr Pepper. "This work?"

"Thank you, yes." Sawyer took it, set it in the walker. "I'm going to pick my things up, man. Y'all need your space, and I need to be with my guy."

"Pick them up?" Jan looked between them. "Like move out? Already?"

Should he jump in? Let Saw handle it? Hide under the kitchen table?

"You're moving?" Hawk came down the hall. "I'm guessing you snatched up Jax, huh? He had your number from the start. Congrats, man."

Jax watched as Saw and Hawk exchanged a handshake and a hug, and he could feel Jan's eyes on him.

He shrugged at Jan. "He's at my place every night anyway, and you guys don't want two dogs here, right? Plus the whole love thing kind of makes this the right decision."

"Yes, that pesky love thing always drives people to want to be together." Jan was actually smiling.

He smiled back. "Right? It's like you have no other choice."

"Well, there are choices. I hope this is a good one."

"I know, Jan. You'll worry. You always worry. You're a worrier." Jax winked at Jan.

Jan shook his head as the doorbell rang. "True that. That's the ramen. I'll be right back."

Jax felt Saw's eyes on him, his soldier cowboy always thinking about him.

He slid right over, as if Saw had his own gravity. "Hungry? Why don't we go sit?"

"Sounds perfect. You're good, sugar?"

"I'm great. I've got you, right?" He leaned closer, asking for a kiss.

"Always." Saw gave it, scarred hand strong and steady where it cupped his jaw.

"One thing I know," Jan said, carrying in the bag of takeout. He ran a hand down Hawk's arm. "Is that cowboys are good for their word. If Saw says always, I guess I better be happy for you both." Jan set the bag down and started unpacking containers.

"It sounds like a plan, Mr. Jan. I'm here to stay." Saw

didn't look away from him, and Jax felt like the center of the world.

"Come on. Let's sit." He rested a hand on Saw's where it gripped the walker. He'd tried a bunch of things, and this was the closest he'd come to holding hands. He wanted the contact, and he knew Saw would also.

"Dining room, Jax. We're being adults tonight."

Jax laughed. "Ooh. Adults. I haven't been an adult in a long time."

"Nope. We tend to eat in bed," Saw whispered. "Like... hrm...adults?"

"Oh, bed is very adult at our place." He pulled out Saw's chair and put the Dr Pepper on the table.

"It's not like you ever slept in your bed before," Jan teased, setting containers of food on the table with Hawk's help. "I'm surprised you weren't using it for storage."

He looked at Saw. "It's true. I slept on the couch. When I slept. Which... well, you know how that goes."

"The couch is too small for us to both sleep hard. We need to stretch out." Saw managed not to look worried or embarrassed at all. No, his soldier was proud to be with him.

Jan passed behind Hawk and placed Hawk's hand on the back of the chair at the head of the table. It was so subtle and easy he wouldn't have noticed if he hadn't been looking right at it at the time. "So there's coconut green curry in front of Hawk and some edamame, then your vegetarian ramen, Jax. And then I just tried a few random things. Help yourselves."

Jan disappeared for a second and came back with sodas for everyone else. "Sprite for you, Jax. All good."

"Looks great to me. You have to try my ramen, baby. It's so good."

Saw tried some. "I appreciate the Cokes, y'all. I'm on

some muscle relaxants, just low dose to help healing, but I can't alcohol on top of them."

"We don't need to alcohol. I like a beer. I like a Coke too." Jan gave Saw's hand a pat. "Also, you're one of the family now."

"Thank you. Thank y'all for everything from the room to the friendship to introducing me to my man."

"You're welcome." Jan started serving up food. "Of course I do wish you were staying longer. The empty room means Hawk will be looking for his next stray cowboy. Am I right, Champ?"

"I'll just invite Sky and Beck and all the kids, darlin'."

Oh, burn.

"Touché." Jan snorted. "But Buck might never forgive you."

Hawk snorted, losing his noodles. "He might. He doesn't mind kids, but three? That's an ask."

"An ask? That's torture. It's a good thing they have a lot of land up there. They can set them free to run all day." Jan shivered. "Kids."

"I hope you know I'm joking, Saw." Jan smiled at Saw, and it made Jax smile too. "I love being able to help when we can. I'm really impressed with how you've adjusted to the city. It's not a small accomplishment."

"I'm getting it. It'll be easier when I get my service dog. And when we find a bakery, I'm going to get to learn somewhere new."

"We're going to start a bakery. Our own business," Jax added before Jan could ask questions.

"What? That is amazing. Your own bakery. You've been talking about that as long as I've known you. Are you baking now too, Saw?"

"I'm learning. Mostly, I can do books and help with

things. Jax is the baker. I'm the one that fixes the broken bits."

"We're going to be partners. It's perfect." He patted Saw's thigh.

"Jax's big worry is the books, so you're stepping into just the right spot. Though I recall you're an expert banana masher." Jan winked at Saw.

"Spectacular. I also wash dishes like a pro. A dish pro."

"Oh, that was my job on the occasions that I dropped by to see Jax. He makes a lot of dishes."

"Shut up." Jax laughed. "Thank you for the ramen. I know it's not your favorite thing, Hawk."

"No worries." Hawk's mouth was full, so how bad could it be?

"I got him a sub for when he's tired of the noodles. My stubborn cowboy." Jax loved the way Jan looked at Hawk, like he'd hung the moon. He knew Jan would do anything for Hawk, just like he would for Saw. Anything.

"They're just messy. I don't like messy food." Hawk actually blushed, which made Jax glance away. "Except for spaghetti and meat sauce. I've learned to love that here."

"Mmm. Spaghetti I could do Impossible meat." Jax slurped up some noodles and soup.

Jan chuckled. "What are you craving, Saw? We'll have that next time."

"Fried chicken and mashed taters with corn." Saw didn't even hesitate.

Jax hummed his approval. "You had me at potatoes."

"Hawk, where did we get the fried chicken last time? Some place you found. Will that work for Saw? Or do we need to look around some more?" Jan shrugged, grinning at Saw. "Mine was... not good."

"It's hard to make. You need a big fryer, I think." Saw grinned. "I'll totally buy the next supper. It's my turn."

"*We'll* buy," Jax corrected. "Looks like you'll be sampling fried chicken for the next few days. And I can have cole slaw and mashed potatoes.

"So you guys are settled then? I mean, from over here... from the outside, this all seems really fast, but I know it's different when you're the ones living it. This business and everything, you guys are on the same page? You're good with staying in New York, Saw?"

He tried to remind himself that Jan's heart was in the right place, but he wasn't a kid, even if he acted like one sometimes. And he wasn't—well, okay he was impulsive, but not this time.

"I have been all over, and I like it here just fine. There's a ton for Jax and me to go and see, good work to be done. I'm ready."

He loved that, that solid, sure, steadiness.

Jan nodded. "Glad to hear that. I'm grateful to you, Sawyer. Jax is my best friend, and he deserves someone like you."

"And I deserve someone like him, so we're even up." Saw tapped his thigh.

"So... Hawk. How should we celebrate? A dinner cruise? A show? A trip?"

"Let's go to the beach. When do you want to go? Tomorrow?"

"The beach?" Jax looked between Jan and Hawk. "I want to go to the beach."

Jan smiled at him. "Tomorrow sounds good to me. Saw?"

"I'm a go-baby, all the way. Let's hasta." Saw grinned at him. "When we have a bakery, we won't be able to just leave, you know."

"No, not for a long time. The closest we'll get to a vacation is the shower." The beach would be fun. They hadn't been out of the city together at all yet.

"So we should take the bull by the horns and do it. Our little fling." Saw's eyes twinkled at him.

Jax took Saw's hand, sliding a thumb over ridges he'd learned by heart. "Where, Hawk? Jersey Shore? Long Island?"

"Wherever Jan wants to go..." Hawk paused. "They all look the same to me."

Jax snorted a laugh, but then covered his mouth quickly. That was supposed to be funny... right?

Jan started with a low chuckle, but it grew into a loud laugh. "You can laugh, Jax. That was a joke."

He puffed out a breath and let the giggles out. "Oh, thank god."

"Damn, sugar. That was cute as all get out." Saw leaned over and kissed his cheek, the caress leaving a warm spot.

"By morning, I'll have found us a place in Montauk for a night or two. Hawk will arrange transportation for us. Does that work for you guys?"

"Yes! I wonder where my bathing suit is. I think I have one..." Somewhere. Hm.

"If you don't, you can buy one there."

"I have one!" Saw grinned at him. "You'll finally get to see me in it. It's Batman!"

"Batman! You've been wearing a Batman bathing suit to PT?" His goofball. He couldn't wait to see Saw in it.

"Who wants to wear a boring pair of trunks to PT?"

"So we're settled then. We'll clean up here and send you home so you can get your baking done. And then Hawk will have a car pick you up in the morning, as soon as I've found us a place."

A car. A place. He'd argue or offer to pitch in, but there wasn't any point. Jan and Hawk were loaded. He and Saw could buy dinner maybe. Otherwise, they'd just get to enjoy the generosity.

He wasn't jealous. He didn't need swanky. But he wasn't going to argue with the chance to enjoy it.

"Sounds great to me!"

"Me too. I like the idea of a joint vacation with y'all." Hawk nodded, like that was that. "We're family now, right?"

"Right." Jan and Hawk were all the family he'd had until he met Sawyer. But now Saw was the center of his family. His heart and soul. The center of everything. "I feel like I'm all grown up."

All grown up and taking a beach vacation with his lover. Like he was finally... real.

16

Lord have mercy, this was a sweet place—wheelchair ramp into the house and down toward the beach, nice kitchen, two good-sized bedrooms with their own baths. Spiffy.

Sawyer went to Hawk who was getting Buck water while Jax and Jan were hauling in bags. "You sure y'all don't need me to pitch in, buddy? I ain't a mooch."

"Shee-it. We know. We got it. It ain't no thing, and starting a bakery is."

"Well, I appreciate it. All the way."

"Jan wouldn't have invited you otherwise." Hawk chuckled. "Where's a good place for this bowl?"

"To your left about two steps should be fine."

He loved how Hawk knew just what he meant.

Jax scooted past him with their bags and an armful of groceries. He set the groceries down and kissed his cheek before heading for their bedroom. "Most of that goes in the fridge."

"On it." He headed over to the fridge once Hawk was out of the way, started the process of unloading while he whistled.

"Come on, love. Let me show you the view." Jan took Hawk's hand, led him to a large window, and started describing the beach and the water in detail.

"Pretty neat, how he does that, huh?" Jax drew a warm hand down his arm.

"It is. It's sort of like how you know how to touch me." Sawyer shot his Jax a warm grin, then put the Cokes and the milk away.

"If you mean everywhere, then yeah. I know." Jax winked at him.

"Yep. What do you want to do first?" They'd slept pretty good in the car, to be honest.

"Beach." Jax looped an arm through his and kissed his shoulder. They'd worked out a graceful dance around his walker and Jax could make it feel like it wasn't even there. "I want to go lie on the beach with you. Take a walk and find shells, and swim and get some sun."

"Okay. I've never done it with the walker, but—"

"Jan and I have a surprise for you." Jax looked utterly tickled shitless. "Come to the bedroom."

He followed Jax down the hall, curious, but more than happy to let Jax have this surprise.

Sitting in the bedroom was a walker with huge, wide wheels. "We rented it from a medical supply. It's a beach walker. You can take it down into the water, sit and dangle your feet, everything."

Sawyer stood there in shock, lips parted. "Well, I'll be."

He hadn't even known he'd needed something like that.

"Well, I asked Jan for help... he's so good at this stuff. I didn't even know there was such a thing. But isn't it cool?"

"It's amazing. Seriously. Thank you, sugar. This is perfect. Let's get wet-friendly clothes on and go wander."

They'd need to nap again in a bit, but he found himself excited and ready to explore.

"You got it." Jax pulled out their suits and they changed, both of them grinning and giggling like kids. "Jan said if we stay between the jetties, we'll stay out of the current. I'm not a real strong swimmer so that sounds like a plan to me."

"I can swim, but let's go for safe." He hadn't swum in the ocean in a long, long time.

"Batman! Those are hot, soldier cowboy." Jax stuck a finger in his waistband and gave it a snap. "Should we go show off?"

He grabbed a shirt and tugged it on, hiding some of the scars and giving himself a layer of protection. "I got me some of them water shoes for the pool. I should wear those, huh?"

"They might help, yeah." Jax pulled a T-shirt out of his bag and pulled it on too, then slipped on a pair of flip-flops. "Let's find towels."

He nodded but left Jax to that while he put on the shoes. He was getting better at that. He really was. It was weird, how things that had once been easy, were hard.

Jax came back with the towels before he'd gotten the second one on. "Hard, huh?" Jax slid a hand over his back, then started to unpack their bags into a little dresser across from the bed.

"I'm getting better at it. I am." He chuckled softly. "I think you can really see improvement in my hands."

"For sure. Art's plan is a good one. And I have no complaints about your hands, baby. None."

Okay, didn't that make him feel like a thousand bucks? "None? Good. I'll have to make sure you get to learn everything about them."

"I'm looking forward to that." Jax knelt by his foot and

helped, without doing it for him. "Let's plan on a lesson later."

"Perfect. I'll need a bonus PT session." He stroked Jax's hair. "Thanks, sugar."

There was nothing like this man. Nothing. He was stupid in love.

Jax stood and offered him a hand up. "Ready to try out your new wheels? See if you can do some doughnuts in the sand? I could sit on the front like I'm riding on your handlebars."

"I was born ready." He stood, testing the walker. "Oh. Bouncy. I approve."

This wasn't made for city sidewalks. No, this was for rough, odd terrain. He liked it.

Jan and Hawk were behind closed doors in their room as Jax led the way out. "I guess we take that path? Hang on." Jax ducked out the back door and returned in a flash. "Yep! It's a little bumpy, but it's wide enough. And not far from the ramp."

"I can handle it. Grab some water, huh?" He maneuvered out the door, proud of how he was handling it, how he wasn't freaking the fuck out about being on the sand again.

"Yep, I'll catch up." Jax left him for a minute, long enough that he made it to the path on his own.

The wind was blowing, the scent of the ocean was strong and so different, and he felt... like he was beginning to be inside his own body.

"Okay. I have water, and Jan gave me a bag of pretzels. They'll be down soon. Come on." Jax skipped a few steps down the path, then turned and waited for him, wind blowing his hair around.

"You ought to be in pictures." He grinned and shot a

photo with his phone. It almost looked like Jax was a mermaid or some such.

"Yeah?" Jax laughed and posed for him, hands on his hips, turning his face up to the sunshine and the wind. "How's this?"

"You're the most beautiful man I've ever seen," he admitted. "I'm a lucky man."

He wasn't sure why he had lucked out and found Jax single, but he had, and he was going to take it.

"Oh, stop. I'm just me. But I appreciate that." Jax stepped off the path and into the sand where he kicked off his flip-flops. "Did we get a gorgeous day or what?"

"It's beautiful." And the walker was stable, so he felt like he could do this. "I've never been to the ocean up here. I've been to Wilmington and then to the Gulf."

"I've been a few times. Never *here*. I mean Montauk. This is... wow. Nice. Is the Gulf warm? The water here is chilly." Jax slipped in beside him with that hand on his as the walker rolled along.

"It is, yeah. Lots of jellyfish. But it's not cold at all." He loved Gulf shrimp, a cold beer, a bonfire.

"Jellyfish?" Jax made a face. "How's the footing? You okay? I bet if we go down closer to the water it will be easier where the surf makes the sand flatter, you know?"

"It's pretty damn good, but let's go down to the water." He chuckled and angled toward the shore. "Is that a song? Down to the water?"

"Uh." Jax looked like he was really thinking hard about that. "I don't know. Is it?" Jax stopped to set out their towels and waters.

"Fuck if I know." Lord, if he got down there, he'd need help getting up. Good thing he had three guys that would do that for him.

Jax must have seen him looking and leaned close. "No worries. We've got this. And Jan's bringing umbrellas!"

"Umbrellas. Cool." That made it feel like a movie or something. Made it feel more special, and he approved.

Jax led him down to the water. "Mmm. Sand in my toes. You're smart though. Those shoes will keep the rocks off your feet when we go in. Sometimes they feel like little razors."

"Yeah, I don't want that. I can feel the sand though." His heartbeat sped, and he forced himself to relax and breathe. Familiar but somehow new things made his body react, but he'd been in enough therapy to understand that, to accept the rush of adrenaline.

He felt Jax look over and study him a second, but if Jax noticed, he didn't mention it. "Let's stay here and get our toes wet for a bit. You want to sit? I can help you turn that thing around."

"Sitting sounds good." He offered Jax a grin. It was good to be with someone who got him, understood.

Jax offered him a shoulder to steady himself with and then started to turn the walker around. "I remember when I was a kid, running on the beach made my calves ache. It's different than walking on solid ground."

"It is. It's a good challenge. Beach sand is a little different than the desert."

Jax moved so he could sit. "Yeah, I bet. No ocean breezes in Iraq. No one goes to the seashore to try to make a difference."

"Yeah." For a second, he couldn't breathe, and he made himself focus on the water, watch the waves and suck air.

"Hey. Sawyer?" Jax took his hand. "What's wrong?"

"Sometimes—" Jax deserved to know. "Sometimes, new things confuse my brain. It's no big deal. But I have to breathe and calm myself down. PTSD. I try not to be obvious, but—I've got a therapist that I talk to, and the dog will help."

Jax knelt by his walker-seat and looked up at him. "PTSD is a big deal. It's okay. We have lots of time for your brain to catch up. And you could be worse places trying to catch your breath." Jax's words were light but his lover was watching him much more seriously. "Can I help?"

"Just be patient with me? I have to deal with my brain shit. I can't just... hold it in."

"No, no you can't. You shouldn't. I'm not afraid of it, you know. I don't know a lot about this stuff, but whatever it is, I'm here for it. For you. Okay?"

"Thank you. I love you, huh?" He needed Jax to know that.

"I love you too, soldier cowboy." Jax smiled up at him and kissed his knee. The waves rolled in and splashed over them. Jax got pretty wet kneeling in the sand, but he didn't hear any complaining. "Sawyer? Can I ask you a hard question?"

"You can ask me anything." He might not be able to answer, but that was how it worked.

"Jan and I were talking and... he told me about your friend. And I just wondered—and you don't have to answer if you don't want to, but I wondered... why the army?"

God, there were a thousand answers to that. Maybe more. "My heart was broken. The service was a place where I didn't have to think or feel or anything if I didn't want to."

Jax rested his hands on Saw's knee, watching him, seeing him. "Was he more than a friend?"

Saw looked behind him, making sure Jan and Hawk weren't coming. "This is between you and me and the bedpost, but I wanted him to be. We were fuck buddies, but it had potential. I saw Ollie die. Like I was holding him when his eyes went dead. I was the last thing he saw; my name was the last thing he said. Ever."

Jax took his hand and tangled their fingers. "That... that's horrible. It sounds like that's what he wanted too. I'm so sorry."

"I was too. I was fucked up, so I ran away. I was a kid. Like honestly—not old enough to drink, even—and I grew up quick. I didn't have time to think about before, until I was in the hospital, and then I had nothing but time." And that was that. Ollie was gone. His normal was gone. He was here.

Jax nodded, stroking his fingers gently. "I understand that. Running away. It's a lot for anyone, but for a kid? It's a little scary to look at all the things that brought you here."

"Everything happens for a reason." Sometimes, that reason was that you made bad decisions. Sometimes, the reason was you were a lucky bastard. Sometimes, the hand of God offered you a bone, and if you were smart, you took ahold of it.

"Well, you're mine now. I'm glad I'm one of your reasons." Jax kissed his fingers.

"I am too. I needed to be someone's reason." More than anything, when it came right down to it.

"You know... we don't have a name for the bakery yet." Jax smiled at him and squeezed his fingers. "And, I mean, Ollie is maybe the cutest name ever."

He tilted his head, his belly drawing up as he fought the urge to burst into tears. "You think?"

"If you like it. I have a concept, a plan, I know exactly what I want it to be, but I've never been able to come up with a name." Jax's look was so sincere and hopeful. "And then you said things happen for a reason, so... maybe this is why."

"Ollie's Bakery. That's... that would be a way to honor him. I would appreciate that."

"Yeah? Then we have a name." Jax sat up tall on his knees and tugged him closer for a kiss. "Ollie's. I love it. I love you."

"I love you, sugar. Swear to God. I will have your back forever." He would make sure Jax had the life he wanted.

"I believe you. I don't always know whether to believe people, but I believe you. You make everything easier for me." Jax settled again and rested his head on Saw's knees.

He reached down and petted, letting his hurt hand do the work. It was getting better. He felt better.

He felt like he'd worked through another knot in his soul.

"You boys look so sweet." Jan dropped a bottle in his lap. "Sunscreen. Jax can be seen from space he's so white."

"Shut up," Jax mumbled, not moving a muscle.

"I'll lube him up. I don't want him hurting." He squirted lotion in his hand. "Move your hair, sugar."

"Good man." Jan patted his shoulder and headed for Hawk down the beach a ways.

Jax moved his hair out of the way. "Space is a slight exaggeration."

"Still, sunburns suck. I've seen some bad ones. A little pink is fine, but..." Shit, soldiers could be stupid.

"Yeah, I know. I don't want a sunburn. But I still like to look like I've been at the beach, you know? I guess you know a lot about sunburn working in a desert for so long."

"More than I really wanted to know." All of them had seen things they didn't want to see.

Jax turned to look at him. "Hard, huh?"

"Some of it. Some wasn't. I have lots of memories. I was

deployed twice." He felt guilty about the fact that some of it? Some of it had been fun.

"People always talk about the bad stuff. What part wasn't?"

"The guys—I had good buddies. We played a lot of basketball and a shit ton of cards. We laughed a lot, because what else could you do?" He'd celebrated new babies and learned a bunch about food. He'd cried over missing holidays, but he'd flown to Tokyo with his friends and spent two weeks there, staring at the neon lights.

"That's great. Do you keep in touch with any of them?" Jax bit his lip. "Oh. Is that a bad question?"

"It's not, no. I have a couple that I email. One nurse in Germany—James is his name, you'd like him. Real straightforward guy. There's a guy in Colorado—Lemon—he married his CO and everything. They are trying to adopt babies." He grinned, because James thought that Jax was hot as hell, which was encouraging as anything.

"They sound like good people." Jax turned again so he could get the other shoulder with the sunscreen. "You know, we haven't talked about stuff like that—marriage and kids—not for real."

"We haven't." Lord have mercy, he'd never had such heavy damn talks outside. Felt nice, though. Like the ocean wasn't listening. "We ought to. If we have a bakery, a home, those things are big. I like the idea that you'd get my benefits, should something happen to me. I like the idea that you'd have the right to speak for me if I couldn't speak for myself." He paused, stroking the lotion down Jax's arm, loving the feeling of Jax's skin. Then he smiled. "I love the idea of standing before God and saying that I'm yours, no matter what. You?"

Jax blinked at him. "Uh. Wow. I didn't care one bit about marriage until just now."

"Well, we should talk about it. I'm not pushing, but I'm hooking my wagon to yours. It's not a pie crust promise. I intend to be with you forever." He was sure about that. The next one, he wasn't sure about. He could be convinced either way. "Are you interested in kids?"

"The only baby I ever thought about was the bakery." Jax shrugged. "I never thought anyone would want to marry me so marriage wasn't even on my radar, and really never thought about kids. I guess I just didn't think I could have that kind of family."

"Well, I'm not ready for kids. Not yet. Someday, maybe. Now, I need to get stronger, get a dog, and we have a bakery to build." He held Jax's gaze, loving the way Jax made him feel whole. "When you're ready to marry me, we'll make it happen."

"Sawyer, I'm yours. We can make it happen any time, any way you want."

"Good deal. We can get us a license when we get home. What are your positions on rings?"

Jax's eyes lit up. "Well, if we're getting married, then I get to give you one, right?"

"You do." He was all over that, especially the excitement he was reading from his Jax.

"Then I think my position is fairly positive, soldier cowboy. What's your position on cake?"

"I love cake. I've never met a cake I haven't liked." He did like the ones without fondant on them best.

"Then you'll get a ring and cake too. Do we pick them out together? Can we get a limo? I've never been in a limo."

"We can get a limo. Do you want a party? We could

invite Jan and Hawk and anyone you'd like." He nuzzled Jax's temple. "Thank you, sugar."

"I don't really have anyone else to invite. Let's... not. Let's go somewhere."

"Okay." Anything. All Jax had to do was ask. "Mexico somewhere or like here somewhere?"

"Anywhere you want. Mexico, San Francisco, London... I've never seen anything." Jax stood up. "Do you want to swim?"

"I want to try, yeah. We'll see how I do." He wasn't sure how it would work, but dammit, he was going to give it a shot.

"Okay, so... maybe we walk in together? What do you think?"

"Hey! Lovebirds!" Jan called and waved at them. "Ramp!"

He looked around and discovered a ramp that went right into the water. This place was amazing. "Ramp! Look, Sawyer. How cool."

"Oh, excellent. Let's do it." He could manage that, no problem. They got moving, walking down the long ramp, and the water was chilly, lapping at his ankles.

"Cold, huh?" Jax shivered but kept moving. The ramp stopped about knee height, so they were going to have to figure it out from there. "Um. Lean on me?"

"I can do that." He dared to steal a quick kiss.

Jax grinned and kissed him back a lot less quickly. "I've been wanting to do that. Thank you."

"Guess what." He couldn't stop smiling. His soul was pure joy. "You're going to marry me."

"I am. Even better? You're marrying *me*." Jax ducked under one arm. "Ready?"

"Yes, sir. I was born ready."

17

J ax stumbled down the narrow hall in the rental house, shaking his head at himself. Nothing like having to pee in the middle of the night and forgetting where the bathroom was. He'd gone down to the little one near the kitchen, forgetting there was one attached to his room.

That was how often he traveled. He wasn't used to waking up in strange places.

This was neat house, the kitchen and living room had a view of the ocean, and he could see the waves in the moonlight. He could hear them, too. Even from the bedroom.

He did his business and cleaned up. Maybe he'd wake Saw up to come see the beach at night. It was so cool.

He was going to marry Saw. Rings and cake and all. It hadn't been a down-on-one-knee proposal, but it had been romantic in an extremely Sawyer-esque way.

It was totally in character for them. They did everything their own way. They'd do this the way that worked for them too.

If only Gram were around to tell. She'd be so excited for

him. His grandparents were so in love, but he never thought it would happen to him. The whole idea just made him smile. Like he was right now.

"Jax... be careful. Be careful, sugar..." Sawyer was talking hard to, well, not him.

He answered anyway as he climbed back into bed, because... well, he didn't know what else to do. He used to talk in his sleep. He didn't think he did anymore, at least Saw hadn't said so. "I'm good, baby. I just got lost on the way to the bathroom."

"Shh. You have to be quiet. Stand still. Be quiet."

He chuckled. "It's cold out here, I'm coming in. You're not even awake." He fluffed up his pillows and pulled up the comforter. Sea air was damp and chilly at night.

Saw grabbed him and held him, and that's when he felt Saw's heartbeat. It wasn't slow and steady like normal. It was pattering like a hummingbird's wings.

"Saw?" Man, Saw had him tight. He took a breath himself, trying not to get too worried. He did have one arm free and he reached for Saw's face, stroking his cheek. "Hey, Saw? Wake up, Sawyer. What's the matter?"

Sawyer's eyes popped open, the look terrified for a second, and then that fear popped in a rush. "Fuck. Fuck, I —dream. Bad dream."

God, that look though. What kind of dream makes someone look like that? "Okay, it's okay. I'm right here." He wriggled free and got an arm around Saw instead. "Breathe, okay? Your heart is pounding like you ran a marathon."

"You were on the dirt. I was trying to protect— Oh, damn. That sucked." Saw pulled in a huge breath.

Saw's heart was still racing, so Jax just stayed really close. What else could he do? "Oh! You said... I heard you. You told me to stand still. Are you okay? You're shaking."

"I'm good. I am. I'm sorry if I woke you up." He shook his head and pulled in another breath.

"You didn't, I was... it doesn't matter. You're safe, I've got you. Do you want to tell me? What were you dreaming about?"

"You were on the dirt and something was going to hurt you, and I wasn't going to let it. I was going to save you, no matter what."

"You're a good man. Thank you for saving me." He kissed Saw's forehead. "But I'm okay."

"Good. Good. I think I need a glass of water or something, sugar. Maybe a sit on the porch."

The porch. Perfect. "Oh. Right. I was coming back to wake you up. You should see the moon on the water. It's so pretty. Come on." He slid out of bed and pulled a shirt on. "We can bring a blanket."

"Cool." Saw sat up, abs rippling. That was pretty, no matter who you were.

Jax dug through a drawer and found sweats and a T-shirt for Saw and set them on the bed in easy reach. He did the same with Saw's slippers. He was trying not to worry, not to read too much into one nightmare. He felt like there was something Saw wasn't telling him, but he didn't know whether to push or back off. Google was so stupid when he tried to figure out how he could help with Saw's PTSD. Everything depended on the person, on the circumstances, on where their head was... It was useless. He ended up more confused than he started out.

The only good advice he got was to listen, to be in the moment. That part was easy for him.

"Thanks, sugar." Saw was stronger now than he had been, and Jax was glad that the therapist wasn't solely focused on Saw's legs. It mattered to his lover that his hand was improving, and it mattered that no one was promising something improbable.

"Can't have you freezing your balls off. I like them." Jax slid Saw's walker over and put the brakes on.

"Me too. They're a nice size, not too dangly, pleasantly sensitive." Damn, Saw managed that with a straight face.

Jax rolled his eyes and laughed, quietly because he didn't want to wake up the whole house. "They taste good too."

"Mmm... listen to you." It earned him a hard kiss, though, and a smile.

The kiss made him feel better, smoothing over some of his worry. Whatever Sawyer needed, he was here. It would be okay. "Yes, listen to me." He got out of Sawyer's way and hauled the big comforter off their bed.

They got to the porch and settled together on the bench, wrapped up in the blanket. Saw's eyes went wide at the sight of the ocean. "Look at that, sugar."

"I know. I could just watch the waves in the moonlight all night." He covered them both with the comforter and snuggled in. "Close your eyes and listen. That's cool too."

"It is. Thank you for—" Saw's voice went husky. "For everything."

Jax nodded. "I love you. You know this isn't... I want to be here for you. You know that right? It's not like I want you so I'll just deal with whatever else. I want to help you... get better. All of you."

"I want to get better too. I mean, that's what the therapy is for. To help me heal." Sawyer squeezed him. "Shit, I've never talked about some of the shit we went into today. It's —it's hard, you know? To not just pretend there's no feelings in me, but that's not fair to either one of us."

He shrugged. Emotions were okay. He'd always been

told that. "It's not good for you. They're feelings, you know? Honest ones, real ones. I think... I think it's like... there's such a small space for all of those big feelings inside, but once you get them outside, there's more room. It's easier. You can fill that space with good things."

"I like that." Saw took a deep breath and let it out. "I'm happy here with you. I'm excited about our future. The bad shit happened. I won't ever lose the scars from that, but that's okay."

"It's okay. They make you beautiful. They make you my soldier cowboy." Jax leaned in hard. "My Gram had some scars. Some pretty ugly ones."

"Was she the baker?"

"No, my grandfather was. He was amazing in the kitchen, and I learned so much from him. My grandmother was like you. Smart. Good with numbers."

But why did he go there? He shouldn't have said anything about her. It was just depressing, and Saw didn't need more of that. "There was a fire in their apartment building. My parents lived up a couple of floors." He looked out over the water. "I... was at school."

"Oh, Jesus. Your granny was hurt? What about your folks? How old were you?"

"Young. Six. First Grade." He sighed. His memories of that time were so jumbled up and strange. "Mom got burned. Gram never told me the story, but I picked up pieces of it. I think she was trying to get upstairs. Gram raised me after that. It was a long time ago."

"I'm sorry. So many people don't have family close by. I was lucky to have my momma for a while. I still have my baby sister, Jo. She's going to love you."

Saw was his family. Jan and Hawk. Casper. He talked to

his food processor a lot so it might as well be family, right? "She's a nurse, you said? Or going to be?"

"She is. She's in nursing school, and she's a sweet, happy little lady. She loves people, and she works hard."

"I can't wait to meet her. Will she come see us get married? She could stand up for you. Jan could stand up for me."

"I'll fly her up. She'll be over the moon. She flew to Germany to be with me in the hospital. Did you know that? Terrified and not speaking a word of German."

That made Jax smile. "I'm glad you weren't alone the whole time. That would have been awful for you."

"I can't wait for you to meet her. Just..." Saw stopped, eyes wide in the darkness. "Don't let her cook."

His snort turned into a giggle that turned into a big laugh. "Oh. No kitchen for Jo. Gotcha."

"Nope. Not even for a PB and J."

Jax could feel Saw's chest rumble as he chuckled, but it was hard to hear over the waves. His soldier cowboy bounced back quick, he had to admit. The panic, though, that had been real.

That was scary. And it probably wasn't the last time. But Saw had so many more good days than bad ones, and now that they were living together, he would be there for Saw every single time. The memories could fuck with Saw's head, but he'd make sure they didn't fuck with Saw's life.

Somehow. He would.

"This is beautiful. I could watch this for days."

Jax chuckled. "I could too if it was warmer. You ready to climb back into bed?"

"Come on. I'll hold you for a while." Saw levered himself up and overbalanced a little, managing to catch himself on his walker. "Oops."

"Oops. Gosh, and I was starting to think you were perfect." He grinned and tugged on the blanket, rolling it up in his arms.

"That's me. Señor Perfecto." Saw winked at him. "Monsieur Parfait. Herr Perfekt. Uh..."

"Sleepy. You're sleepy, Mr. Parfait." He giggled his way back into the house. "Oh. Shh."

"Right. They're morning glories... no, uh, what's the opposite of owl?"

"Uh. Mouse? Silly people that sleep at night. Are you hungry?"

Saw grinned at him, eyes twinkling. "God yes. You? We could make pancakes."

"We should. Perfect." He turned on a light and started looking for flour, sugar, vanilla. "We can make extra and Jan and Hawk can nuke them for breakfast."

"Good deal. What should I do to help?"

"Um. Find a griddle or a frying pan?" He tried to whisper, but he kept forgetting. Hawk and Jan took the upstairs bedroom, so he'd just have to hope they were far enough away. Surely they had a door they could close, right?

"On it." Saw was exceptional at getting around on his walker while seated.

"You kind of look like a crab, zooming around like that," Jax teased.

"Oh, I like that. I should get a glittery red walker to help the illusion." Saw made pincher motions with his good hand, and Jax shook his head.

"Nope. Both hands, stud."

"Right." Saw grinned at him and managed to actually pinch his hip with his scarred hand.

"Hey! I felt that!" Jax grinned at him and gave him a kiss.

"Nice. You made good progress this week. I know Art is tough on you, but I'm so proud of you."

"I have to tell you, I was feeling guilty about backing off on the legs, but they feel better."

"Guilty? Why?" He found a whisk and some milk and started mixing things together.

Saw blinked and looked over. "I—well, I guess... I guess I thought I was supposed to go and go, you know. Do anything and everything? I'm learning about letting shit back off, even when my brain keeps saying, you have to push. I'm not Rocky. I don't get the magical training montage."

Jax nodded. "Okay. I get that. Does having real plans help? I mean, you don't need to do everything anymore, right? Just what you need to get what you want."

"Shit, just realizing how much less I hurt now than two weeks ago is a goddamn revelation. And I think, maybe, I'm walking just as well. Or better?"

Oh Saw was asking, was really wanting to know what he thought.

"I think..." What did he think? Saw was happier, that's what he thought. Motivated, smiling more. "Specifically walking? I think maybe about the same, but you're getting around better. Like walking like other people do is less important than getting the job done just as well." Like the little crab thing with the walker that Saw was just doing. Who cared if Saw walked from here to there. He got there, right?

"I just want to be able to be me, with you." Saw winked at him, waggling his eyebrows. "I'm hurting less, and that's a good thing for my soul."

Jax leaned over and kissed Saw's cheek. "It's a good thing

for mine too, if I'm honest. It's not always easy to see you hurting, you know? Even when I know it's good work."

"I hear you." Saw turned his face to get a real kiss.

"Mmm. You do. You always do." He gave Saw that kiss, happily. He was so lucky. He didn't know why. He never used to be. "All I had was bad luck until I met you."

"Well, I'm glad I broke the streak, sugar. You deserve that."

"I'm glad you did too." He gave Saw another quick kiss and went back to mixing. "Pancakes."

"Skillet!" Saw handed that over and went for the butter and the syrup. "Did we grab any blueberries?"

"Ooh. Yum. I have no idea. You want to look?" He put the griddle on the stove and turned on the heat. "Tomorrow, we'll keep our normal schedule, sleep in. It's our vacation, right?"

"Yep. I like the idea of watching the sun come up over the water. I bet it's pretty." Sawyer dug through the fridge. "Do you get inspiration for cupcakes from stuff like the beach?"

He froze for a minute and looked at Sawyer. "No. But I should. What a great idea! Sand and starfish and... shells."

"Mmm...cinnamon-y sand! I like the idea of that." Saw's smile grew bigger. "Or a flip-flop for the summer. A... what are those things... Oh! A sand dollar cookie on top."

"We're doing this. Flip-flop cookies. Sand dollar cupcakes. Sandy cupcakes with little beach umbrellas in them. You're brilliant." He helped look for blueberries and they found them at the same time. "Ah-ha!"

"Hooray! Blueberry pancakes for the win!" Saw opened the container and popped one in his mouth with remarkably little trouble.

He didn't want to point that out, because Saw wasn't

four. He didn't need every accomplishment pointed out, that would get so annoying. But he smiled, because it was good, really good, and dumped half of the container of blueberries into the batter.

He started pouring batter, and they had a stack of perfect pancakes in no time. Saw even flipped a few. They weren't as pretty, but they were going to taste just as good, and they were the first ones Jax pulled off the stack for himself.

"Jan got the good syrup. The Vermont stuff."

"Oh, I love that shit. There's something special about maple syrup. It goes with pancakes, waffles, bacon, French toast…"

He nodded. "And you can bake with it too. Cupcakes, cookies, fudge, frosting, hard candy… and you can put it in some breads too."

"Mmm…maple isn't super beachy, though. Maple makes me think of fall and Thanksgiving and—" Sawyer stopped, like someone had turned off a faucet, then their eyes met. "We got Halloween together. Thanksgiving. Christmas. We get that, sugar."

He nodded slowly, not trying to stop his growing smile. "We do. And we can do whatever we want together." He reached under the table and caught Saw's knee. "But if you like family, I bet you didn't know we have that too."

"We do. We got Jan and Hawk, Jo. Who else?"

"Hawk's family. He has a hundred gigantic brothers, and they all have wives and kids and… he and Jan hauled me out there for Thanksgiving *and* Christmas. It was wild. *Wild.*" He'd had fun though.

"No shit. You got to meet them all? They're fantastic folks." Saw took a big bite of pancakes with a hum.

"Met them, made salt dough ornaments with the kids,

hid in the barn with the dogs... that was a lot of company." The pancakes were just what he wanted. They were tasty and sweet and filling. "You know what's cool? When I marry you, I'll have a sister."

"You will. We'll have to call her tomorrow, tell her the good news." Saw didn't look the least bit worried about that. No, that was happiness.

"We can start our own traditions. Bakeries are busy at the holidays so we probably can't travel much. But wait until you see New York at Christmas. It's pretty neat." He'd take Saw to Rockefeller Center to see the tree.

"Folks can come to us. We'll have a good twenty years before I've seen all the neat stuff at home, and by then, there will be new neat shit."

He laughed. "Twenty years. We'll be old. We'll be paying people to run our place by then!"

"Yep. And we'll run around like goofballs and laugh together."

And that didn't sound strange at all, did it? That they would be together in twenty years.

"Traveling. Seeing things. Anywhere. Everywhere." He popped a big bite of pancakes into his mouth. "Mhm."

"It'll be great. You, me, whatever dog I have then."

"Dogs? Kids? Maybe your service dog will have a friend. Twenty years is a long, long time. Sometimes, I have a hard time with twenty minutes." He watched his handsome lover. His handsome fiancé! He put his fork down and leaned back in his chair. He was so full. His heart as much as his stomach.

"Shit, twenty years is just a bunch of twenty minutes strung together."

18

"Jo? Jo, honey, you busy?"

"Are you Facetiming me? Really? My face isn't on."

Saw rolled his eyes. Girls. God. "I want to introduce you to someone."

"What? Who? I need to do my hair!"

"Jo, this is my fiancé Jax. Jax, this is my goofball sister, Jo." They needed to meet and find out about each other, and shit. "We're at the beach. It's cool."

"Oh, don't get me started." Jax leaned into the frame and smiled. "Nobody has good hair at the beach. Hi, Jo!"

She blinked and then squealed, the sound loud enough that the seagulls went flying. "Your fiancé? You're getting married? OMG. Give him the phone. Are you cute?"

Jax plucked the phone from his fingers. "Me? No. Not even on a good hair day. Right now, I'm also a little sunburned. You're adorable though."

"OMG! You are *so* cute! Look at all that hair! Jealous!" Everything Jo said was punctuated with an exclamation point.

Jax turned and leaned on Saw so he was in the video.

Well, his shoulder and his chin anyway. "Is this like, you didn't know I existed and suddenly I'm a fiancé? Or has Saw filled you in on the crazy midnight baker he's moved in with?"

"Of course I knew you existed. He only talks about you, like, all the damn time, but he never takes selfies with you or anything!"

"I know, he doesn't think about pictures. He's a bore like that. I can fix this." Jax flipped to his messages and texted Jo a phone number. "That's my cell. Now you can harass me for pictures. Because I do take them. Has he told you how good he's doing here?"

"He has. So you're Jax. I'm so glad to finally know you."

"I am Jax. And me too, Jo. Saw is so proud of you. I can't wait to meet you in person. What's your favorite dessert?"

"Strawberry pie. I love a strawberry pie." She beamed at them both. "When's the wedding? Can I be there? I have a pretty dress, and I've never been to New York."

"Yes. You have to come. But I have no idea. All I said was yes." Jax sat up and looked at him. "When's the wedding, soldier cowboy?"

"When can you be here?"

"December. School's out on the eighth, and I have practicals this time. If y'all can't wait, that's cool, but I have my four-point-oh right now. I can't lose that."

"No. No, we can't have that. You've worked too damn hard, honey." Saw would work it out.

"December is okay with me," Jax mouthed at him. Then Jax looked back at the phone. "We'll get back to you, don't worry. There's no rush and we can't do it without you there. You're family."

"Then December I'm free, and I want to come see you

and meet Jax and see your home!" Jo sounded like she was over the moon.

Jax leaned on him again and handed him his phone back. "December then."

"Apparently. December is a great month." He grinned at Jo. "Love you, baby girl. Work hard. Learn all the things."

"Every goddamn day, Sawyer."

"Good girl." He winked at her. "Bye."

He hung up and winked at Jax. "That was her."

"She's so cute! I love her." Jax's head landed on his shoulder. "It must be hard to have her so far away."

"Yes, but she's got a life, a boyfriend, a sorority. She's happy." She was living her dream.

"Good. Did you guys grow up close?"

"She's a few years younger than me, but yes. She's a sweetheart—cheerleader in high school, good in school, drill team in college—the whole shebang." He'd been a cowboy, through and through.

"Did she... know Ollie?" Jax traced the scars on his arm with one light finger.

"I brought him home once or twice, but he's some old guy to her, I bet. Not a cute boy." He leaned over and kissed Jax's cheek. "Not like you."

"I'm a cute boy?" Jax snorted and turned his head and pointed to his pouting lips. "Right here needs a kiss too."

"You're my cute boy." The words made him chuckle, and he took a hard, quick kiss.

Jax laughed. "Okay, I can go with that. So, December?"

"December. That'll be a spot of joy in a super busy time, right?" He knew that they would be busy on anniversaries, but he needed Jo to be there, if possible.

"She said the eighth, so, let's do it as early in the month as we can. That way we might be able to squeeze in a day off when Ollie's is up and running. Every day is like a honeymoon right now." Jax squinted out over the water. "Maybe every minute."

"Sounds perfect." He grabbed Jax's hand and held on. He was ten feet tall, so honored, so proud. So fucking happy. "Thank you."

"The night we get home, I have to bake two hundred cupcakes. See if you still want to thank me then." Jax squeezed his fingers.

"I'll fill them." He was still splotchy on the whole icing bit. Okay, but learning, that was him.

"I'll take it." Jax stood and offered him a hand up. "Beach walk? I want shells."

"Beach walk." He liked this—walking on the sand. It was a challenge, and it was actually fun.

"Oh. Who's texting me? Everyone I know is at the beach." Jax pulled his phone out of his pocket and looked at his phone.

For a long time.

"So... do you have PT or anything on Wednesday?"

"No, sir. What's up?" That sounded... distressing.

"Well, I found a realtor and she wants to talk to us on Wednesday." Jax glanced up from his phone, a goofy smile growing on his face.

"Oh. Oh! Really? Cool." He let himself smile right back. "Exciting, right?"

"I think I'm terrified. And excited." Jax's eyes lit up. "This is happening, isn't it? Like, for real?"

"Is everything okay?" Jan and Hawk were making their way down the beach toward them.

"Yes. Very. Yes. And crazy too. We have an appointment with a realtor." Jax bit his lip.

Hawk clapped his hands together. "For an apartment?"

"For a bakery," Jax said softly like he might jinx it.

"What?" Jan threw his arms around Jax. "Really? You've got a commercial realtor?"

"We do." He chimed in, grinning as wide as Jax was.

"It's ridiculous. This is ridiculous. I can't believe someone took us seriously." Jax shook his head. "Nuts."

"Why wouldn't they? We have a business plan, a going business, money, and I am a veteran. We're a great bet."

"Saw is right. You're a safe bet and a good investment. If you need some backing cash, you let us know." Hawk gave Jan's arm a pat. "We'll celebrate at dinner."

"Sounds good to me, but Jax promised me a walk on the beach first. Do y'all want to come?" Saw stood, balancing himself on the walker, finding his stance on the sand.

"Thank you, but no. I'm taking Hawk sightseeing. But we'll see you on the deck to grill around six?" Jan smiled at him and gave him a wink.

"Perfect." Saw reeled Jax in for a soft kiss, letting it linger until the nervous tension eased. "Let's wander, man. Tell me about what we're going to look at when we get back."

"Store-fronts that could be bakeries." Jax bent and picked up a shell, blew the sand off it. "But right now, we're just on vacation."

"We are!" They were doing a lot more than that. They had decided on a wedding date. They had decided to start their lives.

He had a second chance.

19

"Okay, that's three. I give up. You're hurting and I'm over this." Jax shook his head. They'd seen three properties. The first one was never going to work, the location was awful. Like, scary. The next two were super nice, but one was too expensive and the other landlord didn't like their lack of credit history.

They'd seen two other places with the realtor two days ago, and neither of those were going to work out either.

And nobody cared about their business plan, not even the realtor. It was just about money. She was nice maybe, but if she didn't see things like they did, who would?

He was done.

He pulled out his phone. "I'm getting us an Uber."

"Okay, sugar." Saw didn't seem to argue. "There will be the right place. I know there will."

He shook his head again. "No. Now's not the right time, I guess. I don't know what I was thinking."

"Stop it. We aren't just giving up. We'll take a breath, a break even, but I'm not giving up."

"I should have known better. I'm like a bad luck magnet.

I swear. Car will be here in five." Saw might not be giving up, but he was. Saw had this weird way of never giving up. But he didn't have that... thing. Drive. Gene. Whatever.

"Nope. Not bad luck. These weren't the right bakeries. We don't need the wrong one!"

"They're all the wrong one." He paced a couple of steps away, trying not to get mad. Upset. He didn't like being upset. "We're not getting any of them, Saw. I know you're all Mr. Optimism, and for you, that's good, but for me, that's silly!" It was better not to get his hopes up.

"Why?" The question wasn't angry. It was just a question.

He frowned. "Why what?"

"Why is it silly? I don't understand."

"Because it's *me*. Good things don't happen to me. Nothing I want ever happens. I wish I'd never said anything about wanting the bakery. It was better as a happy dream I knew would never happen." He was the happiest he'd ever been after he'd met Saw but before he'd told anyone about his dreams. Why hadn't he just kept that to himself?

The car pulled up, and Saw stood and grabbed his walker. "I happened to you."

Jax stared at him. Shit. He was so stupid. "Well, yeah. You did. You're better than good. You're a *great* thing." He jumped up and opened the car door for Saw. "You're the best thing ever. I don't even need any more good things after you." Stupid. Why didn't he think before he said stupid things?

"Then maybe this is the start of the getting what we want. You and me." Saw smiled at him. "Hold my walker? My legs are shaking a little."

"Got it." He steadied the walker for Saw. The start?

Maybe. Other than Saw, the start had been pretty rocky. "Maybe."

"Thank you." Saw got into the car with a sigh, and when he'd put the walker in the back and climbed in, Saw took his hand. "Do you want to go eat or go home and nap?"

He leaned against Saw. "I don't know. Are you hungry? I don't think I'm hungry. I don't feel great. I have to make cupcakes later..."

"So let's go home and nap, so that we can order Chinese and make cupcakes later." Saw grinned at him. "There are going to be more bakeries. Have faith."

He shrugged. "I do, in you, but that's all." He didn't think there would be more bakeries. He wasn't even sure he wanted to look anymore. He was tired of being told no.

"That's fine. That's enough for me."

How could Saw just be so... okay? Why wasn't he more pissed off?

It didn't make sense.

He turned on the seat to face Saw. "Why doesn't this upset you? I mean, I know it's not your thing like it's been mine, but why are you not mad? I am. I'm really fucking upset." He kept as calm as he could, but he couldn't stop the tears or his hands from shaking.

"Well, I guess because I expected to have to look a long time? The guys I know from the service could look at thirty houses before they found the right one." Saw leaned in, and those eyes were twinkling. "And it's kind of exciting, looking at things with you, planning with you, figuring out all the things."

"With me? That's exciting?" It was a little. Maybe that was a better way to look at it. "Like an adventure..."

"Yes. I am learning a ton, seeing the city, and exploring with you. I like learning things with you."

He sat back in his seat again. "I like that too. You're so... relaxed. You don't worry. You just... do things."

"Yeah. My therapist says that it's a defense mechanism, that it's how I learned to cope."

"Maybe I need some of that coping stuff." The car stopped. They were home.

"You just need more good luck." Saw eased himself up out of the car, swaying dangerously for a second.

"Got you." He moved up right behind Saw and stood close, not helping really, but letting him lean, and not giving him anywhere to go but forward with his walker. "You good?"

"Yeah. Sore. Ready to snuggle in our bed together and have a big glass of water." Saw started slowly moving toward the door.

"Me too. I'm toast, man." He stayed very close as they went inside and got on the elevator. "You did great today though. We did a lot of walking. You're getting stronger all the time."

Dragon Lady Schwartz was waiting for them as they got off the elevator. "Someone said you were going to get a dog. You can't. They have fleas."

"It's a service dog," Saw explained. "He won't have fleas."

"And he'll be legal and approved by the landlord and everything. Have a nice day!" He stood between the Dragon Lady and Saw so Saw could get by. "Maybe thank him for his service, instead."

"Give peace a chance!" she hollered, and Saw just cracked up, laughing so hard he had to stop a second.

He burst out laughing too, hard enough he also held onto Saw's walker for a second. "I told you, I can't make this shit up, soldier cowboy."

"It's perfect. I approve." Saw grinned at him, waggling his eyebrows. "I cannot *wait* to get my dog."

He let Saw in and held the door. "Go to bed. Get off your feet. I'll get us some water." He watched Saw for a second. "You good? You want me to walk with you?" He didn't offer help often. Saw knew when to ask, but his soldier cowboy was tired. They both were.

"I'm good. I'm going to make it and try to take off my shoes without falling on my face this time. Goals!"

"I approve. Be careful and give those shoes hell." He chuckled and headed for the kitchen for water. They'd get a nice nap, and later they'd get up, eat something bad for them, and bake.

He was surprised to find himself... okay. Somehow, Saw had done that for him. He was disappointed, sure, but it wasn't the end of times.

It would have been without Saw. Then again, without Saw he probably wouldn't even be trying. Ugh. Things were feeling complicated again. He needed his man. Then everything would be all right.

He grabbed two water bottles and headed for the bedroom.

20

Saw was not going to let this whole weird-assed bakery-hunting thing get him down. He was happy to do the internet leg work, and he was slowly integrating Jax's wants with his needs, and what their budget could do.

It was like a huge puzzle, and Saw wasn't mad at it.

"Oatmeal, chocolate chip, white chocolate almond, sugar, and... snickerdoodles." Jax set a cookie down on his keyboard.

"Snickerdoodles!" he sang like the world's biggest idiot. "Are my favorite!"

That was guaranteed to get a smile.

"I kno-ow!" Jax sang back, the huge smile lighting him up inside and out. "I made an extra tray just for you, my handsome soldier cowboy lover. What are you doing?"

"Researching commercial spaces. Too bad we don't need to have a bakery in Nowhere, Tennessee. Those are reasonable. No customers, but the rent is good."

Jax snorted. "Kinda need people to eat. Just give up. I don't think it's meant to happen right now. Another cookie?"

"Is too, and yes. Yay cookies!"

Jax laughed and brought over two more. "I think we should talk about Halloween costumes and forget this." He knew deep down Jax hadn't given up, but it was hard to keep hearing no.

"Do you usually dress up?" He hadn't dressed up in an eon, but he was willing.

"No. I bake. I bake my ass off for two days, do a huge morning-of delivery and then sleep like the dead for a day. Holidays are like that for me. Gotta pay the rent!" Jax grinned at him. "I just thought you might."

Well, then he wouldn't either. He would watch Halloween while they worked. "I'll help with the baking. I'm getting better at it."

"Jan and Hawk go to some party. They always invite me. You should go have some fun."

"You're fun. We have fun, don't we?" He thought they did.

No. He knew they did. Jax was just being sensitive.

Jax sat with him at the table. "We do. We totally do. And you're really getting the hang of baking too. I just... I don't want you to miss out on all the holidays because of me. I bet you love holidays."

"So we'll decorate, have candy, and watch scary movies together." He was going to outstubborn this down mood of Jax's, dammit.

"Yeah? Okay. That sounds great. Just watch the jump scares, they're hell on frosting." Jax grinned at him.

"Ack! Bloop! Ack! Blop!" He loved making Jax laugh. It suited him to the bone.

"Yes. And sometimes, whee!" Jax slid his arms across the table. "Seriously. It's a mess. I wait out the suspenseful bits."

"Oh, I like that. Good idea." He reached across, letting

his sore muscles stretch, twining their fingers together, oh so carefully.

"Look at those fingers all moving independently. That hand was kind of like a mitten when you met me, you know? You're doing great." Jax closed his fingers gently around his. "It's nice."

"It is. It was the right decision, to work on my hands and arms. I need to be able to lift and squeeze and touch." He liked feeling macho, and he really liked knowing that he could learn all this new stuff about baking. It made him happy.

"You're smart, Saw. And you have a good physical therapist. Wait until you tell him you piped icing spiders and gave them tiny candy eyeballs and licorice legs."

"Oh, I saw these ones on Pinterest where you put a Rolo on a hot cookie and smush it a little and make it a roach." It had been gross and amazing.

"A roach? That's gross! I love it. We should do that just for us to have on Halloween." Jax covered their hands with his free one. "When do you get your dog?"

"Hopefully, we start training around February. I've seen pictures, but they're still in their training, and we'll get a fit during the holidays." He was excited. He'd be more excited with a little space for the pup, but it would be okay.

"A Christmas present! Oh, Christmas. Christmas is complicated. Hawk has all this family... you think you can handle it?"

"Where do they stay?" Why couldn't he? His sister was going to be here first for their wedding.

"Oh, no. We go there. I've been going down late Christmas Eve, after I deliver my Christmas goodies, but I do go. Hawk won't hear of us not going."

"Where are they?" He wasn't going to Texas. This would

be his first Christmas CONUS in a long time, and he wanted to see what it was like here. If Jax wanted to go, he totally understood. He'd hang out with Jo.

"Texas. I don't know, I fly into Austin."

"It's a decent airport." That was his best non-answer answer. He'd talk to Hawk, maybe, see if there was a way to check the weather on this front.

"Wait until you see New York at Christmastime though. It's amazing. Lights and the big tree and people everywhere. Sometimes it snows... What's wrong? You have a weird look..."

"Do I? I'm looking forward to being here for Christmas, you know? It'll be our first together."

Jax's head tilted like was hearing some strange sound. "It's our first Christmas together." He got a big grin suddenly. "We can do whatever we want. You have family. *We* have family."

"We do." And Jax got it. "I'd like to discuss this year, just being us. Here. Just being where we are together and making our traditions. This is my first Christmas home."

"Let's do it. Just us. And Jo, of course. I've got morning deliveries on Christmas Eve and then I take the week off through New Year's Day." Jax looked excited now, happy.

"Then we will be able to just be. Tree, singing, stupid cartoons, laughing." He winked at Jax. "Do we order Thanksgiving in or does Jan?"

"Well, Jan does it here in their apartment. He and Hawk invite anyone who needs somewhere to be for the holiday. Cowboys, friends of Jan's, me, sometimes their neighbors... whoever. It's fun. Maybe we can still do that?"

"Sounds perfect. We'll be busy and tired, and we don't need the stress, right? And it'll be perfect to spend with our chosen family." Because Jax needed Jan, and he knew it.

"That's okay? You're sure?" Jax was trying to downplay how important it was, but Jax couldn't hide it from him. "Jan deals with all the food and everything. I always bring something sweet, but all we really need to do is show up. It's easy."

"Perfect. I'm in." He leaned forward, offering Jax a wink. "Dude, we just organized the whole holiday season in one fell swoop."

"We did?" Jax leaned back in his chair. "You're right, we did. Look at us being adults." Jax laughed. "Gram would be so proud."

"Yeah. Where was their bakery? Here?" He rubbed Jax's hand with his thumb, so proud of himself.

"Hoboken, across the river in New Jersey. It's nice over there. She had an apartment, but there was a courtyard behind the building and a park just up the street. I remember taking long walks along the river. It was nice."

Hoboken. That was a great name, like Kalamazoo or Truth or Consequences. "Is that far from here, then?"

He wasn't sure where things were, exactly. His range of knowledge was growing, but slowly, sort of organically.

"Nope, just across the river. Easy trip into the city. You can even get across by ferry. I used to come in with Gram every weekend that way, the ride is like, ten minutes. It's cool." Jax shrugged. "It's cheaper than the city, but not by a lot."

"So is that an option for you, then? I mean, to widen my search?"

Jax looked interested, like it wasn't something he'd thought of before. "Sure, why not? Maybe there and maybe Jersey City?"

"Okay. I'll do that. I just want something that makes us

happy." Everything he knew about New Jersey could fit in a thimble, but he could so try.

"You're good to me. You're like snickerdoodles for my soul. I can't believe you're still looking. Thank you." Jax stood up and kissed his cheek.

"We're planning a future, sugar. I'm having a ball." He'd never imagined this. "My world is right."

21

Jax rolled out of bed as the sun was going down. He didn't want to leave Sawyer's warmth, but he had to pee and his stomach was growling too. They had to get up soon anyway. He had more baking to do.

They were on the last day of a three-day binge of making cookies and cupcakes for Halloween. Each night, they'd baked, then delivered in the morning, then went to bed just to get up to do it all over again the next night.

One more night and then they had four days off.

He finished in the bathroom, then made a cup of tea and put another hunk of the giant egg bake they'd made before all of this started into the oven to warm up. His man had been waking up hungry. Then he took his tea and wandered over to his laptop, which had been sitting on the little card table in the front room for weeks while Sawyer hunted for bakeries, properties that could serve as bakeries, places they could rent, buy... just all kinds of hunting.

Saw had been so much help with the baking, he hardly remembered what it was like to do it alone. It took less time and was much more fun with Saw around, even just for company when Saw's hands got tired.

Saw was so enthusiastic about doing this with him, too. Bakery after bakery, space after space. He was nonstop.

Beside the computer was a notebook, lines and lines and lines of notes, all in this tiny, blocky handwriting. Every page was titled.

Needs.

Wants.

Options.

Budgeting issues.

Supply issues.

Equipment.

Commute time.

Then came the lists of areas and notes about each property. Toward the back were notes about Hoboken. About his grandparents' bakery. About the area. Costs. Phone numbers and email addresses and lines and lines of information.

It was amazing. So much work, so much detail. It was proof that this meant as much to Saw as it did to him. Not that he needed proof, his soldier cowboy was focused and determined where he would have given up long ago.

But he hadn't given up. He couldn't. Saw had kicked all his excuses to the curb. It had frustrated him a bit at first, but how could he stay that way when Saw said things like they were doing this together, this was going to be their business, it was their future.

It was everything he wanted, and he was happy.

He traced the address of the old bakery. He'd grown up there. Loved it. They'd find something like it eventually, even something smaller to start out.

He took another sip of his tea and woke up the laptop,

which opened up to a document with addresses and links. It looked like something Saw was pulling together either to show him or maybe give to their realtor? It was neat and organized.

He clicked through the links, nodding at some of the things Saw had found.

Then he clicked on one link, and there it was, his Gram's bakery.

For sale.

Whoa.

"What?" For sale? And it looked like whoever owned it had kept it a bakery, or some kind of take-out food place at least. "Saw..." he said softly, then pushed back from the table and ran for the bedroom. "Saw! Saw, you found it!"

"What? What's wrong?" Saw sat up in a rush, eyes wide. "Jax?"

He jumped onto his side of the bed. "You found it. Gram's bakery. You found it!"

"I did." Saw nodded, drew him in. "This morning early. I was hurting, so I was researching while I waited for the pain pill to kick in. I called to go see it."

"You called? Already?" He kissed Saw's cheek. "I'm sorry you were hurting."

"I'm waiting for an appointment. I'm better now. PT sucks some days, huh?" Saw leaned back, let him lean. "I thought we had to go and see it. It's a touch above our price range, but there's even an apartment above, so there's an option there..."

"Gram's apartment too? Oh, no..." He frowned. This wasn't good. What if it was too expensive? What if they couldn't do it? He'd be so disappointed.

"It's a joint deal—so we'd have to rent it out, if you wanted to stay here, but that's doable too. We have options."

"What if we wanted to move there? Can we afford that? I don't think I know how to say no to my Gram's old bakery, Saw. If we can't say yes, then I better not go."

"If we moved there, we wouldn't be paying rent here, right? That's how we'd do it. Is that a good place to live?" Saw blinked at him. "I mean, we're going to see it."

"It's a little farther from Jan, but it's a good place for a dog... the park and everything. The walk along the river..."

"Oh, yeah? That's a bonus. Did you like it? The apartment, I mean?"

"It was Gram's. I sold all her stuff and moved out when she went to the nursing home. I missed it for a while." He'd missed for a long time. It might be old now, or run-down, or maybe renovated by whoever moved in next, who knew? "I liked it."

"Well, we should go see—" Saw's phone rang, and he answered it. "Hey, Terrance. Yes. Yes, we are. Can we come out tomorrow afternoon?" Saw glanced at him, eyebrow lifted.

"What?" He mouthed, getting butterflies in his stomach. Actually nervous butterflies. "Already?"

Saw nodded back. "We'll be there. What time. Two? We can be there."

"Oh my god. Perfect. We can do our deliveries and then go right over..." He tried to keep his voice down, but he was so excited.

"We'll see you there. Thanks, man. I look forward to it." Saw hung up the phone, offering him again. "So. Two. We'll go see."

"Two o'clock tomorrow. It's a good thing we have so much work to do tonight. I wouldn't sleep anyway." He took Saw's hand. "I'm so excited. I hope..." He stopped himself. "I better not get my hopes up, huh?"

"You want to look at all the online photos? I thought it seemed solid." Saw's hand slowly slid up and down his spine.

"Yeah. I started to, but... I just couldn't believe you found it. I can't believe it's available. It feels like..." He took a deep breath. "I mean... you know what I mean."

"I do. I'm excited. I want to see it with you. Go grab my laptop? We can surf together."

"I'll get it. Be right back. I'll bring you coffee too."

He managed it by tucking the laptop under his arm before picking up their two mugs.

Saw made room for him, trying to take one of the mugs and only spilling a little bit on his fingers.

"You got it? Looks like you do." He opened the laptop up. "I hope you don't think I was being nosy. I just decided to poke around and see what you were looking at, and I saw it. Did I ruin a surprise?"

"Nope. I mean, I wasn't going to tell you if it was gone, but I was just up. No stress." Saw sipped his coffee with a happy sigh.

"Did you want to make sandwiches or order some food in before we get started tonight? We have monster cupcakes, Oreo spiders, and six graveyard cakes to make. I wish I had two ovens."

"Rawr! Monsters!" Saw could make some goofy-assed faces, guaranteed to make him laugh. "I'm easy. I don't mind a sandwich at all, and I like tacos too."

Saw was good to him, and made everything seem so easy. "Let's go easy and cheap tonight and tomorrow, after we sleep some and you do your PT, then we can have tacos."

"And we see the bakery! Don't forget that part." Saw waggled his eyebrows. "But first? Halloween fun."

The bakery. He hadn't forgotten. He was just trying very

hard not to get too excited. What if it was too much? Too big? Too expensive? What if it needed too much work, or the apartment was a mess or... anything could happen.

He didn't let himself think about what if everything was okay. Or even perfect. What if it was their first big step together...

"I can't think about it anymore. I'm going to explode. Just... boom. Let's make dinner. Do you need help getting up?" Focus on Saw. Focus on work. Focus on the things that made sense.

"Just stay close? I think I'm good." Saw kissed his nose.

"I like close. I can do close." He kissed Saw's shoulder, squeezed his butt, blew cold air across Saw's neck... anything to make sure Saw knew just how close he was.

"I like the way you do close too." Saw levered himself up, breathing hard, but managing it.

"Looking good, soldier cowboy." He closed the laptop, slid off the bed and picked up their mugs. "Do your thing. I'll meet you in the kitchen." He'd make them sandwiches and he'd pull a couple of snickerdoodles out of his secret stash.

"I'll be there with my icing muscles."

Oh, he liked that. He had been on the squeezing end of those muscles.

"My favorite muscles!" Well, almost his favorite. The other muscles they needed to be more naked for.

He laughed at himself and headed for the kitchen.

22

Lord have mercy, Jax was so ramped up that Saw was barely keeping him off the ceiling.

He prayed this bakery was okay and available, because he would move heaven and earth to get it for Jax. He'd already spoken to Jan and Hawk, and so he knew he had some investing wiggle room.

Saw was making this happen, dammit.

Jax was all smiles on the ferry ride and knew his way around, so they found the neighborhood easily.

"I haven't been back here in ages. It all looks so different. Nicer." Jax squinted up toward the top of a building. "Expensive."

"Revitalization is a thing, huh? It's cool. Look at that park. I can see walking my dog there." Saw forced himself to stay relaxed and easy in his skin. As easy as he could, given that he was nervous to death.

"I know, I used to walk with Gram there too. It's way greener than I remember." Jax had a hand over his where it rested on his walker. It was the closest they could really get to holding hands as they walked, and Jax just did it like it was the most natural thing in the world.

"Yeah? This is a good neighborhood, and it needs a bakery." Because people needed a good local place.

"It needs our bakery." Jax bounced a little, then gasped and pointed. "Right there. Oh, wow." It was a simple glass storefront with an awning that had seen better days. It looked just like it had in the picture.

Still, paint, a good cleaning, a new awning, some plants outside—it wasn't scary.

God knew they'd seen scary.

"Let's go look in the windows."

Jax went with him, and they cupped their hands to look in through the big window. "That looks like a pizza place. Was this a pizza place? But if that was a bakery case instead of a counter, this would be just like I remember."

"Well, we'll have to get one." Surely that wasn't the end of the earth. He'd been researching refrigerated cases already.

Jax nodded. "And new ovens maybe. We'll have to see when we get inside. Are we supposed to go upstairs first? Or wait out here?"

"He's meeting us—" The man he recognized from the website turned the corner. "—here. Now. That's him. Terrance."

Saw waved, and the realtor waved back, all smiles. "Hey. You beat me here."

"I know the neighborhood. Hi. I'm Jax. This is amazing." Jax stuck out his hand, and Terrance shook it.

"It's a great place. Needs some TLC, but what doesn't? It used to be a bakery, but it was running as a pizza joint for a couple of years. There's an apartment above as well, so that's a good investment opportunity."

Or a good place to live. He liked the idea of one set of stairs. "Is the apartment accessible?"

"Yes! There's an elevator in the back. It's super tiny, but it's there. It used to be a closet, but Gram had it made into an elevator when Gramps got sick." Jax glanced at the realtor. "Uh. I think. I mean it was there…"

Terrance's head tilted. "You know the space."

Jax blushed. "My uh… my grandparents owned it. The apartment and the bakery."

"Oh? Then you really know it. Excellent. Well, let's look at what changed."

Hopefully, it was cool, that Jax knew about it.

"You go first. I'm talking too much," Jax whispered to him.

"Sure. Remember he's working for us, babe. Breathe." Saw wasn't worried. This had happened for a reason, dammit. "We'll be fine."

Terrance opened the door, and the scent of flour and yeast was faint, but Saw imagined it was sunk into the soul of this building.

"We'll start in the shop."

They walked through, and Terrance told them about what was working and what wasn't and let them look around.

"New ovens here, and new bakery case here, register, a couple of little tables over there… just two. And Ollie's on the window." Jax stood at the counter. "Right?"

He smiled at Jax. He would do anything to keep that smile on Jax's face. "Yes. Paint. New awning. A hard scrub. Want to see the apartment?"

"Yes." Jax didn't wait for the realtor. He knew the way. He went toward the back, opened what looked like a closet door, and pulled a little gate out of the way. "After you."

"That doesn't hold more than two. I'll take the stairs." Terrance gave them a wave.

"It's cool, right? Tiny, but cool."

"It's perfect. Just right for me. Are you pleased with the state of the bakery?" He thought it was doable, and he hoped the apartment was in decent shape.

"We'll have to buy the big things, but we can clean it up easy and it might be cool to use found things for the tables and chairs and just paint them. And Jan told me when we were talking that he knows a guy that does the window thingies." The elevator was slow, but they got there. Jax pulled back the gate before he opened the door. "This should be interesting."

"It's going to be fun. I want to see where you used to live." Saw leaned and kissed Jax's cheek.

Terrance opened the door before Jax could. "Was the ride okay?"

"Just like I remember. Slow and squishy." Jax stepped out into the apartment. The elevator opened into a short hallway with two decent bedrooms and one pretty big bathroom, and up front was the kitchen, the living room, and a third, smaller room that might have been a study or a den.

"Wow. This is totally different...but I remember it anyway."

Much like the downstairs, it needed some scrubbing and some paint, but it was going to be way more room than they had now. "Which bedroom was yours?"

"The little one. The one on the left there was theirs and the one across the hall was sometimes their office and sometimes they rented it out."

Jax looked at the realtor. "Are a lot of people looking at it?"

"There have been a few people, yes. Investors." Terrance met Jax's eyes. "But the owners are in the neighborhood. They may be willing to give someone with history here a better chance."

"Well, nobody has more history here than me!" Jax leaned against the kitchen counter. "It's not in bad shape."

"It's not. It's a good size, a good neighborhood..."

"Do you like it? We should talk about it?" Jax bit his lip, looking hopeful but unsure.

"Can you give us a couple of minutes to explore, man?" Saw asked, because he wanted to just tell Terrance they'd like to make an offer, but they needed to chat.

"Of course. You can wander both spaces, I'll wait outside." Terrance pulled out his phone as he headed through the back door and down the stairs.

Jax pulled out his phone and tapped a few things, then held out the screen for him to see. "That's what I have saved..."

Saw blinked at the number, which was easily quadruple what he'd imagined. Okay. Okay, then. They could play ball here, especially with Jan's backing. "I can match that. Wanna buy a bakery?"

"Yes? Yes! Yes, please. Are you sure? You like it?" Jax looked like he might rocket into space any second.

"Yes. I'm sure. Let's do it. If we work it, we can make Christmas money." It was a risk, sure, but what wasn't? He'd never been a baker, but dammit, he would figure it.

For them.

"We can work it. I can keep baking at home while it's getting set up. You think we can be open by Christmas?" Jax was leading him back to the elevator.

"You start on the ovens. I'll start on the rest." First, they had to get their collective shits together and buy property.

Jax took a bunch of pictures with his phone before they got on the elevator and took even more downstairs in the shop. "Jan isn't going to believe this."

Neither did he, but it was happening. "Hey, Terrance? We'd like to make an offer."

23

Jax heard the phone ringing from somewhere, but it was dark and... oh. Sleep. He was sleeping and the phone was ringing. He should answer the phone. "M'kay," he mumbled, trying to sit up before he was even awake and not at all sure he was actually moving. "Got it. I got it."

"Hello?"

Wait. Who was talking? Was he on the phone? "'lo?"

"Yes, this is Saw. Uh-huh."

Oh thank goodness. Saw got it. He blinked his eyes open to find he hadn't moved one tiny bit. His head was still on his pillow.

"Cool. Cool. Yes. Go for it. Yes. Thirty days? Can we lease for a month, get in there? Yeah? Perfect."

Lease for... what? He rolled over and looked at Saw, his sleepy brain not putting the pieces together. "Who is that?"

"Terrance, sugar. Uh-huh. Uh-huh. Yeah. Email it. Yes, that'll work. I'll tell him. Good deal."

Terrance. And it sounded like really good news. He sat up and waited for Saw to hang up, watching as the butterflies grew in his stomach again. He really wanted good news, more than he had let himself admit.

And he'd admitted a lot.

"Hey, sugar, you up?" Saw didn't turn to look, but he did roll his shoulders and stretch.

"I'm up. I'm right here." He scooted closer to Saw, fitting right along his lover—his fiancé's back. "What did he say? Is it ours? It sounded like…"

"It's ours. We close in thirty days, and we're renting the space starting Monday, so we don't miss the holidays." Saw's heart was pounding hard.

"Oh my god." He tucked an arm over Saw and hugged him hard. "Oh my god. You found my Gram's bakery and you made it ours…" He didn't totally understand when his eyes filled with tears. He wasn't a crying kind of guy, but he didn't fight it either. "You did that for me. For us."

"For us." Saw held him tight, letting him cling. "We can start our lives. We just need ovens, right?"

"I might need to get Bessie a friend." He laughed softly. "I can't believe it." He kissed Saw's shoulder. "I love you. We're really doing this." He had his dream, he had his man… "Next stop, two zillion pumpkin pies!"

"Pumpkin pies. Pecan pies. Apple pies. Rolls. Thousands of rolls."

"So many rolls." He laughed again as the tears were clearing up. "I'm so relieved. I'm so happy."

"Then my work here is… well, just starting." Saw started chuckling at him.

"If we make it to January, we're golden." And he was determined to make it to January even if he had to bake pies in the pizza ovens. He'd even find a day or two to marry the man he was holding onto like a life buoy right now.

"We'll make it, sugar. You and me, we got will and each other. What else do we need?" Saw paused. "Well, lots of sugar and flour."

He slid over Saw, carefully helping Saw stretch out on his back. "That ought to do it."

"Yeah..." Saw grinned up at him, eyes laughing. "You got a wicked smile on, sugar."

"Mhm. Do you like it?" He slid his hands from Saw's waist to his shoulders and back, teasing those pretty little nubs along the way. "I'm just trying to be grateful."

"I like it." Saw swallowed hard, wetting his lips. Suddenly, the air in the room was electric, the buzz making the hairs on Jax's skin stand up. "I like it a lot."

"I think I'm going to kiss you." Saw's beard had been getting shorter and shorter, but it was still long enough for him to tug a little, and he did, giving Saw a flirty smile.

"Ooh... daring. I think I'd like to feel that." Saw's hand was hot as a brand where it landed on his hip.

That little buzz was still there, making him ache in a good way. A really good way. "Okay, then." He leaned down and gave Saw a kiss, and the buzz turned into a roar he could hear in his ears and feel in his veins.

Saw responded so well, cock filling against him, letting him know that Saw was right there, as eager for this as he was.

He stretched out long, kissing his way over Saw's chin to his neck, his shoulders, and lower, tasting skin. Scarred or not, it was all the same to him now. It was just Saw.

"Love you, sugar." Saw's hands dragged over his skin, long and slow and easy.

"Love you." Saw was the best thing that had ever happened to him. The best thing that ever would happen.

The bakery was a miracle really, but his man was still better. He reached between them, slipping his fingers under Saw's briefs.

"Mmm... You have the best ideas, Jax." Saw's grin tasted so sweet.

"Don't I? We need to celebrate... each other." Jax pushed his fingers into Saw's curls and slid them down to play with his lover's balls. Saw loved that, like all the scarred skin around them made them that much more sensitive or something.

His lover spread as best he could, letting him in, giving him space to play.

"You got something for me, soldier cowboy?" He bent to a pretty pink nipple and drew it in between his lips.

"I've got everything for you, sugar. Anything you ask for." The weird part was that Jax believed it. Anything he asked for, his Saw would arrange.

Jax reached for the lube. "That's what I want. All of this. Everything."

"Hell, yes." Saw's eyes burned into him, sharp and hungry. "Every inch for you."

He was glad they'd tested weeks ago. Rubbers were just one more thing Saw had to fumble with, and it took all of that awkwardness out of this equation. He slicked Saw's perfect cock, stroking just enough to get a soft moan, then reached back to get himself ready. "Want you so bad."

"Need you." Saw's callused hand carefully wrapped around his prick, loving on him, petting him.

"Love your hands." They were stronger than ever. He lined himself up, one hand guiding Saw's prick just so.

"Love you. Please, sugar. Please." Oh, Saw was so sweet.

"All yours." Jax sank down slowly, groaning with the

burn, never happier than when he and Saw came together like this. "God. The way you fill me up."

"So tight. I ache for you..." Saw's hand tightened around his cock.

He made some weird noise—he always made weird noises and Saw never cared—and started to move, giving Saw what he needed. What they both needed. That touch, Saw's grip demanded his attention. Saw could make everything and everyone go away with a touch like that. So all that mattered was them. And this.

"Love." Saw's eyes were fastened on him, clinging to him.

"Yes, love." He nodded, bracing his hands on Saw's chest and moving faster.

When Saw's eyes crossed, he knew he'd done the right thing.

But it was also his last really coherent thought. He just about lost his mind trying to push his cock through that tight fist and ride Saw's thick cock at the same time.

Saw did his best to help, rocking up into him, giving him all he had.

"I..." He didn't know if he'd been riding for a minute or an hour when he felt that knot start to come loose in his belly. Everything was just Saw and breath and hot fucking words. He tried to warn Saw, but he wasn't sure if any words actually came out of his mouth. He arched back and took Saw in to the hilt, humping down hard a couple of times before that heat seared through him, threatening to rip him in two. "Saw!"

"Got you..." Saw stroked him through his orgasm, then began humping, moving as best he could.

His head about exploded, but he rode Saw's perfect cock hard, making sure that his man got everything he needed.

Being able to make Saw shoot made him feel almost as dizzy as his own orgasm did.

"Love! Love you!" That wildness, that frenzy—that was his and his alone, and the heat as Saw shot was even better.

Jax shivered as he worked Saw through his orgasm, watching his lover's face and admiring his expression. He hung there, panting, body still trembling. "Love you, love you."

"Good." Saw laughed, the sound echoing inside him. "So good."

"Uh-huh. Whoo-boy." He slid off of Saw and flopped onto his back, grinning at the ceiling.

"We're buying a bakery." Saw sounded a little stunned. "And an apartment."

"My grandparents' bakery. And our new home." He curled his toes and stretched out long, giggling. "This is terrifying."

"We're going to have so much to do." Saw's hand was heavy on his belly. "I'm excited."

He nodded. "Me too." He wasn't anxious, even though he should be. Saw was confident, and that made it easier.

"We should know in a bit when we can pay a month's rent and get the keys and set to work."

"When we wake up, I'll grab my notebook and we can make lists." Saw knew he lived by lists. His notebook had everything he ever needed to remember. Orders and shopping lists, bills, phone numbers... he'd make a whole new section for the bakery.

"Perfect. You just tell me what you need, I'm on it. Utilities, moving, all the fun stuff."

"Not going to think about it now, though. I'm still buzzing." He covered Saw's hand with his. "Go back to sleep, soldier cowboy."

"I love you, sugar." Saw sighed, and his smile was pure satisfaction.

He knew that. He worried about a lot of things, but he didn't worry about that.

Ever.

24

S aw sat in the bathroom of their new apartment and
sobbed.

His body screamed—every single inch of him was in
agony after the last week of moving, and if he could give up
and die to stop the pain right now? He would.

How had his body gone from being able to do anything
he'd asked of it to this? How was he going to manage this?

"Sawyer?" There was a light knock on the door. "It's
January. Hawk and Jax have gone to return the truck Jax
rented. Don't ask me why a blind man volunteered to help
return a truck, but that's Hawk for you. Can I come in?"

He shook his head, trying to breathe. "S-sure, man.
What you need?"

Jan opened the door slowly. "I don't need anything. I just
heard you in here and thought you might want some
company."

"Sorry. Please, man. Don't tell Jax. He can't know." But he
was hurting so fucking bad.

"What's going on?" Jan started to sit on the edge of the
tub but discovered the zero-entry shower they'd put in and

smiled, then leaned against the counter instead. "Great shower."

"It is, huh? Just hurting. My body's wearing down."

"It's been a long week. I'm pretty sore too from all the moving. I can only imagine how difficult it's been for you. Why don't you think Jax should know?"

"He stresses, you know?" And Saw worried that it wouldn't take much to push Jax from his high to a low.

"Oh, I know. I've known Jax a long time. He stresses everything—his clients, the bills, what we're having for dinner on Sunday nights... that's Jax. He doesn't stress over you though. You make him happy."

"Good. That's what I want." What he needed right now was to stop hurting a little. "Can you help me, man? Please?"

Jan nodded. "What can I do? Do you have meds? Do you want to go lie down?"

"I can't open the bottle." He needed a pill and to have a few minutes on the sofa, he thought.

Jan looked around and reached for the bottle on the edge of the counter. "This one, yes? Just one?" He opened it up. "Let me get you some water."

"Please. Thank you. It's awful big." And he was crazy tired.

Jan put a pill in his fingers and brought him a fresh bottle of water, which Jan also opened for him. "You overdid it this week. I get why. Jax will understand too. But I don't think keeping how you're feeling from him is a good idea."

"It's not my job to make things worse for him, and we have so much to do. I just—you know. You're in love. You want things to be okay."

Jan took the water bottle and put the cap back on it. "Where do you want to move to?"

"Couch?"

"Sure." Moving was slow torture, but Jan was patient and just kept talking. "Being in love means protecting your man sometimes, but it's your job to be honest. That's love, too. I know you think you're sparing him something, but you're not."

"I hate this. I hate being broke, man. This wasn't what I used to be like."

Jan helped him settle on the couch and put his open bottle of water in reach. "Have you told Jax that?"

"Told Jax what?" He didn't follow.

"How you feel. That you hate this, that you feel broken... all of that stuff?"

"God no. Have you met my guy? He's got a lot on his mind, man."

Jan sat with him, watching him from the other end of their new couch. "Saw. You're just suffering through all of this and not telling the truth to the man who loves you more than anything in the world?"

"Telling him doesn't fix it. He helps me, a lot, but right now, he's in flux." And he wanted to be able to do this.

Jan shook his head, brow furrowed. "Flux. Well, you're not wrong, but you're not his therapist, Saw. He's a grown man, and he's going to have to figure out how to handle all of this. I think he will. And I think you need to give him more credit. He'll step up if you need him to. He can do it."

"He's amazing." And he loved Jax enough that it ached. "What do you think of our new place? I'm going to be painting a lot."

"It's a great place. Jax is very proud of it. Have you decided on colors?" Jan took his cue and let it go, but he could sense a little disapproval. Jan was protective of Jax. It was hard to argue because that was out of love too, but it was different. Jan was a friend, not a fiancé.

"No. I know the bakery is going to be a bright white with a red trim, but that's all." Something clean and bright, something nice.

"That will look great. I can help paint if you need it. Hawk won't be that helpful, but he can order pizza and beer with the best of them."

His phone chimed, and he gingerly pulled it out of his pocket.

JAX:

Picking up dinner, home soon <3

woo

"They're on their way back with food." Which was good, because he was a little sparkly around the edges.

"That's why Hawk went. He wanted to buy dinner." Jan chuckled. "That man of mine." Jan glanced at him. "How are you feeling? Did the meds kick in?"

"They're starting to. It's down to a roar. Can you tell?" He winked because he knew Jax would know he'd had to take one.

"Well, you texted Jax so I figured your fingers felt a little better, but... no. Not really. Do you have a heating pad or something, maybe?"

"Oh. God... I don't know where it is..." He panicked, because he was never going to rest without it.

"Hey. That's something I can do. I'll find it. Bedroom boxes maybe?" Jan got up and walked past him. "Think about what else you need while I'm looking."

"Warm socks and sweats, please." The jeans were killing him.

"Got it." Jan ducked into the bedroom, and he could hear boxes being shifted and opened.

Saw leaned his head back, forcing himself to relax.

"Heating pad, sweats, toasty socks. Easy to find, Jax packed them all together in one box, along with a pillow and some other things. It looks like he wanted you to sleep well."

"He's good to me. Just leave the clothes over on my walker? I'll get Jax to help."

"Sure." Jan left the clothes on the seat of his walker. "Heating pad now, or later?"

"Now, please." That was so he could eat, especially if forks were involved.

Jan handed it to him and found a place to plug it in. "You'll probably want an extension cord eventually, but this works for now. Why don't you rest until they get here? I can amuse myself."

"It means a lot that y'all helped." He didn't have any friends here yet, but it would happen.

"We were happy to. Moving is stressful and a lot of work. We'll get out of your hair soon, I'm sure you and Jax want to enjoy your new place alone, but Hawk will insist everyone eat first." Jan pulled out his phone and glanced at it. "They're almost here. Walking, looks like."

"I know that Jax wants to show off the bakery too. He's over the moon."

"You found him his dream, of course he is." Jan and Hawk had given them a small investment, but never tried to take any credit for helping.

"I want him to be happy. I want him to be proud and confident and to feel safe." It was the most important thing in the world.

"I hope you're looking after yourself, too. When do you get your dog, Saw?"

"Oh, they moved it up! Hopefully, before the end of the

month when my address changes. It should be around Thanksgiving."

"Oh, a good Thanksgiving gift. You and Jax are coming to our place, yes?"

"Yes. I would like that very much." He met Jan's gaze. "We're not going to Texas for Christmas, though. I hope you understand."

Jan smiled at him. "Of course. Jax has family now. He should be with you on Christmas. We'll miss you both, but I'm happy he's got a family of his own."

"Yes, and we'll be heading out on our honeymoon, right after." Even if they didn't actually go anywhere.

"Sounds perfect."

The elevator door opened, he could hear it from where he was sitting. "We're home!" Jax hurried right to him and Jan moved to the kitchen where Hawk was headed. "We found a deli, like a real New York deli, just up the street. Easy walking distance. It's a great place." Jax kissed his cheek.

"Oh, excellent. Did you get me something amazing?"

"Sandwiches on rye bread and big dill pickles." Jax watched him and sat down. "It's okay if you're not hungry right now. You look like you need to lie down."

He smiled and reached out to him. "I want to be with you. And I could stand to eat, huh?"

It helped with the pain pills.

That got him a sunny smile in return. "Okay. I'll bring you a sandwich. Do you like pickles?" Jax got up carefully, not jostling him at all.

"I love pickles." Not as much as he loved Jax, of course.

"Be right back."

He could hear the voices in the kitchen, his kitchen, as everyone got food. Jax came back with a turkey sandwich for

Saw, a cheese sandwich for himself and great big pickle cut in half.

"Here you go." Jax sat the plate down on the coffee table.

"These sandwiches are enormous." January helped Hawk find a seat. "You okay eating on your lap, Champ?"

"Yeah…"

Oh, that wouldn't work. "There are TV trays, Jan… I need them too. Sugar? You know where they are?"

"Oh, right. Yes. Hang on, I'll find them." Jax hopped up and disappeared into a bedroom.

"Thank you, Saw. It does make things easier. Otherwise, I end up feeding Buck, mostly." Hawk chuckled. "Not that he minds."

"No, but this is just easier. I know you know."

"Yes. Thank you."

"I found them." Jax came back with two trays, handed one to Jan and opened one up for him. "Sorry, love. I wasn't thinking."

"You're fine. The truck's back okay? No worries?" He found himself swaying in the chair, ever so gently.

"Oh, yeah. That wasn't too bad."

"Jax did quite well driving it back," Hawk said. "And Buck enjoyed the ride."

"We might need a truck eventually. Not one that big, but a pickup maybe? Getting everything delivered might be expensive after a while."

"Sure. I can see that." He could totally drive, maybe.

"Mm. Oh, that deli you found is a keeper." Jan chewed happily. "Good."

Jax nodded. "The pickles are amazing."

They all got quiet as they ate, and he realized he wasn't the only one that was tired. Shit, they'd moved their whole friggin' lives with two guys that couldn't do it all.

"I think I'm ready for a shower and my pillow." Jan gave Hawk's knee a pat. "How are you holding up?"

"Tired, but I'm managing."

Jan nodded. "We'll head home after we eat. The boys will want their privacy, and Buck has earned some downtime."

It would be great when he got his dog home. He thought it would help him and also Jax some too. This whole thing was a huge learning curve, but life had been since he'd left home.

"I tried to buy you dinner to say thank you, but Hawk wouldn't let me."

"You said thank you. You're welcome. Eat."

Jan snorted. "You heard the man."

"Eating eating la la la."

They all cracked up, the four of them just howling with it.

Eventually they finished up, all of them leaning back in their chairs, full as ticks, except Jax, who was running around cleaning up.

He ought to help, but the pills were in full swing, and all he could do was close his eyes and hope everyone understood.

25

Jax stood in the bakery kitchen admiring the new ovens all lined up where the pizza ovens used to be and ready to get to work. The pizza ovens sold for more than they'd expected, which let him buy a few other baking gadgets too.

Another week or so and they could start stocking supplies and baking a little. A soft opening, Saw called it. A trial run.

He couldn't wait to show Saw. He made sure things were locked up, then ran up the stairs to their apartment. Saw was spending the morning unpacking the last of their boxes and then they were going to sit and shop online for some furniture.

The apartment was awfully quiet—no music, no TV. Nothing.

Weird.

"Saw? Hello?" Did he go out? Jax poked his head into the kitchen but didn't see Saw there so he headed for the bedroom.

He found Saw curled up on the floor, walker turned

over, his lover panting.

"Saw!" He hurried over, heart pounding with worry but knowing he couldn't panic. "Hey. Hey, I'm here. Are you hurt? Can I move you? I think I should move you. Saw?"

"I fell. I'm sorry." Saw's expression was pained, sore.

"Don't be sorry, I'm here now and I want to help, okay? Let's see if we can get you onto the bed." He knew whatever he did was going to hurt. And he was ready to call for help if they couldn't do this.

"Okay. I'm sorry. I just... My arm wouldn't hold me up." Saw reached for him, holding on with trembling hands.

"I know this hurts. I'm so sorry." He just did what he needed to do and got Saw free of the walker, then carried him to bed, without even thinking for a second that Saw might be heavy until after it was done. "Okay... wow."

"I'm sorry. I'm sorry, love. I didn't mean to scare you." Saw had tears in his eyes.

"I'm sorry I didn't hear you go over. But I'm here now." He kissed Saw's forehead, hoping it might help. "You're hurting. You need your meds. Try to relax. I'll get them." He didn't know if Saw had hit his head or hurt himself or something, but the meds would help and then he could see.

He set Saw's walker back upright, then went to the kitchen for the meds. His heart had stopped pounding, and he was actually pretty okay now that Saw was safe and talking. He grabbed the bottle, filled a glass with water, and pulled a straw out of the drawer by the fridge. Sometimes when things were bad that was easier for Saw. "Got 'em."

Saw was sitting there, tears on his cheeks, and he wiped them off when Jax walked in.

"Hurts, huh? I'm so sorry." Jax set everything down and lifted Saw gently, scooting in behind him to help him sit up a little. "Did you hurt yourself? Do you think you hit your head?" He held a pill for Saw to take—sometimes Saw's hands hurt too much for little things—then picked up the water with the straw in it.

"Thanks." Saw drank deep, draining the glass. "I don't think I hit my head. I just... couldn't hold myself up, you know?"

That was weird because Saw had been working on his arms and his hands and they were strong. "I guess maybe you're tired, huh? I'm tired too." They'd take the rest of the day off and rest. Sit on their new couch and watch their new TV before they furnished the rest of the place.

"Are you? My muscles are protesting bad..." Saw leaned hard against him, heart just pounding.

He curled an arm around Saw gently and hugged him. "We've been working hard. Maybe you're doing too much? All this unpacking, it's not important. It can wait. You should rest when you need to." He would rather live out of boxes than see Saw hurting like this.

"I feel like I ought to be able to..."

To what? Do more? Keep up? What was Saw so worried about? "Ought to what? You don't even have your service dog yet. You're still doing rehab and stuff. Don't put pressure on yourself."

"I guess... I want to be more help, you know." Those poor overworked muscles shook hard, vibrating underneath him.

"I know. I'd kind of like to look more like Tom Holland, but we have to work with what we've got." He grinned against Saw's cheek.

"Butthead. I think you're perfect. I don't want Tom Whoever."

"Well, I think you're perfect too. I don't want you hurting yourself because you're working too hard. You're shaking,

Saw. I can feel you shaking. I know you're in pain. And I know this can't just be because of today."

"Moving's hard work." Saw rested harder against him.

"We've got this. You and me. We're not actually perfect, but we're enough. Okay?" This trembling was scary, and he hoped Saw's meds kicked in soon. No way was he going to be anything less than what his man needed though. Saw was his to take care of.

"You and me. How's it going downstairs? Good?" Saw began to relax. He could feel it, and it was gratifying as hell.

"Really good. The installers got the ovens in and glass cases are being delivered tomorrow. I'm going to break them in with a batch of cookies tomorrow to make sure they're all working right. That's easy work." Jax was going to make sure Saw relaxed tonight and if Saw didn't decide to take tomorrow off on his own, he'd insist himself. Give Saw's poor body a rest.

"Snickerdoodles?" That hopeful question made him smile.

"You know it." He kissed Saw's temple. "It'll be the first thing I bake in our ovens. What else would I do?"

"You're good to me." Saw took a long, deep breath, then let it out.

"I love you." Saw's heart had slowed down enough that it wasn't pounding against his chest anymore and that deep breath had to mean the meds were kicking in.

"I know. Can you stay a minute? Please?" Saw was melting, going heavy.

"I'm staying. I'm right here." He still didn't know how he hadn't heard that walker fall over, or Saw calling for him or anything. But he was going to be right here this time when Saw needed him.

"Thank you. I just need a few minutes; then I'll get back to it, huh?"

He snorted. "We're taking the rest of the day off. Pizza and movies. Don't even bother arguing."

"Yeah? You're sure? I'm not trying to slack, but... I hurt pretty good, sugar."

"I know. You're not slacking. You're resting. We have to listen to your body, okay?" He hugged Saw a little tighter.

"My body is an asshole that yells a lot."

He chuckled and nipped at Saw's ear. "Your body is amazing, and I love every inch of it. It's maybe a little bit mad, and I guess I can't blame it."

It had been blown up. That was a problem.

"Yeah, that seems a little unfair."

"I'm sorry about the walker. When you have your dog, that won't happen again, you know. He'll come get me. Or *she* will. I'll know you need me right away." Until then, he was just going to be very careful about leaving Saw on his own when he was tired, that was all.

"Yeah. That's the point, right? To have a safety net."

"Yes. That's exactly the point. And they won't let you work so hard you hurt yourself either." Oops. So much for not getting into things while Saw was trying to rest. "Go to sleep, soldier cowboy. I'll be right here."

"I'm not sleepy. I just want to be with you a minute. To hold you."

"Correction. I am holding you." He laughed gently. "And I like it." He'd stay right here for as many minutes as Saw wanted him to.

"You are. Me too. Liking it. You. Us." Oh, Saw made him smile.

"Are you feeling a little better? What were you trying to do when you fell?"

"Unpack some clothes. I just wanted to get some work done up here, you know? And we need to put that dresser in the right place."

He looked around the room. The dresser was probably not in the best spot for Saw to move around it. "I'll move it later." Maybe he'd call Jan and see if Jan had some time tomorrow.

"Yeah. Maybe I can help. Not right now." Saw sighed for him, the sound gusty.

"All I want you to do is rest. You've only just stopped shaking." That was scary. But he was keeping it together. He could lose it later, like on the phone with Jan or something. He could handle this.

"You're good to me, sugar. Do you like our new home?"

He loved it. Saw had to know that. "You know I do. We're going to be so good here. I hope you like it too."

"I love it. It's ours." And with those words, Saw was out, just sound asleep. Boom.

He tried not to laugh, but a giggle slipped out anyway. Sleep was good. And since Saw was using him as a pillow, he had a great excuse to not get up. He leaned back in the pillows and closed his eyes, grateful for pain pills, but more for the man in his arms.

26

S aw was so fucking nervous he couldn't breathe.

He was about to meet Poppy, his service dog.

Poppy.

She was a two-year-old Belgian Malinois with the prettiest markings, the brightest eyes.

"Breathe." Jax squeezed his hand and rocked into him lightly. "She's going to be worried about you if you don't relax."

"I'm sorry. I'm excited." Not scared. Not even worried. He'd had dogs all the time he was growing up. He'd worked with dogs in the service. But he wanted to see her. Make sure she was *his* dog.

"Excited is good. You still need to breathe." Jax was excited too. He could tell because Jax couldn't sit still. "I feel like you've been waiting forever."

"I feel like that's exactly right." Saw hated waiting. He wanted to get everyone home and start a damn routine.

A handler came in with Poppy on a leash. "Hey there." She stopped walking and Poppy sat at her side. "I'm Kate, this is Poppy. I'm just going to let her get used to guests for a minute. Did you get here okay?"

He glanced at Poppy, who gave him distrustful stare. "Can I give her a cookie?"

Jax chuckled. "We got here fine, thanks. He's excited."

"Sure." She handed him a little pouch of treats, then unclipped the leash. "She's all yours."

"Thanks." Saw thought he might be in love. "You want a cookie, Miss Poppy?"

She tilted her head, her nose working hard.

He waited, making himself be patient and easy. He knew how to do this, and they weren't just going to grab her up and take her. That wasn't good.

She inched toward him and took the treat, then backed up a step.

"Good girl," Jax said softly.

Poppy chewed the treat, then stretched her neck forward, looking for another.

He fed her a few more, and then she was close enough to pet, and she wiggled for him, nosing his hand.

"There you go. Well done." Kate gestured for Jax to come with her and they went and sat on a bench. "Just give her some love."

Saw muttered to Poppy, stroking her ears, offering her love and pets. God, she was soft, and her tail wagged, nice and slow.

"Good. So she isn't real sure right now if she's supposed to be working, so make it clear. If she is, come get the leash. If she's not, take off her harness. Up to you."

"What will make her more comfortable?"

"Probably working. She'll be working on her way home, right?"

"Yes, for sure." Kate held out the leash, but didn't get up. When Jax started to help, Kate put a hand on his knee. "Sawyer, you can come get it, or you can ask her to if you like."

Right. Right, he was the boss. He could do this. "Poppy, leash."

Her head tilted, and she went right for her leash, grabbing it, so he continued. "Bring it."

She brought it to him and instead of dropping it, she nosed at his fingers.

"Good girl." He clipped her leash in her harness. "Sit."

That fuzzy butt hit the floor. Boom. God, that was cute.

"Great. Now run through some of your commands. And if you need to sit or are in too much pain or anything, remember not to hide that stuff from her."

They managed to do everything from 'down' to 'under' to 'go through'. She was amazing. "You're so smart, baby girl. You are amazing."

"She's great. And so pretty." Jax was grinning, and he knew Jax would want to pet her too, but that would have to wait until they got home.

"Can we go home? I'm wearing down." And he wanted to get this done. They'd done the home visit, the paperwork, everything.

"Yes. Of course. We'll see you back in a few days for some more training. You have the schedule?" Kate got up and Jax followed her over.

He sat on his walker, letting Jax deal with this part for him. He winked at Poppy. "You about ready to go home?"

Poppy sat beside his walker but looked up at him, tongue lolling and tail wagging. He was sure that was the doggie version of *hell, yes*.

"Yeah. Me too. I bought you a couple beds, a bowl, toys. You'll have a tiny yard and a park..."

Poppy turned her head and sniffed him—his knee, his thigh, his hands, his back, like she was looking for something, or trying to learn about him. Then she sat beside him again, obviously focused.

"Okay, we got it. Thank you so much." Jax had an envelope with him when he came over. "I've got paperwork and schedules and all kinds of fun stuff. Are you ready?"

"I am. Let's go, Miss Thing. I swear, I'll do good by you." He meant it, down to the bone.

Poppy stood as he started to get up, staying close but not getting in his way.

"We'll see you back soon." Kate saw them out and the door to the office closed softly behind them.

"Hey, you. It's just us." Jax kissed his cheek.

"Yeah. I'm a little freaked out." Just because he'd wanted this and worked for this and moved here for this, and now it was real.

"Good freaked out, I hope." Look at her. She's beautiful."

Poppy nosed his fingers where they gripped the walker, then crossed the hallway to the elevator buttons.

"She's smart too." Jax grinned at him. "Tell her down."

"Down button, girl."

She pushed the button, tail thumping.

Jax laughed. "Look how happy she is to be helping."

"Dogs need jobs, huh? Even if that job is to love on you." Saw's heart was pounding fast, and he was so ready to get home and settled in their life.

The elevator doors opened and Poppy went in, turned around and walked out again, standing in the way so the doors wouldn't close.

"Let's go, soldier cowboy." Jax followed him in and Poppy sat at his side.

"Right. Let's introduce her to her new home. I hope she's

not too scared." He'd sit with her all day if he needed to. Thankfully, they were up most of the night.

"I don't know. She seems pretty focused right now. Our place is cozy. She'll like it. I know she will. Her bed is in the perfect spot too." They'd put it under the front windows where it got sun and she had a great view of the street and the park.

"Right? Lots of things to watch while she's sleeping. That was a brilliant idea."

"Shut up." Jax snorted, and that made him giggle, which made Jax giggle, and by the time the elevator stopped, they were laughing.

Poppy watched them both like they were crazy, and that just made it funnier. In fact, he could barely breathe by the time the doors opened.

Poppy took a couple of steps forward and barked once at them like she was in charge and they needed to get with the program.

"Right on, Poppy. Let's go." They stepped out into the chilly fall air. "Woo. It's cold."

"It's like winter is trying to show up early this year. Do you have a coat? Gloves? You need good gloves for your hands." Jax stayed close as they headed for the subway.

"I have my jacket from the Army..." That was a coat. "I could use gloves though, and boots that work on ice. No falling for me."

"Nope, no falling. I can teach you how to walk on ice, but I don't think your cruiser will learn very well." They got to the curb and Jax stuck his arm out. "Look! He's free!" The cab pulled right over. "We deserve a cab. We can teach Poppy the subway when we're less tired."

We, which he knew mean him, but Jax never made him feel bad about anything.

"Sounds perfect, sugar. Thank you." He got in with Poppy while Jax stowed the walker. His service dog. "Good girl."

Poppy wagged for him and rested her head on his knee.

Jax climbed in and gave the driver their address. "Are you hungry? We can eat before our nap. I think I'm making a cake tonight and a bunch of petit fours."

"Oh, yeah? I'm going to start hunting for a delivery van and putting some ads up for Christmas—cookies, mostly?"

"A lot of cookies, and also sugar cakes and cinnamon buns and coffee cakes for Christmas morning. People love gooey Christmas sweets." Jax smiled at him. "I like Christmas sweets too."

"Mmm... me too." He'd remember that. "What's a sugar cake?"

What do you want for Christmas?

"Ooh. Have you never had one? It's an eggy, buttery potato bread covered in sugar and cinnamon and baked until it's gooey and amazing." Jax sighed. "They have to rise for like an hour and a half though, and I only have four cast-iron pans so they take forever. I sell them frozen because I'd never get them done otherwise. I'll teach you. You're going to love them."

He didn't quite follow, but sugar and cinnamon and gooey sounded right up his alley, so he'd take it.

They were quiet until the taxi pulled up right in front of their place. The bakery had a warm glow to it when it was closed. Jax had placed a few lights just so.

They stayed open until one p.m., Monday through Friday, and they were open for pickups until noon on Saturday. It was a decent schedule, and left them time to make deliveries and for Jax to bake. So far, the locals seemed to enjoy having a bakery open, and the pastries were flying off the shelves.

Poppy sniffed around the sidewalk as they got out of the cab. Jax got his walker out of the trunk. "She might need to pee. Should I take her and meet you upstairs?"

"I'll come with you." He wanted to be able to take care, to make Poppy comfortable and at home.

"Okay, good." Jax looped Poppy's leash over his fingers. "I'll come with *you*, then."

"Excellent. We'll have a little wander." They headed toward the back area. "Go potty, Poppy. We'll go for a real walk without your vest."

Like an angel, she squatted and peed.

"Good girl!"

"That's proves it. She's the smartest dog ever." Jax laughed and hugged his arm.

"She's amazing. Seriously. And so beautiful."

And his. A friend, a helper. A good dog.

Thank god.

27

"He's almost ready and he looks amazing." Saw's sister Jo ran down the last few stairs and into the bakery. She and January had spent the morning turning their new favorite place into a neat little spot for a wedding. Jo spun around in her pretty green dress, which matched his bowtie and January's tuxedo jacket. "I haven't seen him that dressed up... maybe ever."

"Is it time yet? I'm so nervous." Jax had stuffed his hands into his pockets so no one would see them shaking. They were good nerves, but he still just wished they could get started. He needed Saw here so he could relax.

"Almost," January put a hand on his shoulder. "Breathe. You're fine. He's excited too."

"You look pretty, Jo. I'm glad you're here for him. Us. All of it." He chuckled and rolled his eyes at himself.

She beamed at him, then launched into his arms, squeezing him tight. "He's so happy, Jax. You make him so happy."

He laughed and hugged her back. That was literally

everything he wanted. Just to make Saw as happy as Saw made him.

Hawk came walking in from the kitchen with the JP who was officiating for them. "I hear happiness. Someone must be getting married?"

He snorted. "If Saw would ever get down here."

"He was getting Poppy in her finery." Jo winked at them. "It's so damn cute."

"Jo, did you see Buck's green bowtie?" Jan pointed to Hawk's service dog. He was bigger and burlier than Poppy, and so well suited to Hawk.

"So damn sweet!" Jo was just hugging and loving on everyone. "I love it here. I love you guys. I—Oh, Saw... look at you!"

Saw stood there in his uniform, smiling at him, so warm and happy. "Oh, sugar. You're fine to me."

"Wow." They were really doing this. And Saw was so handsome he was practically glowing. He'd never seen Saw in his dress uniform, and the sight was stunning—he stood tall and proud, medals on his chest. "You're beautiful."

Saw stood taller, offering him a sparkling smile. "Am I? I'm glad you approve."

"The whole room approves, Sawyer." Jan stepped up next to Jax, and Jo moved to Saw's side, walking with him. "You look great."

"Thank you. I'm happy." And didn't that seem like the truth? His soldier cowboy was beaming.

"I can't believe you dressed Poppy up." Poppy had on a green velvet collar, and she was wagging hard. It was the cutest thing ever.

"This is the best day ever." Jo took Saw's arm, and some of the medals tinged and jingled.

"Yes, ma'am. I'm so glad you're here, baby Jo." Saw beamed down at her, and Jax saw tears in those pretty eyes.

"Shall we start, then?" Their JP was a friend of Jan's, a handsome older man with a friendly smile. "Everyone looks ready."

"I'm ready." Jax pulled Jan over to stand with the JP. He wasn't nervous now that he could see Saw's smile. Everything was perfect.

"I'm rarin' to go." Saw chuckled softly. "Let's do this thing."

Hawk started some music, something he and Saw had picked out, and Jan waited with him as Saw took the few steps to cross the bakery floor with Poppy on one side and Jo on the other.

Poppy wagged, Buck barked, and Jo started giggling, the sound almost hysterical. Saw patted her hand, then shook his head. "Y'all all be good."

The little gesture Hawk made got Buck to quiet down right away, but Jo was still giggling when Saw reached him.

"Hello, my handsome soldier cowboy." He smiled and went in for a kiss, but January stopped him.

"Not yet."

"Oh. Right." He chuckled and straightened up. "I'm rushing things."

"You can kiss me anytime, sugar. My life's fixin' to be wrapped up tight with yours."

Saw, for all that he liked to pretend that he wasn't that amazing, could say the best things. Better than that, he meant them.

The JP started talking and he said some amazing things as officiant about love and luck and journeys and... other things, but Jax was so focused on Saw that he barely heard it. He'd never seen Saw in all of his military finery and it was amazing. Saw was so handsome and looked so important.

He wanted to get to their vows and say what he felt and hear what Saw wanted to say.

The best part was that Saw never glanced away from him, never once. It was as if they were in another space, a dimension that was quickly shrinking to only them.

Jan tapped him on the shoulder, smiling. "Go on."

"Sorry. Saw's just..." He looked up at Saw. "You're just so beautiful. I got distracted."

"Isn't he?" Jo was just beaming, and Jax noticed that she and her brother had the same smile.

"Okay. So." He took a breath getting lost again in Saw's eyes. "If someone had told me that one day the Universe would bring you to me, I wouldn't have believed them because I've never had that kind of luck. I would have laughed because good things just don't happen to me. *Didn't* happen to me. But I knew something was happening the first time you mashed bananas for me, you wanted so much to help—even though you didn't know me at all and your hands hurt—and I just knew that it had nothing to do with luck. You found me, you found my bakery... through all your PT and your rehab, the meds and the walker... you were patient with me and determined and you gave me a home. You stopped my head from spinning. You gave me reasons. It wasn't luck. It was you. It is you. And it's always going to be you. I love you more than anything."

That was a lot. He never said that much at once, but he never had so much he wanted to say. "More than anything."

Saw cleared his throat, eyes shimmering. "You're my people, and I will spend my life making you happy. You got my word. I'll do whatever I need to. I love you, sugar, and I have your soul to protect. I swear to God."

The room was silent for a moment, and he was glad because Saw's words were big too.

"Wow, you guys." Jo sniffled.

"Let's get to the good part, then. Do you..."

"I take Saw to be my husband. Yes."

"And I take Jax to be mine."

Jax laughed and leaned in for that kiss.

"I pronounce you husbands!"

Saw cupped his head in one hand and took a deep, hard kiss, not holding back one bit. He knew he was crying, he could feel the tears, but he let it happen because they were so real. As honest as he could get.

He heard applause around them and the dogs were barking, and music started playing again.

"My husband." Saw smiled against his lips. "Wow. My husband."

That smile made Saw shine.

"*My* husband. Even more mine than you were when you woke up this morning." It was hard to believe that was possible.

"Yeah. December tenth is an amazing day." Saw held his hand, fingers squeezing gently. "I love you."

"I love you."

Jan cleared his throat.

"What?" Jax chuckled. "Are we boring you?"

"No." Jan pointed out the bakery's front window at a long, black limousine. "You're keeping the limo waiting."

"The—" Saw looked as confused as he felt. "What's going on?"

"Y'all are going on a honeymoon! I'm keeping Poppy here, and Jan and Hawk say they'll hang out with me." Jo bounced. "You have a night of pampering and champagne!"

"What?" Jax looked around, then back at Saw. "Really?

Hawk laughed, the sound deep and happy. "Steak for Saw and anything that you want. Go on. Go get in the limo."

"Are you sure, Jan?" Saw seemed utterly shocked. "I mean... thank you."

"We better be sure because it's all paid for."

"I should... we should pack something?" A toothbrush? Something?

Jan snorted. "It's one night. The limo is taking you there and bringing you home. You don't need a thing."

Jo laughed, swinging a little sack. "Sweats, socks, comfy shoes, ditty bag. "I'll be here when you get home tomorrow, big bro. Go, go, go!"

"I love y'all! Be good to my dog!" Saw started moving toward the door.

"Thank you! You're sneaky, but I love you too!" Jax ran past Saw and opened the door. The limo driver got out of the car and let them into the car. He even took Saw's walker and put it in the trunk himself. "I can't believe this."

"I can't either. We have amazing friends." Saw sat there, holding their sack of soft clothes in between his legs.

"This car is humongous." And despite that, they were sitting right next to each other, so close there was no daylight between them.

"It is. I—I can't believe we're just leaving. Just leaving all our people at our house."

"I think we got thrown out of our house." He laughed. "So, you know what? I'm going to enjoy it all because when we get home it's Christmas baking until we want to hate Christmas."

"And then we get to do Super Bowl and Valentine's!" Saw teased, because they already had three Super Bowl game orders from Saw calling sports bars.

"You're a nut." He was hoping they could get a week or so

of beach time in somewhere warm and tropical, but they needed to make some money too, so maybe a real honeymoon trip would have to wait. That was okay. He had Saw one way or the other.

Saw and a real Christmas tree with a rainbow light-up star and ornaments, fairy lights around the window, carols on Spotify.

Wedding rings on their fingers.

They pulled up in front of a swanky hotel he'd heard of but never stepped foot in. He wasn't even sure he could afford to stand on the sidewalk.

This was going to be an adventure.

28

Saw wanted to go see the holiday lights. The windows. The ice skaters.

He wanted to, but it wasn't going to happen. They were busy from the time they woke up to the time they crashed on the bed.

Cakes.

Pastries.

Cupcakes.

Cookies.

Pies.

Breads.

More cookies.

It was insane.

Saw would never ever bitch, but it did make him unhappy that they were missing the holidays.

Jax didn't seem to miss it. He was a cookie machine. He made batch after batch without even commenting on how much work it was.

In fact, they hadn't really talked much at all the last few days, other than "pass me the sugar" or "can you get those out of the oven." It was baking and napping and quick showers. Saw got out a couple of times a day with Poppy, but Jax just stayed in the kitchen.

Saw took Poppy out around one a.m., sitting in the bitter cold and wishing it would snow. He'd always wanted to live somewhere it snowed. Poppy did her business and didn't seem to mind the cold much, but even she had had enough after a bit and nudged his fingers.

The bakery door opened, and an oven mitt flew out of it, flames lighting up the sidewalk as it hit the ground. "Heads up!" Jax followed and jumped on it with both feet, stomping out the flames.

"Oops!" His eyes went wide, and he wasn't sure he ought to ask, but he had to know. "What happened?"

"Left it too close to the burner I was melting chocolate on." Jax stared down at the charred mitt with wide eyes, wringing his hands and breathing hard. "Jesus."

"You all right, sugar?" He levered himself up off the bench. "Did you burn yourself?"

"No. No. I'm okay. I'm totally okay. I've never set anything on fire before. Whoa."

Poppy circled them both, herding them toward the door.

"No? I have. Lots of things. I'm sort of amazing at it." He was going for lighthearted.

"What if I'd burned down our house?" Jax rubbed his eyes. "Wait. How are you good at setting things on fire?"

"I was in the service a long time, sugar..." And it had, in a sense, been his job.

"Oh." Jax laughed. The sound was a little tight, but it was still a laugh. Jax picked up the mitt carefully and let Poppy coax him to the door. "Right. Well. That scared me."

"I'm sorry. Do you need a hug? A beer? An orgasm?"

"I have cookies in the oven, but I'll take a hug." Jax

locked the door after they got back inside where it was much warmer.

He wrapped Jax in his arms and held on tight. "Happy fifth day after our wedding."

Jax chuckled.

"What? It's a thing? I intend to celebrate it until I can't remember how many days it's been." That was good, wasn't it?

"I'd just lost count of the days. Is it five already?" Jax hugged him back. "Happy fifth day of being my husband. It hasn't been all that romantic, has it?"

"No, but it's been us, and I love us, so that's cool." And he meant it.

"Christmas Eve isn't that far off and time is going to fly. And then we'll go… wherever we want to go." They talked about going, but they hadn't ever discussed where.

A timer went off and Jax kissed him quickly before hurrying to the ovens. "Cookies."

"Save the cookies!" he cheered, and Poppy barked like she was agreeing.

Jax moved around their new space easily, putting cookies up to cool. "I'm going to shut this down. We don't have any early deliveries, and even if we did, everything for the next two days is done. And you know what? I'm tired."

"Well, then, let's go upstairs. We'll have a long shower and relax together." That sounded like heaven to him.

Jax shut off the ovens and covered the dough to put in the fridge. "Yes. We need a break. I tried to burn the place down after all." Jax sighed heavily. "Unbelievable."

"Oh, sugar. You had a little accident. That's all." He caught shit on fire a lot more.

"It wasn't little. It was fire, and it freaked me out, okay?" Jax turned off the kitchen lights.

"Okay." He didn't want to argue about it, and honestly, he thought it was a little funny. He had a hundred stories of soldiers causing trouble, making mischief, but he reckoned that Jax wasn't interested in "no shit, there I was" stories.

"Okay." Jax nodded and led the way to the elevator. They'd figured out a way to fit all three of them in. Poor Poppy got a bit squished but never complained.

Damn, he felt like he'd done something wrong now, and he hadn't. Had he?

Fuck.

"You want a sandwich or something? We got turkey."

Jax shook his head no and leaned against him. "I'm just grumpy. All I want is you."

"Well, you have me. Grumpy or not." He kissed Jax's temple. "Love you."

Poppy hopped out as soon as the elevator doors opened onto the apartment.

Jax kissed him, fingers tugging at his shirt and keeping him there another minute.

Oh, that didn't taste like Jax was mad at him. Not at all, and he approved.

Jax looked happier as the kiss ended. "I love you too." Jax closed the door after they left the elevator and kissed him again. "Still offering orgasms?"

"I am." He winked over, going for lecherous. "Still interested?"

Jax's nodded comically. "Yeah. Yes. So interested. All-day interested."

"Oh, all-day interested is good, but I know better." He slipped Jax a kiss with tongue, teasing and playing. "But you are stop-baking-cookies interested. That's hard-core."

Jax nodded begging another kiss and untucking Saw's shirt. "I'm give-up-on-cookies-forever interested."

"Oh, that's special." And he'd take it without the sacrifice, thank you.

He carefully worked on Jax's buttons, humming under his breath as he did.

"You're beautiful." Jax's fingers settled on his abs and pushed up to his chest.

Poppy walked in circles around them, tail thumping against his legs. She wanted him to sit down.

"I'm yours. Come to bed. I want to touch you." Love on him. Adore him.

"Yeah." Jax led him to the bedroom, then tugged his shirt off and tossed it, showing off smooth skin. Jax wasn't muscled at all—instead of being cut and hard bodied like Saw's army buddies, Jax was softer, smoother, barely a scar on him.

Jax was the sexiest man he'd ever seen. He dragged one hand down Jax's belly, the skin there like silk.

"Mm. Sit and let me help you with your jeans. I want what's under them." Jax helped him sit and went after his fly.

"Mmm... that's a lovely sight—your hands on my jeans." His body was eager to harden, his cock to fill.

"I like my hand on your jeans. And your fly. And... what's under your fly." Jax's fingers brushed against his cock, still hidden by his briefs.

"Mmhmm..." His cock jerked, and his legs parted.

Jax pushed his walker aside and knelt, not even taking the time to pull his jeans off. Jax just tugged his cock free and licked around the head, humming like it was the best ice cream cone ever.

"Jax!" One of his hands landed on his lover's—no, his husband's—head, fingers tangling in the soft hair.

"I know." Jax grinned up at him. "You promised *me* orgasms. But you're just so... hot."

"I did. We did. Wanna sixty-nine?" He could give and take, for sure. In fact, he wanted that sweet prick.

"Uh-huh." Jax kissed his belly, then stood up and stripped out of his jeans.

"Jesus, you're fine." He loved the way Jax was put together, the way all the parts worked to become a fabulous whole.

"I love the way you say *fine*. Nobody's ever called me that before. I've only heard it in the movies." Jax was bare in an instant, smiling down at him, and he was still sitting on the bed in his jeans.

It didn't seem reasonable, so he worked his boots off, then his jeans and the rest. They both needed to touch, he thought.

Jax took his hands and kissed each one. "These need a rest. Mouths was a good idea." Jax pushed him back on the bed.

"I'm a brilliant son of a bitch." He stretched out and licked his lips.

"You're a beautiful son of a bitch is what you are. And I'm all yours." Jax climbed up and kissed him again, in that sweet-hot way of his that seemed so innocent and burned him right up at the same time.

His day was getting better and better every second, and he dove right back into the kisses.

Jax broke it off, leaving them both breathless, before turning on the bed and stretching out beside him, giving his thigh a kiss before climbing over him.

Saw hummed and dragged his tongue along Jax's cock, gathering the salty tang of his lover's skin.

"Jesus. Give a guy a second to..." Jax sighed and rocked against the touch, betraying his words.

"Mmhmm..." This was more fun than color TV, and he licked again, making sure Jax felt it.

That time, he got a nice moan, and Jax answered by sucking the head of his cock into a hot mouth. Jax teased his tongue over the slit and hummed around the head.

His heart pounded, and he forced himself not to buck up and drive into Jax's mouth.

He knew Jax loved giving as much as he did, and while this wasn't ever a competition, sometimes with Jax, it felt like one. Which of them would make the other pull up first? There was no telling, it could go either way.

They were both winning this particular battle, no matter what.

He grinned and focused on finding a solid rhythm, taking a bit more of the sweet cock with every move of his head.

Jax did the same, making it a challenge for him to focus. Sneaky fingers, curled around his balls, playing and teasing.

His toes curled, and he couldn't fight his whimper, his shiver. Jax's hips jerked, and he felt the groan before he heard it, vibrating around the head of his cock.

Dammit, that was cheating. There was no way around it. Jax was driving him nuts.

Well, two could play at that game, and he knew what Jax liked. He reached up and dug his fingers into Jax's fine ass and pulled him down, swallowing around his husband's cock.

Jax pulled up with a howl and sucked in air. "Saw!"

Oh, yeah. He groaned and just stayed where he was, sucking over and over, demanding Jax's pleasure.

Jax pushed a little deeper, then pulled up again with a groan. "You... fuck. Your mouth."

Yes. Fuck my mouth. That was exactly the point, and he felt like he was so connected to Jax, both of them creating a circle.

His cock disappeared into Jax's mouth again, even as Jax's hips rocked, pushing that sweet prick farther into his throat. He swallowed hard, encouraging his lover to come for him.

Jax groaned again, the vibration making him tingle. A few more careful but needy thrusts and Jax's spunk filled his mouth. That cock swelling for him.

As soon as Jax stopped shooting, the suction around his prick became near unbearable, and he thrust up into those lips, over and over.

Jax gripped his ass, encouraging him, letting him push deep.

"Sugar... sugar, fuck..."

One finger slid back, pressed against his hole, tapping and teasing before barely pressing in. Jax was so focused it made his eyes cross.

His belly tightened, and he knew he wasn't going to be able to hang on. He didn't even try. He simply let himself go, his entire body shuddering with his orgasm.

"Mm." Jax hummed once the storm had subsided, and slowly turned around to snuggle up against him. "Better."

"God yes. So much better." He nuzzled the top of Jax's head, the tension in his head relaxing.

Jax kissed his chest. "You're amazing. All I wanted all day was you. I was getting so... *mad* that I had so much work to do. That doesn't usually happen to me."

"We are newlyweds, right? We're supposed to be wildly

horny." And this was their busiest season, especially being brand new.

"I think when the holidays are over and we get back from our honeymoon, we should tell the bosses that we need to hire some help." Jax chuckled against his ribs.

"We totally ought to. We can threaten to strike." He winked over, letting it stay light.

"That's it. We can ask for fourteen-hour days and sex breaks."

"Oh, I like sex breaks. Guaranteed blow jobs, periodic shower sex."

"See? We have *great* benefits." Jax yawned over that last word and puffed out a breath, going heavy next to him. "I'd love you even without the benefits."

"Good. Rest. We'll get up in a bit and eat, okay?" They both needed a nap.

"Mhm." Jax was dozing off even without his permission.

Lord help him. They weren't going to survive Christmas.

29

Jax had lost count of how many times he'd wanted to quit in the last couple of weeks and today he didn't care if he never saw another Christmas cookie for the rest of his life. But in a few hours, it would be Christmas Eve, and as much as he'd appreciated being included, for once he didn't have to get on a plane and pretend he wasn't exhausted at a big Texas Christmas dinner.

He and Saw had put in crazy long days and seen dozens of Hoboken sunrises, but this one would be the last one he intended to see until after New Year's Day.

It had been like a life raft though. The morning after he'd set that stupid oven mitt on fire, he and Saw walked the few blocks to the waterfront and watched the sun come up. After that, no matter what they were working on, they'd taken a break every morning to do the same. They'd count the hours to sunrise and somehow it would all seem possible again. Just two more hours. Just a couple more blocks.

Just one more cup of tea.

"So, those were the last two pickups? It's over?" Saw

seemed drawn and a little gray, but that smile refused to fade. Every time Saw looked at him, Saw smiled.

Jax looked around at the kitchen, which should probably get a thorough post-insanity scrub but was otherwise clean and nodded. "I think so." He knew so, but he was a little afraid to say it out loud.

"Good. I want to go upstairs and turn on Christmas cartoons and sit together and eat pizza."

"It's seven a.m."

"Oh. I guess you can't get pizza for breakfast."

"I'd suggest leftover whatever, but I don't think we ate yesterday." He didn't remember eating anyway. "Do we still have Froot Loops?" The longer he stood there, letting the idea that they were basically done sink in, the more tired he felt.

"I have no idea. I don't think there's milk. How about—a bowl of chocolate chips with orange juice poured over?"

Jax look horrified. "Gross! We better go out. Someone else can make us breakfast. And you need coffee."

"Oh, that sounds good. I could murder a huge omelet or biscuits and gravy or waffles and sausage…"

"Pancakes and bacon or maybe French toast. Or all of it. We don't have to rush back here for anything."

"That's a relief. It's been a wild month, hasn't it?"

It had been a wild year. Not even.

They'd met, moved in together, bought a building, moved, got a dog, opened a bakery, got married…

They owned a bakery. Somehow Saw had found him a bakery that was already home.

He reached out and pinched Saw's arm.

"Ow! Had I dozed off?" Saw's eyes were the size of saucers.

"No. I just wanted to make sure this was all real and I

didn't feel like pinching myself." Jax gave him a wide grin. "You're real."

"I am so real. I am also starving." Saw grinned at him, the expression wicked. "*Starving.*"

"Uh-huh. I've got a ready-made dessert for you later." He pulled off his apron and tossed it in the bin with all the flour and dough-covered kitchen towels. "You good to go? I can get our coats."

"That would rock. Thank you." Saw turned the closed sign over with a satisfying thump.

Poppy lifted her head, then hopped up, tail wagging. "Yes, girl. We're going *out.*" He grinned and ran up the stairs, listening to Saw talk to her while he was gone. He grabbed coats and mittens and scarves, plus a few treats for Poppy and her coat. It was cold out.

The Christmas tree was standing and lit, and it was waiting for them to decorate after they woke up. It was beautiful. It was their first tree.

He had no idea where Saw had found it, or when. It just showed up a couple of days ago, and boxes of decorations arrived a day later. All Saw had to say about it was "Merry Christmas."

He was humming some Christmas song he couldn't remember the name of as he went back downstairs, arms full.

Saw was leaning against the door, eyes on the sky, a smile on his face. "Jo says Merry Christmas, sugar."

"Is she still coming? When does she get here?" It was their first, but Christmas was for family after all.

"She'll be here midday Christmas. She got a great deal on a flight, and she's doing Christmas Eve with her boyfriend."

Oh, he liked that. They could wake up together and take

Christmas morning slow. Make breakfast. Open presents. Smooch under the mistletoe.

It could be their own new tradition, which involved whatever they wanted.

"I got her a car from the airport, so we don't have to stress it." Saw drew him close, his hand solid and strong. "Merry merry, sugar."

"Merry, soldier cowboy." Jax gave Saw a quick kiss. "Put your coat on. I'm starving."

While Saw wrestled with the coat, he got Poppy ready to go. He was always ready to help Saw if he needed it, but the Christmas baking season had been good for Saw even if it had been exhausting. Saw's hands were more agile, his shoulders too, from moving and handling dough and washing dishes. They'd joked it was like baking rehab.

"She's so cute in her coat, isn't she?" He fixed her working harness over the coat and stood up.

"She's gorgeous, aren't you, sweet Poppy?"

She stared at Saw with utter adoration, and Jax got it. Saw was her person.

He looked around the bakery, then shut off the lights. "That's it. We're done. Let's go eat." He opened the door and held it, letting in cold, winter air. "Brrrr!"

"N-n-no shit. Wow. It's like my nose hairs are fixin' to freeze."

He grinned and locked up. "If you're going to live up here, your Texan nose is going to have to get used to it."

"My Texan sister will have to learn to knit scarves. She's smart." Saw waggled his eyebrows at Jax.

"She is smart. I can't wait to tell her." He laughed and put his gloved hand over Saw's on the walker. "The diner, right? It's close." He might be used to cold winters, but that didn't mean he wanted to freeze longer than he had to.

"Yes. Coffee. Pancakes. Sausage. Bacon." Saw moved slow and steady.

He moved at Saw's pace, perfectly happy to take their time. They were both tired. "All of that. Yes, please. And a treat for you-know-who."

"She totally gets a treat. She's a good girl."

It was definitely cold, but it was a beautiful morning— bright sun, blue sky, and the streets were quiet. They got there in good time and had their pick of tables, so they decided on a comfy booth where Poppy could sit on the bench with Saw or under the table and be out of the way.

Coffee arrived without needing to ask for it, and giant diner menus. Jax ordered his tea. "I could eat everything on here."

"Maybe two. But I want breakfast. Things with maple syrup."

"Mhm. French toast and bacon. To start."

The server must have heard them because she came right over and took their orders. He leaned back in his chair and smiled at his handsome husband. "I'm usually headed for the airport about now."

"Are you upset?" Saw nudged his toes under the table. "I mean, to not go? I feel selfish, but I needed you."

"No. No... I am not upset at all. I'm actually relieved not to be traveling, and I'm happy to be spending Christmas with you. I'm selfish too. You're my family now." Hawk's family had always been welcoming, but Hawk and Jan were married and he was... just himself.

"Yeah. We have our own traditions. Ones involving nappage and eating and blow jobs." Saw had the best traditions.

"And Nat King Cole! He's so romantic." He sipped his tea, thinking about the rest of his new family. "Will Jo want

Christmas dinner? Like a roast or turkey or something? Because I'm a great baker but..."

Saw gave him a sheepish look. "So... I asked Hawk, and he told me where I could order a whole Christmas supper... I got extra rolls."

"You did?" He knew his huge smile was probably goofy looking and he didn't care. "Really? As a surprise?"

"Yeah, I figured making a spread was the last thing we'd want to do, so... Merry Christmas, sugar." Oh, someone was pleased with himself.

He reached over the table and took Saw's hand. "I don't think I deserve you, but I'm not giving you up so it doesn't matter."

"Nope. You're stuck with me. Forever. I'm going to be your right-hand man until the end of friggin' time."

"Damn right. What did you do for the holidays before this?"

"I traveled. I was overseas, so a bunch of the single guys and I just went and did." Saw rolled his eyes. "I hated it. I wanted Christmas."

He squeezed Saw's fingers gently. "This is going to be the best Christmas ever."

"It already is."

He had married a poet. How had he managed that? It made him feel ten feet tall.

He had everything he wanted. Everything. A home, a bakery, a husband.

He felt like every day was the beginning of their future together.

30

"Merry Christmas!" Saw had never been happier. They'd slept for twelve straight hours, they'd snacked, they were waiting for Jo, and he was whole for the first time since Ollie had died.

It was a weird but wonderful sensation of fullness. Fullness? Was that a word?

Even if it wasn't, that was what Saw was.

"It's been such a good one so far." Jax grinned at him and held a sprig of mistletoe over his head. "Oh look! Mistletoe!"

"Oh, my!" He clapped his hands on his cheeks, playing along. "I think you're required by law to kiss me now."

"By law." Jax leaned in and kissed him. "Not that I need a law." He got another kiss and Jax slipped an arm around his waist.

It was easy to draw Jax in, rub their noses together, let one kiss become another and another.

Their doorbell rang, and Poppy woofed softly, interrupting them.

"Ooh. Maybe it's Santa!" Jax laughed. "I'll be right back with her."

"Good deal." They had a guest room here, somewhere comfortable for Jo to stay for the holidays, and they had gotten her a coat, scarf, hat, and mittens.

She wanted to go ice skating while she was here, and Saw couldn't wait to take video.

"Guess what I found?" Jax came up the stairs, smiling. "A suitcase!"

"Hooray! I've always wanted a suitcase!" He applauded, then held his arms open for Jo.

"A purple suitcase, because, of course it is." She hugged him hard, obviously as happy to see him as he was to see her. "Merry Christmas."

"I'm putting it in your room, Jo." Jax ducked into the guest room and was back quickly.

"So you both survived the huge baking. Now you're ramping up to Valentine's Day?"

He and Jax both groaned in unison. "Don't talk about baking."

Jo's eyes went wide, and then she started to laugh, the bright, happy giggles filling the room. "Sorry! Sorry. Although I'll be unhappy if I don't get to try those snickerdoodles Sawyer is always raving about."

Jax sighed dramatically, playing with her. "Oh, I *suppose* I could make you some while you're here."

"Not today."

"No, and probably not tomorrow either. Tomorrow, we'll go shopping!" Jax winked at him. "Saw helps us get the best parking spots."

"Are you sure it's Saw? Because Poppy is cuter." Poppy had been sitting quietly by Saw's side since Jo walked in. "She looks so smart. You'll tell me when I can play with her, okay? I don't want to distract her, she's being so good."

"She's not at work, sister. Play away. Her squeaky

reindeer is in the hallway." Saw grinned at her. "Are you hungry? There are bagels in there."

"Hey, girl." Jo dropped to her knees and started loving on Poppy who looked at her completely in love. Jo did look like him, after all. "A real New York bagel? Yes, please. And I want to see what you've done to your place. It's so cute. I love your tree. You guys made it so festive in here."

"Yeah, we didn't have a chance to decorate up here before the wedding, but it's better now. I have the guest room done."

Jo looked up at him and smiled affectionately. "Thank you. It wasn't too bad before, though."

"It needed a little love." And paint. He'd hired that done.

Jax laughed. "A lot of love. It's a guest room. But for you. You're the guest it's for. Go check it out. I'll put a schmear on your bagel."

"You rock like a rocking thing. Thanks! I have to dig out y'all's presents." She hopped up. "Come on, Poppy! I got you a special bone."

Jax watched them go and chuckled at her happy little squeal as she entered the room. "I think she likes it. Nice work, big brother." Jax leaned close, flirting.

"It's her dream room from her Pinterest board." It was all royal blue and lemon yellow with pretty china decorations. It was girly but had been easy.

And maybe it would entice Jo to move up north once she got her nursing degree. Maybe.

"Wait until she sees Rockefeller Center all done up for the holidays."

"Me too. I'm excited. Like a lot." He was tickled to know that they had a week of Christmassing left in them.

"And don't worry about Jo. I baked a big batch of snickerdoodles last night. They're downstairs in the pantry. I didn't think Christmas would be right without the cookie that made you fall in love with me." Jax winked at him and gave him a smug little grin.

"It was a deciding factor, sugar, absolutely. You knew the way to my heart." Jax had believed in him, had believed in his abilities, his heart, his spirit.

"You made the noise go away. My handsome soldier cowboy." Jax rubbed noses with him, then leaned back and snagged the mistletoe off the TV stand. "Do it again."

"Every day until the end of time." He reached up and cupped the back of Jax's neck, bringing their lips together. "You have my word."

Interested in learning more about BA's cowboys and Jodi's gentlemen? Want free fiction and news? Join our newsletters!

What's Up with Jodi
https://readerlinks.com/l/2317334

Spurs and Shifters
https://lp.constantcontact.com/su/A9CRUzp/baandjulia

The Merry Everything Series
Jodi Payne and BA Tortuga

Cowboys and city boys. Opposites attract. Friends or enemies to lovers. The magic of the holiday season.

The Merry Everything Series is a collection of standalone novels set during the holidays when anything can happen, especially unexpected love. They are uplifting, happy ever after stories that will leave you smiling and toasty warm.

For those of you who have read our other series, you'll often find cameos of familiar characters and/or side characters as MCs.

Click below for a link to series. Happy Holidays!

Find the whole Series here!

Happy Holidays, Y'all!

We want to thank you for giving Cowboys and Cupcakes a try. We hope you enjoyed the story.

If you can spare a few minutes to post a review at the retail website where you made your purchase, we'd very much appreciate it!

Don't forget to "like" our Facebook pages and groups to keep up with all the news--new releases, sales announcements, giveaways, sneak peeks-- and of course the rodeo pictures, coffee memes and just general fun. We'd love to have all y'all!

Yeehaw and thanks for reading!

BA & Jodi

ABOUT JODI

JODI takes herself way too seriously and has been known to randomly break out in song. Her men are imperfect but genuine, stubborn but likable, often kinky, and frequently their own worst enemies. They are characters you can't help but fall in love with while they stumble along the path to their happily ever after. For those looking to get on her good side, Jodi's addictions include nonfat lattes, Malbec and tequila any way you pour it.

Website: jodipayne.net

Newsletter: https://readerlinks.com/l/2317334

All Jodi's Social Links: linktr.ee/jodipayne

ABOUT BA

Texan to the bone and an unrepentant Daddy's Girl, BA Tortuga spends her days with her basset hounds, getting tattooed, texting her grandbabies, and eating Mexican food. When she's not doing that, she's writing. She spends her days off watching rodeo, knitting and surfing Pinterest in the name of research. BA's personal saviors include her wife, Julia Talbot, her best friends, and coffee. Lots of coffee. Really good coffee.

Having written everything from fist-fighting rednecks to hard-core cowboys to werewolves, BA does her damnedest to tell the stories of her heart, which was raised in Northeast Texas, but has heard the call of the high desert and lives in the Sandias. With books ranging from hard-hitting GLBT romance, to fiery ménages, to the most traditional of love stories, BA refuses to be pigeon-holed by anyone but the voices in her head.

BA loves to talk to her readers and can be found at http://batortuga.com/ and her newsletter signup link is http://bit.ly/BAJulianews

AVAILABLE FROM JODI & BA

The Cowboy and the Dom Trilogy

<u>First Rodeo, Book One</u>

<u>Razor's Edge, Book Two</u>

<u>No Ghosts, Book Three</u>

The Soldier and the Angel, a Cowboy and Dom Novel

Sin Deep, a Cowboy and Dom Novel

Trouble with Cowboys - a Sin Deep Novel, coming January 2024!

East Meets Westerns

(single titles)

<u>Wrecked</u>

Flying Blind

Special Delivery, A Wrecked Holiday Novel

Temptation Ranch

Seeds and Sunshine

Pickup Man - Coming Spring 2024!

The Merry Everything Series

<u>Window Dressing</u>

Cowboy Protection

Cowboys and Cupcakes

The Higher Elevation Series

<u>Heart of a Cowboy</u>